SPRUCED UP FOR MURDER

A RIGHT ROYAL COZY INVESTIGATION MYSTERY

HELEN GOLDEN

DREW BRADLEY PRESS

ALSO BY HELEN GOLDEN

COPYRIGHT

This is a work of fiction. Names, characters, places, and incidents are the product of the author's imagination or used fictitiously. Any resemblance to actual persons, living or dead, events, or locales, is entirely coincidental.

ISBN (P) 978-1-915747-65-5

Edited by Marina Grout at Writing Evolution

Published by Drew Bradley Press

Cover by Helen Drew-Bradley

First edition October 2022

DEDICATION

*To Mark. My fiercest critic and my staunchest
supporter.*

*You were my mentor, my inspiration, and my friend.
You are greatly missed.*

NOTE FROM THE AUTHOR

I am a British author and this book has been written using British English. So if you are from somewhere other than the UK, you may find some words spelt differently to how you would spell them. In most cases this is British English, not a spelling mistake. We also have different punctuation rules in the UK.

However if you find any other errors I would be grateful if you would please contact me helen@he lengoldenauthor.co.uk and let me know so I can correct them. Thank you.

For your reference I have included a list of characters in the order they appear and you can find this at the back of the book.

1

EARLY MORNING, WEDNESDAY 7 APRIL

"Oh my giddy aunt!" Perry Juke slapped his hand up to his mouth, his face turning pale as he gawped at the body in front of them.

"Oh my giddy aunt, indeed," Lady Beatrice, the Countess of Rossex, replied, gazing at the prone form lying only a few metres away from her. Her stomach twisted at the sight of his lifeless body. Instinctively, she wanted to look away, but like a moth attracted to a light, she was drawn to the scene before her.

He — for it was definitely a man with his stocky frame and shaved head — was lying on his front, his arms and legs splayed out, looking rather like he had fallen from a great height. Blood obscured the right-hand side of his face. A patch of what looked like red wine had soaked into the green and black Persian rug underneath his body. The grey marble table, which was normally by the side of the olive-green leather Chesterfield, was lying askew on the floor. One corner was covered in something dark and sticky.

"He must have fallen and hit his head on the table. Is he dead? He looks very dead," Perry said, scanning the room as if searching for someone to confirm the body was, indeed, dead.

Lady Beatrice raised her hand to her chest to still her racing heart.

The press is going to love this.

A dead body at Francis Court, found by a member of the royal family — this was gold.

She raked her slim fingers through her long auburn hair. If only she hadn't been guilted by her mother into accepting her sister's request to take on the interior design of the refurbished Events Suite, she would be upstairs in her apartment right now, enjoying a leisurely coffee and snuggling with her dog, Daisy. Shaking her head, she returned to the matter in hand. There was possibly a dead body in front of them, and it had to be dealt with.

I suppose one of us needs to check for a pulse.

She turned hopefully to Perry.

2

THREE MONTHS EARLIER, MID-AFTERNOON, SUNDAY 10 JANUARY

Lady Beatrice peered over at her son, who was sitting on the edge of his seat next to her in the back of the car. It struck her how grown-up Sam looked in his Wilton College uniform. His blazer, still a little big for him but with room to grow, something which he would no doubt need if the last few months were anything to go by, was still shiny and new, not yet exposed to the wear and tear a thirteen-year-old boy was about to inflict upon it. Earlier, when they had left Francis Court, he had been so excited to tell her of the clubs he wanted to join — photography and music production, and the sport teams he wanted to try out for — cricket and tennis. Looking at him now, she marvelled at how calm and collected he appeared.

She, on the other hand, had butterflies in her stomach and a right leg which would not stay still. Saying goodbye to Sam, the boy who had been her entire world since the day he was born, was turning out to be harder than she had expected.

How will I manage without his smile to brighten my day and his joyous enthusiasm for life to keep me going?

She could feel the tears prickling at the back of her eyes.

Come on Bea. Stiff upper lip and all that.

She turned away from Sam and discreetly pinched herself on the inside of her arm. The sudden nip refocused her brain and helped dry up the tears.

Grabbing Daisy, her West Highland Terrier, she tried to give her a hug, but the little dog only wanted to see out of the window and squirmed in a 'get off me mum' sort of way. Sighing, Lady Beatrice gave up.

Shhhuuuu. The glass panel dividing the front and the back of the Daimler slid open.

"My lady, Mister Sam, we will turn off the main road shortly. We should be at Wilton in approximately five minutes," Ward said, as they turned off the main road, following a narrower route flanked by fields of sheep on one side and cows on the other.

Daisy, wanting to get a better view, went to launch herself through the now open glass partition and onto the front seat of the car. With the lightening reflex of a mother who has to pluck their child from the jaws of disaster, Lady Beatrice grabbed Daisy just in time and pulled the terrier onto her lap. There was another *shh-huuuu* and any hope Daisy had of escaping was dashed as the glass partition slowly closed.

"You're not going anywhere, young lady," Lady Beatrice scolded. Laughing, Sam leaned over to pat Daisy on the head.

"No," Lady Beatrice cried. Jerking his hand back, Sam stared at his mother, his eyes wide and questioning.

"I'm so sorry darling, I didn't mean to shout." Grabbing his hand, she smiled at him. "But Grand-mama gave me strict instructions when we left Francis Court: we are not to get dog hairs all over your new uniform. Neither of us wants to get in trouble with Grandmama, do we?" She tilted her head to one side and was relieved when he shook his head and grinned.

As they approached the entrance of Wilton Col-lege, they slowed. Sam shuffled further forward in his seat and craned his head to look out of the car window. Lady Beatrice, whose right leg was now tapping up and down as if keeping in time with a particularly challenging piece of music, took in the elaborate and imposing wrought-iron gates ahead with a feeling of dread. There was a gaggle of press standing around them, cameras at the ready. Daisy shook with excitement.

Lady Beatrice turned to her son and smiled. "Ready?"

He beamed back at her and grabbed her hand. "You'll be fine Mum, I promise."

3

MORNING, MONDAY 11 JANUARY

The Society Page online article:

Lady Beatrice—What Will She Do Now?

Yesterday, Lady Beatrice, the Countess of Rossex (35), the youngest daughter of the sixteenth Duke of Arnwall and HRH Princess Helen, the Duchess of Arnwall, dropped off her only son, Samuel (13), at the exclusive boarding school, Wilton College, in Derbyshire. He joined his cousin, Lady Sarah Rosdale's son, Robert Rosdale (14), who began his studies at Wilton College last year.

Samuel, whose full title is the Right Honourable The Viscount Millock, is the son of the Earl of Rossex, James Wiltshire, and the only grandson of the Earl and Countess of Durrland. James Wiltshire was only 24 when he was killed in a car accident six months before Samuel was born. His car was found embedded in a tree only five miles from The Dower House where he lived with Lady Beatrice. A female passenger, Gill Sterling (27), the wife of Francis Court's estate manager, Alex Sterling, was also in the car and died later in hospital. Fourteen years later, it still remains a mystery why Mrs Sterling was in the car.

So, what now for Lady Beatrice? Apart from attending official royal family events and the occasional charity fundraiser, she has kept herself out of the public eye since her husband's death and concentrated on raising her son. Now Samuel is away at Wilton for the next few years will she continue to hide herself away at Francis Court, or will she re-emerge in the public arena?

4

VERY EARLY MORNING, THURSDAY 14 JANUARY

Lady Beatrice woke up with a start, her brain scrambling to identify the noise that had dragged her from slumber. Heart racing, she half sat up in bed, then relaxed. It was just her phone.

As she looked over to her bedside table where her mobile phone was lit up and vibrating, Daisy let out a deep sigh and snuggled down even deeper into the duvet.

Reaching over, Lady Beatrice picked up the phone.

"Hello darling, are you awake?" Her Royal Highness Princess Helen, the Duchess of Arnwall, asked.

Lady Beatrice looked at the time displayed on

the front of her phone. It said six forty-five. She shook her head.

There should be a law against ringing someone before seven-thirty.

"Hello Mother," she replied, her voice still husky with sleep. "I am now."

"Oh, darling, I am so sorry. Did I wake you? I forgot you don't rise early now you have nothing to do." The princess was the master of giving an apology and having a not-so-subtle dig at the same time.

Lady Beatrice ignored the comment. It was too early, and she'd not had a coffee yet. "What can I do for you, Mother?"

"Well, to start with, I am going to send Naomi down to you with a coffee, so you are not quite so spiky." Her voice muffled, she shouted, "Naomi, can you rustle up a large black coffee and take it over to Lady Beatrice, please? I seem to have woken her up, and she's not thrilled with me."

Lady Beatrice covered her mouth, trying not to laugh. "All right, Ma, I'm sorry I was rude, and yes, a coffee would be lovely. Thank you."

Keeping her phone to her ear, Lady Beatrice slipped out of bed, being careful not to disturb Daisy who was laid diagonally across the duvet on her back, legs akimbo, gently snoring. She grabbed her dressing gown from a hook on the back of the door and padded into the adjoining sitting room. She drew back the curtains to reveal a grey and wet January morning. Peering out of the window, she could barely see where the drive split in two, one leg veering off to the Old Stable Block on the left and the other following the path to the circular route leading to and from the main entrance.

Sitting in the middle of the court was a grand seventeenth century water feature called the Cascade. Built in 1692, it had two sets of twenty-two stone steps, one facing south and one facing north, over which water flowed from a set of fountains on the top. It would be another forty-five minutes before sunrise when the fountain switched on, so it currently sat quiet, giving the whole scene a slightly eerie look.

Lady Beatrice sighed with pleasure and sat down on the sofa facing the window.

"So, Beatrice, I need you to do something for me."

"What would that be, Mother?"

"I need you to accept a lunch invitation from your sister today and listen to what she has to say with an open mind. Can you do that for me?"

"Um, all right. Is that it?"

"I need you to listen, darling. Not the 'polite

listening' you have perfected over the years of public engagements; I mean *properly* listen. Sarah has a proposition for you, and I think you should accept. But I know you, darling. You will throw up barriers about why you can't do it. But you *can* and it will give you something to do now Samuel is away at school."

Lady Beatrice didn't like where this was going. *What on earth is my sister going to ask me to do?*

There was a knock on the door, and she called out, "Enter." Naomi came in carrying a silver tray and placed it on the low coffee table in front of her. A silver coffee pot sat next to a wide fat porcelain coffee cup alongside a plate containing croissants and pain au chocolat — her favourite.

Thank you, Ma.

"Thank you, Naomi," she mouthed at her mother's maid. The short, plump woman smiled in return, gave her a quick curtsy, and left. Lady Beatrice poured herself a coffee and gulped down a mouthful; the hot black liquid made her feel more alive.

"I'm worried you are going to end up without purpose now Sammy has gone, darling," her mother continued, "aimlessly wandering around Francis Court like a human ghost."

A what?

"Mother, Sam has only been gone for three days. I hardly think I've gone into decline in such a short time. And what on earth is a human ghost?"

"You know, like a ghost, wafting around the place, scaring the public, but human. Anyway, that's not the point. You have already told your uncle you don't want to take on an official role within the family, so you need to decide what you *are* going to do, darling."

But Lady Beatrice was enjoying the unstructured nature of having no responsibilities since Sam went away. Having spent the last thirteen years running around after a growing boy, she deserved to have a more relaxed routine, at least for a little longer.

"Mother, you know I'm not ready for a public life on my own. I don't want to be press fodder again."

"Yes, I understand that darling; I know the whole James thing was horrid for you. But it was a long time ago, Beatrice, and you really need to move on with your life. You can't let it stop you from having a fulfilling purpose."

Lady Beatrice smiled. No one would ever give the princess a job as a counsellor. 'Pull yourself together' was no longer an acceptable response to mental trauma. But she knew her mother meant well.

"Can you tell me what Sarah wants me to do?" she pressed her mother. "Then I'll be better prepared when we meet."

"Fine darling, but you have to act surprised when she asks you, all right?"

"Yes, I promise."

Lady Beatrice picked up the pain au chocolat and moved it onto a side plate. She didn't normally eat this early, but the pastries were too tempting. Like a bolt of lightning, Daisy shot across from the bedroom and came to an abrupt stop by the side of her chair, quivering in anticipation, her gaze glued to the pastry in Lady Beatrice's hand.

How does she do that? From asleep to alert in ten seconds.

Lady Beatrice broke off a piece of the chocolatey pastry and popped it into her mouth. Daisy whimpered to remind her she was still there and waiting. Shaking her head, she whispered, "No, Daisy, it's not good for you." Huffing, Daisy jumped onto the sofa and curled up beside her.

"We only have two more scheduled events before we close the Events Suite. We then have twelve weeks for it to be refurbished, redecorated, and dressed. I still don't agree with Sarah that it's tired and outdated, but I lost that argument and it's going ahead despite my misgivings." The princess sniffed. "Anyway, Sarah is going to ask you to do the interior design for it all."

Lady Beatrice's mouth fell open. She had not been expecting that. Picking up her coffee, she took another giant gulp.

"We will have a grand reopening on the first of May," the princess continued. "It will be a proper paid job, darling, with a brief and a budget, and you will need to present your ideas to Sarah for final sign-off."

Lady Beatrice fiddled with her wedding and engagement rings, which she had moved to her right hand a year after her husband's death. Looking out of the window, through the dimness she spotted a small herd of fallow deer huddled under a clump of trees to the left of the long drive. About a dozen in number, the herd was only a fraction of the population on the Francis Court estate.

"Darling, are you still there?"

Reaching over, Lady Beatrice refilled her cup from the pot. "Indeed. It sounds interesting Ma, but I have never done a proper paid interior design project. I'm not sure I can."

"Beatrice, stop!" her mother hollered. "Of course you can. You did a beautiful job of Caroline's suite at Knightsbridge Court. And, of course, you did Grandmama's apartment here. She loves it. Your own rooms look fabulous — in keeping with the house, but modern and inviting. Look how you moved a few things around in my sitting room last month, adding some cushions and bringing up some artwork from storage. It feels like a whole new room. You have a natural eye for these things, darling."

"Thank you, but they weren't *proper* projects. I did those because I love interior design, and it's enjoyable to keep my hand in. The Events Suite is a serious proposition, Ma. With the rates Sarah charges to hire it out, the interiors need to be perfect. And they are public rooms. Guests post pictures of them on social media, and Sarah uses them for promotional purposes. It is an enormous responsibility."

"I know, darling, but you will work with Sarah, which will be fun. You won't even need to leave Francis Court, and I'm sure we can keep your involvement low key as far as the press is concerned."

Lady Beatrice stared into the darkness. *Can I do this? What happens if it goes badly? It's an enormous task...*

"Darling, you've gone again!"

"Sorry." Lady Beatrice sighed. "My biggest concern, besides whether I'm good enough—"

The princess huffed at the other end of the line. Lady Beatrice ignored her.

"—is the time frame. Twelve weeks isn't long, and it's a lot for one person, especially with all the ordering and organising required."

"Try not to worry, darling. Sarah has a solution to give you some help. Please keep an open mind and go to lunch with your sister, all right?"

"Yes, Mother, I will."

"Thank you, darling. This is an exciting opportunity for you. I'll speak to you later."

"Thanks, Ma."

Lady Beatrice put the phone down on the table and, pulling her dressing gown belt tighter, she tucked her legs underneath her. *What to do?* Excited at the thought of working on a professional interior design project, she also felt overwhelmed by the responsibility. If it went wrong, then it would be a spectacular failure and a public one at that.

Her phone vibrated.

Sarah: *Hey sis, can we do lunch today at The Station? I'm in Fawstead for a meeting with a po-*

tential supplier for a cheese & wine event next week. I should be done by 12:30. xx

Well, that was quick. Her mother must have called her sister immediately after they'd finished.

Stretching out, she pulled a sleeping Daisy towards her. The dog sighed before settling her head on Lady Beatrice's lap. Stroking Daisy's head, the rhythm soothing, she thought about their conversation.

Her mother had a point. *I need to do something.* And she loved interior design. This could be a great opportunity to test her skills in a safe environment. Sarah and her mother wouldn't let her fail. But whether a failure or a success, this project would launch her back into the limelight. *Am I ready for that?* Would the press continue with their unrelenting speculation on James's accident and his relationship with Gill Sterling? It had happened fourteen years ago, but they couldn't let it rest.

You cannot let it stop you from having a fulfilling purpose. She hated it when her mother was right. She picked up her phone.

She would go to lunch and listen to what Sarah had to say.

· · ·

Bea: *That sounds great, see you there. xx*

When the Daimler pulled up outside The Station in Fawstead, Lady Beatrice unzipped her jacket and made sure her T-shirt was tucked tightly into her jeans. As Ward walked round and opened her door, she took a deep breath and smoothed down her long hair.

Click, click, click. The noise dominated the air as she unfurled herself from the back seat.

How do the press even know we're meeting here? The restaurant probably tipped them off. Even though The Station already had a three-month waiting list and an exclusive clientele, the extra publicity of having royal guests for lunch added to its prestige.

Eyes darting around, Lady Beatrice extended her leg over the curb. Her foot landed on a tartan patterned carpet on the other side. Then the shouting started.

"Lady Beatrice!"

"Over here, Lady Rossex!"

"This way, please!"

Here goes…

She plastered a smile on her face as she stepped

out of the car and focused on the restaurant entrance ten metres ahead of her. Her heart beating fast, her legs wobbly, she tried to ignore the cacophony surrounding her.

She slowly made her way forward.

Her mother frequently expressed her opinion that the approach to The Station was ostentatious. Staring at it now, Lady Beatrice couldn't help but think that maybe she had a point. The wide carpeted walkway covered by a pointed, multi-coloured glass canopy held up by silver metal columns on either side certainly provided a striking first impression. However, from a practical view, the open sides with their red roped posts laid out to keep the press from blocking the entrance, offered guests (and the carpet) little protection from the rain. And Fawstead, being on the east coast, had its fair share of rain. As her mother had put it, "Who wants to step onto a soggy carpet and squelch all the way to the door?" Fortunately, today, the carpet was dry.

"Lady Rossex, it's so good to welcome you to The Station today," the restaurant manager said as he presented himself in front of her, holding his arm out to guide her up the plaid avenue. Following him, she shielded her eyes with one hand as the lights flashed in her face. *Click, click, click.*

"Lady Beatrice, over here!"

"Can you look this way, my lady?"

"Lady Rossex!"

"My lady, this way!"

As she reached the enormous glass doors that led to the restaurant she took another deep breath, then turned to face the press. The glare from their lights made it almost impossible to see. Giving a brief wave, she smiled. *Click, click click.*

Ignoring the cries for more, she rotated on her feet and followed the manager into the peace of the restaurant's foyer. *And breathe...*

Hearing a slight commotion, Lady Beatrice shifted in her chair and peered around the pillar blocking their table from the curious eyes of the other diners. She could see the restaurant manager heading in her direction, followed by her sister, who was taking off her coat and handing it to him. She rose as Lady Sarah rounded the pillar and held her arms out.

Kissing Lady Beatrice on both cheeks, she said, "Sorry I'm late, Bea." She turned to the manager, waiting patiently by her side. "Please, can you make sure we're not disturbed, Mr Watts?"

"Of course, Lady Sarah," he said, holding out

her chair as he wrestled with her coat, trying not to drop it.

Sitting down opposite her, Lady Sarah smiled at her sister and, leaning over, took her hand. "Thank you for coming out to meet me for lunch. I don't know how the press found out. I hope it wasn't too awful for you?"

Lady Beatrice smiled. "It was fine. Mr Watts looked after me, and I noticed Ward had hung back with the car until I was safely inside." Taking a sip of her sparkling water, she sighed. "I don't know why I still find it so daunting going out in public these days. I used to do it every day when James was alive."

Squeezing her hand, Lady Sarah said, "I think you've just answered your own question, Bea."

Lady Beatrice nodded. She had embraced her public duties back then, loving that it allowed her to meet inspiring people and learn new things. And although an inconvenience — and occasionally, when they'd wanted some time alone, a downright pain — she had mostly coped well with the attention of the press. She'd accepted it was part of her job and acknowledged that without the publicity, many of the good causes she felt passionate about would not get the support they needed to survive. But she'd also had James by her side. And even when they'd had separate engagements, when she got home, she'd been able to share the experiences with him, both the good and the bad. *Pull yourself together Bea, your sister is about to offer you an exciting, if a little daunting, opportunity. Move on...*

Lady Beatrice smiled and squeezed her sister's hand before pulling away and picking up the menu. "So, did your cheese meeting go well?"

Lady Sarah puffed out her cheeks and leaned forward. "I think I may have sampled too much," she whispered.

They both giggled.

5

MORNING, FRIDAY 15 JANUARY

The Society Page online article:
Royal Ladies Who Lunch

Yesterday, Lady Sarah Rosdale (38), the eldest daughter of HRH Princess Helen, the Duchess of Arnwall, met up with her sister Lady Beatrice (35), the Countess of Rossex, for a cosy lunch at The Station in Fawstead, the most fashionable place to eat outside of London.

Lady Sarah looked stylish in a cream Max Mara wool wrap coat over a green Balmain button detail knitted dress paired with black Stuart Weitzman suede knee-high boots. Lady Beatrice looked rather more edgy in a black Brunello Cucinelli suede biker jacket over a fitted red Balmain tee with slim black jeans and the highly sought-after Gucci black Frances biker boots which retail at £895.

So what were the sisters discussing? Well, a little dickie bird tells us Lady Beatrice is considering taking on the redesign and refurbishment of the Events Suite at Francis Court. As it is Lady Sarah who runs the events management at Francis Court, the two sisters could be working together soon...

"Morning," Lady Beatrice greeted her brother, Frederick Astley, Earl of Tilling (Fred to his friends), over breakfast the next day. He was fussing Daisy who, like the attention-seeking diva she was, had already flipped onto her back and exposed her tummy for him to tickle. Lady Beatrice rarely made it to breakfast, preferring a coffee in her rooms, but when Fred had rung her late last night to ask if she wanted to meet him in the Breakfast Room in the morning, she had jumped at the chance.

"Morning." He rose to kiss her on both cheeks. "So how are you getting on without Sammy to keep you busy?" he asked as he sat down again.

"I'm doing fine, thanks. I miss him a lot, of

course, but he seems to be settling in well," she replied as she lowered herself onto the chair opposite.

Smiling, she remembered how a recent Tatler article had described Fred as having 'the looks of a Disney prince and the demeanour of James Bond.' They'd ribbed him a lot over it. But all joking aside, it was a fairly accurate summing up of her older brother. Fred was an enigma. He worked for the Foreign Office, having left the British Army two years ago, but she didn't *really* know what he did there. Her father, when describing him to members of his club, Brooks, called him 'a sort of ambassador for the UK'. Her maternal grandmother, Queen Mary The Queen Mother, called him 'a roving fixer', whatever that meant. When she'd asked Fred herself, he'd given her a vague answer of 'some diplomatic stuff' and then he had changed the subject. He spent a lot of time in London, where she presumed he went to work in a government office. The rest of the time, he flew off to various meetings around the world.

Fred patted Daisy on the head. "And are you keeping up with this little lady's training without Sammy here?"

Sam had been doing some advanced training with Daisy under the expert eye of Adrian Breen, the head of security at Francis Court. Previously, Breen had been with Fenshire police, initially as a dog handler but later teaching officers and their dogs detection techniques and search and rescue. Sam, unlike his mother, talked to anyone and everyone around the estate, and during his recent school holiday had been discussing it with Breen. The first Lady Beatrice had known about it was when her son had informed her of how well Daisy's first training session had gone.

Before he'd left for Wilton, he'd taken his mother down to the beach early one morning to show her what they could do. It had impressed Lady Beatrice when Daisy found Sam on command. Then even more so when she obeyed the order, 'Daisy, get help'. Afterwards, she'd promised to carry on with Daisy's training while he was away.

Her brother grinned. "I can tell by the sheepish look on your face, little sis, that you've done nothing yet, have you?"

"Um, no, not yet, but it's only been a few days since Sam left. I'll start it soon." She crossed her fingers under the table.

"Well, you better had, or I'll have to report back to Sammy that you've already broken your promise." He took a piece of toast from his plate and popped it into his mouth. "So what were you and my evil twin talking about over lunch yesterday?"

As he tucked into his breakfast, she told him about Sarah's offer.

"And what did you say?"

"I told her I needed some time to think about it."

"And now I bet you're canvassing everyone in the family to see what they think?"

Lady Beatrice rolled her eyes at him. "Am I so predictable?"

He smiled back at her and shrugged.

She didn't understand why her family found it so odd that she asked them for their opinion before she made major decisions. She valued the input of those around her. They knew her, and she trusted them.

"What did Caro say?" Fred asked, referring to their cousin, Lady Caroline Clifford, and one of Lady Beatrice's closest friends.

"She loved what I did with her apartment and said I have a natural talent for interior design. She thinks the timing is perfect. In fact, she said I would be a chump to say no."

He chuckled. "So she's not sure then?"

Lady Beatrice leaned over and punched him on the arm.

She took a sip of her coffee, then said, "What do you think, Fred?"

"I agree with everything Caro said. In fact, I will go further and say if you don't say yes, I will disown you as my sister."

"So, you're not sure then?" she asked, hastening out of his reach.

"What about Sammy? Have you asked him what he thinks?"

"Of course." She nodded. "I spoke to him last night." She smiled at the memory of her waiting for her excited son to tell her all about his first photography lesson before she could get a word in edgeways. "You can imagine what he said."

"Something like 'go for it, Mum'?" Fred knew his nephew so well.

"Yes, that's almost exactly word for word what he said." They both laughed.

"And what do you think, Bea?"

"It's a tremendous responsibility," she told him, playing with her rings. "Sarah has suggested lending her executive assistant to help me. She says I will then have some moral support and someone who is super organised. Perry Juke has a brilliant eye for design, especially with fabrics, which will be valuable."

Fred nodded. "I agree. He will be a real asset. I'm amazed Sarah is okay to let you borrow him."

"I imagine Ma had something to do with it. She is so desperate for me to do something other than mooch around here like a lost soul. I suspect she told Sarah to release Perry for the project duration, so I have no excuse not to say yes."

Fred picked up his glass of orange juice and raised it in a toast. "Well played, Mother."

6

MID-MORNING, FRIDAY 15 JANUARY

Lady Sarah Rosdale had a spring in her step as she exited the east wing of Francis Court. She'd just received a text from her sister saying she'd take on the project. Skipping down the stone steps, she paused. There was only one thing she needed to do now, and it would not be an easy task. She needed to persuade Perry Juke to work with Bea for the duration of the project.

The few times they'd come into contact, he'd complained to her that Bea had ignored him. Perry *did not* like to be ignored.

Lady Sarah shook her head. Her sister and her executive assistant were chalk and cheese. Open and flamboyant, Perry was happy to be the centre of attention. Whereas Bea, reserved and guarded, was always keen to blend in. But they were both hugely observant and creative, with an enviable sense of style. Lady Sarah was sure they would complement each other. *I just have to convince Perry now.*

Moving on again, she approached the large glass doors of the restaurant. She checked her watch. It was nine-fifty. Breakfast service would finish soon, and the staff would set up for lunch. Not that they were likely to get many of the public in on a bitter January day like today, even if it was sunny. Only the gardens were open at this time of year and the public preferred the cosy atmosphere of the Old Stable Block Cafe to the more formal setting of the Breakfast Room. No matter, the staff would enjoy the food they made, their perk of having a free breakfast and lunch.

As she came level with the doors, they flew open. A woman burst out, her head down, and slammed into her. Teetering on her feet, Lady Sarah shifted to keep her balance. She reached out and grabbed the woman before she fell over, too.

"Ellie, what's the hurry?" Lady Sarah asked as she steadied them both.

"I'm so sorry, Lady Sarah," Francis Court's catering manager said with a catch in her voice. "I didn't see you."

Lady Sarah tilted her head, trying to get a look

at her face, but she couldn't see it under the long fringe of Ellie's mid-length brown hair.

"Are you all right, Ellie?"

"I'm fine, my lady, but I'm in a hurry. I have a meeting, and I don't want to be late. Please excuse me."

Frowning, Lady Sarah said, "Of course, Ellie, off you go."

As Ellie rushed ahead of her along the terrace and down the stone stairs towards the Old Stable Block, Lady Sarah wondered if she should call her back, but Ellie's body language had been screaming, *leave me alone*. She would leave it for now, but check in on her later.

About to continue on her way, she halted when the doors from the Breakfast Room opened again and this time Alex Sterling, the estate manager, came charging out. He looked around scowling, before spotting Lady Sarah. With a tight smile, he said, "Good morning, Lady Sarah."

She smiled back. *Ah, that all makes sense now.* Alex and Ellie's relationship was the worst kept secret at Francis Court. They must have had an argument. "Good morning, Alex. Are you looking for someone?"

He hesitated. "Not especially, my lady. Please excuse me. I need to get over to the staff cottages to see about some damage to the Harris's cottage after the weekend's storm."

"Of course, Alex, please carry on."

Giving her a curt bow, he strode off towards the long drive, which led to some of the staff cottages.

Lady Sarah looked over at the Breakfast Room doors, waiting to see if anyone else would come dashing out. Nothing happened. She checked her chignon of brown hair was still intact, then headed off across the terrace and down the stone steps towards her office. Within a few minutes, she was walking across the cobbled courtyard inside the rear of the Old Stable Block towards the management suite. To her right, someone had parked a tractor with a trailer attached outside a large, open barn referred to as the gardening shed.

Sighing, she shook her head. She had spoken frequently to Seth Padgett, the head gardener, about ensuring they didn't park the gardening vehicles in view while the grounds were open to the public. Even though the roped off courtyard had a large *Private* sign displayed, the public could see into it. As she had pointed out to him, it only took a few extra minutes to park them in an adjacent building. Annoyed, she marched into the barn to have a word with whomever had left the vehicle outside.

As she entered the double-height building, she

squinted in the subdued light. She could just make out the outline of two men standing at the far end. She strode towards them, then stopped and frowned, having recognised the back of the man talking to the head gardener.

She shook her head in confusion.

Alex had just been heading towards the staff cottages in the opposite direction. *How did he get here without passing me?*

As she moved closer, the *click, click* of her high-heeled Jimmy Choo court shoes alerted the men to her presence, and they turned towards her. She smiled. It wasn't Alex, after all. It was Pete Cowley, one of the gardeners. She was astounded at how similar they looked from the back — same stocky build, same height, same shaven head. It was only when Pete turned and she saw his beard that she could see it wasn't Alex.

"Lady Sarah," the other man said, giving a brief bow. "What can we do for you?"

"Ah Seth, Pete, can I ask one of you to move the tractor and trailer out of sight, please? We have talked about this before, Seth. It looks untidy if the public sees them outside."

"Of course, my lady, my apologies," the head gardener replied.

Pete interjected, "Lady Sarah, sorry, it's my

fault. I was popping back to pick up some fertiliser. I only expected to be a few minutes, then we started talking about the plans for the kitchen garden planting and I lost track of the time."

He smiled at her, and she smiled back, feeling bad about having come in all guns blazing. They were lucky at Francis Court to have such a dedicated team of gardeners; she didn't want to upset them. "Of course, Pete, I understand. If you won't be much longer, it can stay where it is. Please carry on."

She followed the light out of the gardening shed and into the courtyard, where she turned right and continued towards the offices.

Perry Juke was finishing an email when he looked up from his computer screen. The elegant form of Lady Sarah Rosdale was purposefully walking his way. After quickly hitting send, he closed his laptop, ready to give her his full attention.

"Hello Perry," Lady Sarah greeted him as she halted in front of his desk. Clearing her throat, she asked, "How is your morning going?"

Lady Sarah always started a conversation with a well-appointed personal enquiry. They were both aware that it was something she did to be polite. She wanted to connect with her staff on a more personal level rather than rushing straight into business. Whether she was interested in the answer was unclear. Sometimes Perry considered giving her a detailed report of his morning, but he never did. He enjoyed working with Lady Sarah and didn't want to upset her. Today, he could tell from the way she was biting her bottom lip that she had something she needed to get off her chest. It would be cruel to make her wait.

"It's been fine, thank you, Sarah."

She smiled and gracefully lowered herself into the chair opposite him. "So, Perry, I have a favour to ask you, and I'll be honest, I'm not sure you'll be ecstatic about it. But if it helps, I don't think it will be as awful as you think it will be." She interlocked her fingers and placed her hands on her lap.

Perry stroked his clean-shaven chin. Lady Sarah had blurted out the sentence without appearing to take a breath. "Okay, I'm getting worried now, Sarah"—he leaned in towards her—"what on earth do you need me to do?"

She crossed her arms. Before she could open her mouth to reply, Perry continued, a smile spreading over his face. "Do you need me to pose naked for the latest promotional photos for our wedding brochure? Because you know I'll do it if you ask me, don't you?"

She uncrossed her arms and broke into an enormous grin. "I know you will, you floozy." She laughed. "But it's nothing like that." She shifted in her seat. "I've asked Lady Beatrice to do the interior design for the new-look Events Suite."

Perry stiffened, his back rigid against his seat. "Really?" He raised an eyebrow and stared at her. "I wasn't aware she took on proper interior design projects as substantial as this."

Lady Sarah cringed. "Well, she hasn't before, but she did study interior design at university and has worked on quite a few jobs for members of the family. She recently refurbished Lady Caroline Clifford's apartment in Knightsbridge Court. It looks marvellous."

Perry pushed his chair away from his desk and crossed his arms and legs.

Shrugging, she continued nervously, "Anyway, she said yes."

Perry cleared his throat. "Well, I'm sure you know what you're doing, Sarah, but why are you telling me?"

Lady Sarah shifted in her seat again. "I want you to work with her, Perry. We have a little over twelve weeks before the grand opening on the first of May. We can't expect her to get this project completed on time without some help."

Perry uncrossed his arms and legs and moved his chair forward. He leaned in. "When you say 'work with her'"—he air quoted the words—"do you mean help her with design choices and ordering goods? Or do you mean be at her beck and call for the next three months, doing all the donkey work?"

He reclined and recrossed his arms.

"I see you working as a team, Perry. I believe you and she will do well together. And you are amazing with fabrics, so you'll have the chance to contribute to the overall look," she replied in a soothing tone. "This could be a great opportunity for you to get some design work under your belt."

Perry sighed. "And is she okay with that? Will she listen to me and let me contribute to the design? Because I'm not sure she even knows who I am, Sarah."

"Of course she knows who you are," Lady Sarah said in a pacifying voice.

Perry shook his head. "The most I've ever had from her has been a nod of her head and an insincere smile."

Lady Sarah raked her teeth over her bottom lip. "Perry, I'm sorry you feel that way. She really is lovely when you get to know her, I promise. She's just wary of people she doesn't know, and she goes into 'meeting the public' mode, which can come across as aloof and disconnected."

Perry huffed.

"You'll be surprised at how well you two will get on. Just give her some time." Leaning over the desk, she put her hand on the sleeve of his beautifully tailored Paul Smith suit jacket. "And you would do me a great favour, Perry."

Lady Sarah squeezed his arm gently and smiled, then she dropped her hand and smoothed down the skirt of her dress.

Perry moved back in his chair and put his hands out, palms up.

"Okay, Sarah, I'll do it for you. But I'm warning you now, if she treats me like her personal slave, I will never speak to you again!"

Crossing the Old Stable Block courtyard, Perry Juke was grateful the working day was over. Since his conversation with Lady Sarah that morning, he had been keen to go home and talk to his partner, Simon. If anyone could put it into perspective for him, it was Simon. That was why they were such a strong team — Perry, the spontaneous, over-the-top showman and Simon, his anchor, who never crushed Perry's personality but gently reined him in for his own good.

He rounded the north-west corner of the Old Stable Block and turned right, passing in front of the garden centre, gift shop, and cafe. It was five in the evening, and they were all unlit and shut up for the day.

Approaching the west wing of the main house, he ran up the stone stairs leading to the lower terrace framing the front of the house. He reached the French doors and peered into the Garden Room.

Dark-green striped wallpaper met walnut wooden panelling halfway down the wall. There was an eclectic selection of sofas and chairs arranged around coffee tables and rugs. There was a smattering of lamps, trays and candles on occasional tables and sideboards, and an art deco cocktail cabinet by the window on his right-hand side.

Sarah is right, it looks tired and out of date — like the theatre set of a country house farce.

If he was honest, he would love to be part of transforming it into something current and fabulous. *If only it didn't involve working with Lady Sarah's stuck-up younger sister.*

Continuing along the terrace and past the Smoking Room, he descended the stone steps back onto the gravel path. As the icy wind whipped across him, he stuffed his hands in the pockets of his Rubinacci blue cashmere Ulster coat. Turning left, he worked his way along the path leading to the north side gate. When he approached the security office, there was a *click* of the lock releasing, and he pushed open the metal gate in front of him.

"Goodnight, Mr Juke. I've signed you out." Jeff Beesley, the late shift lead security guard, raised a hand from the open window of the office.

Perry responded in kind. "Thanks, Jeff. Have a quiet shift."

Striding along the gravel path that connected Francis Court with the village of Francis-next-the-Sea, he inhaled the salty air as he reached the village green. The slight headache he had been nursing all afternoon disappeared. He turned left at the corner of the road, then walked past three cottages. He was about to open the gate to the fourth, Rose Cottage, when he caught a movement in his peripheral vision.

He turned his head in time to see Ellie Gunn hurrying across the green. To Perry's surprise, she didn't turn right towards Daffodil Cottage, which she had rented from him since she'd left her husband three years ago. Instead, she headed for The Ship and Seal, Francis-next-the-Sea's only pub. As she disappeared into the warm inviting glow he thought about asking Simon if he fancied popping over to the pub to join her.

Just then, a blue BMW turned into the pub car park. Alex Sterling unfolded himself out of the driver's seat and made his way inside. *No doubt off to meet Ellie. Maybe I won't suggest going to the pub then. I don't want to disturb the happy couple.*

Turning, he scampered up the path to Rose Cottage. As he entered the house, the comforting smell of homemade bread enveloped him. He smiled.

He was home.

A glass of merlot in hand and a plate of Simon's homemade beef lasagne in front of him, Perry leaned across the dining table, took Simon's hand in his and planted a light kiss on his partner's fingertips.

"Thanks for this, love. It looks delicious, as always."

"After I received your call-to-action text earlier, I had to do something," Simon replied, squeezing Perry's hand and smiling at him.

Letting go, Perry tore off a chunk of focaccia

from the still warm loaf in the centre of the table. As they ate, he told Simon of Lady Sarah's request.

"That's great news. You love interior design, and it will be prestigious to have your name attached to such a high-profile project." Simon raised his glass to his partner. "I'm very proud of you."

"I knew you would see the positive aspect of it, love, but didn't you hear what I said? I'll have to work with snooty Lady Rossex."

"Why do you call her that? I thought you rarely had anything to do with her," Simon said, taking some bread for himself.

"But I see her around Francis Court, and she rarely engages with any of the staff. She wanders around with her cute dog, too good for the likes of us." Perry stuck his nose up in the air and sniffed. He took another mouthful of lasagne.

Simon sighed. "I think you're being a little unfair. Maybe she's simply shy and guarded around people. After everything she went through with her husband's death, I wouldn't be surprised."

Perry's eyes lit up. "Did you have any dealings with her when you were investigating her husband's death?"

"No, not directly." Simon shook his head. "It was only my second case since I'd transferred to CID. But I did feel sorry for her. She was even younger than me, and her husband had died in un-explained circumstances. Did you know he was supposed to have been in London overnight and wasn't due back until the next day?"

Perry nodded. "I read that somewhere."

"So she was in shock and overwhelmed. On top of that, she was pregnant, although she said nothing at the time. The press coverage was extensive and relentless. They wanted to know the ins and outs of the investigation and persisted in speculating why Gill Sterling was in the car. It must have been really hard for her to deal with."

Perry put his fork down and wiped his mouth with a napkin. "Well, when you put it like that, yes, I can see why she wanted to keep to herself. But it has been fourteen years. You would think she'd be over it by now."

"The entire experience probably had a lasting impact on her, especially since the PaIRS guys were rather tough on her."

"Who are the pairs guys?"

"Sorry, they're the Protection and Investigation (Royal) Service. They're a division of the City Police who protect the royal family." When Perry nodded, Simon continued, "Between their questioning and the press being camped out here for months, it must have been awful for her and the family."

Perry let out a low moan. "Okay, I'm sorry. I hadn't thought about it like that." He gave Simon a tentative grin. "But now that you've firmly put me in my box, if I promise to play nice with her, can we have dessert, please?"

Laughing, Simon got up and went to the fridge. He returned with a most spectacular chocolate mousse cake topped with whipped cream and chocolate chips.

As Simon placed it on the table, Perry's phone buzzed.

Lady S: *Will you meet me and Lady Beatrice at the Breakfast Room at 8:30 tomorrow morning so we can start? I'll buy you breakfast...*

Perry gazed at the pile of chocolate heaven in front of him, his mouth watering. A huge grin spread across his face. He picked up his phone.

Perry: *I would be delighted. See you in the morning.*

7

EARLY MORNING, TUESDAY 6 APRIL

The Society Page online article:

The Duke and Duchess of Arnwall and Family Join the Rest of the Royal Family for the Traditional Easter Celebrations at Fenn House.

Charles Astley, The Duke of Arnwall, and his wife, HRH Princess Helen, along with their three children and their families, spent Easter Sunday at Fenn House with King James and Queen Olivia. Members of the royal family, as is traditional, walked the short distance from the house to the church for the Easter Sunday service.

After the service, they stopped to say hello to the crowds that had gathered along the route. It was the first time Samuel Wiltshire (13) has greeted members of the public, and the crowds were clearly pleased to see the king's great nephew and the future Earl of Durrland in person, many offering him flowers and flags.

The Astley family stayed for most of Easter Sunday at Fenn House, enjoying a five-course Sunday lunch sourced from local producers, including lamb raised on the Fenn House estate. The Astley family returned to Francis Court in the early evening.

The renovation and refurbishment of the Events Suite at Francis Court is now almost finished with just two rooms, which did not require structural changes, left to complete. We look forward to seeing the final look at the official opening on the first of May.

With Daisy at her heels, Lady Beatrice advanced across to the Old Stable Block Cafe buried in her Moncler quilted parka, her hands in her pockets. She marvelled at how she had acclimatised to being in the public areas at Francis Court without feeling on edge all the time. Before she had started on this project, she could count on one hand the number of times she had been in the cafe since it had opened six years ago. But over the last few months, she had challenged herself to walk around the grounds of Francis Court, sometimes with someone else but sometimes just with Daisy. And, she admitted now, her mother had been right. *Isn't she always?* When she walked with confidence, asserting her right to wander around her home, she found the public respected her privacy.

As she opened the door to the cafe, Daisy darted in and ran straight to Perry, who was sitting at a table in a side alcove. The cafe was quiet, even though it was lunchtime. With the house closed until the first of May, and following a wet and windy start to April, it was only the dog walkers and season ticket holders who visited the gardens on a day like today.

Removing her coat, Lady Beatrice headed to where Perry was sitting. Seth Padgett, Joe Fox, the gardening apprentice, and Pete Cowley, were having a coffee and sandwich at a table on the other side of the alcove. By the time she arrived, Daisy was already sitting by Perry's side, her gaze on the uneaten sandwich on his plate. On the table, in front of an empty chair opposite him, sat a large black coffee.

"Hello, Perry. Sorry I'm late. I came here via the north side entrance so I could see what state the outside of the Garden Room and the Smoking

Room are in. Is that for me?" She pointed to the coffee. He nodded, and rubbing her hands together she sat down. "Thank you. That's very thoughtful."

How different things are between us now compared to our first meeting. Then, Perry, who'd been sitting bolt upright opposite her, looking immaculately dressed in a stylish blue Ted Baker suit, had been stony-faced and unsmiling. He'd given her the distinct impression that he was only there as a favour to Sarah, remaining polite and business-like throughout their breakfast. He had insisted on referring to her as Lady Rossex, even after she had asked him to call her Lady Beatrice. Today, he had ordered her a coffee, just as she liked it. Watching him offering Daisy a piece of meat from his chicken salad sandwich, she couldn't help but smile at how far they had come.

Perry patted Daisy on the head and straightened up. "How is it looking along the front of the terrace?"

"The good news is they look like they've finished cleaning the leaded windows and touching up the frames of the French doors. They look amazing. The bad news is the ugly tarpaulin tent is still in front of both rooms."

He nodded. "I think that's because the restorers

don't want debris getting on them while they're wet, especially in this wind."

"Indeed. Although I was hoping they would be dry by now. We need to start in one of those rooms tomorrow if we're going to finish on time. I can't imagine how we'll manage if we can't move the sofas and bigger pieces of furniture out through those French doors." Shaking her head, she grabbed her coffee, taking a big gulp.

Holding up a finger towards her, he said, "Give me a minute." He picked up his radio. "Charles, this is Perry Juke, over."

There was a crackle from the handset, followed by a loud whine. Seth Padgett shouted *sorry* from the next table and turned down the volume on his radio.

"This is Charles, Mr Juke. What can I do for you, over?"

"Charles, when do you think you will be done with the French doors in the Garden Room and Smoking Room and the tarpaulin removed, over?"

"Mr Juke, we've finished. We're just waiting for everything to dry thoroughly and then we can take the tarp down. It should be completed by lunchtime tomorrow. Is that okay, over?"

Perry looked at Lady Beatrice and she mouthed 'perfect' to him.

"Charles, that's great. Thank you, out."

Lady Beatrice smiled. "Thank you, Perry. So do you agree we should start in the Garden Room? We can mark up everything early, and then Alex can organise a team to move the furniture and distribute it as we did with previous rooms. They can take the smaller pieces first and move the larger items once the tarpaulin has gone."

"That works for me, my lady. I'll give Alex a ring when I return to my office. I'll also ring the decorators and set them up for Thursday. The paint and the wallpaper for the Garden Room are here already, so they can start straight away once the room is clear."

He slipped Daisy his last bit of sandwich and she gobbled it up. As he moved his chair out from the table to cross his legs, she jumped up onto his lap.

"Aw, Daisy." He kissed the top of her head. "I wish I could believe you want to sit on my lap because you love me, but we both know you're after the crumbs on the table. You're a food monster, little girl — albeit an adorable one." He rubbed the top of her head and she attempted to lick him. Daisy had become notably attached to Perry over these last few months, and not just because he'd shared his food with her.

"Food monster, indeed," Lady Beatrice responded, shaking her head. "She's obsessed."

Perry laughed as Daisy continued to try to lick him. With the noise of chairs scraping on the floor, Seth, Pete, and Joe stood up from their table and headed towards the door.

"Oh, Seth," Perry called out. All three men stopped and turned towards him. "We're planning to move the furniture in the Garden Room tomorrow, starting at ten. I'll confirm with Alex later, but we're hoping you, Joe, and Pete will be free to help."

"Yes, Mr Juke," Seth replied. "We're ready to go. Alex has already warned us we'll be needed to move some furniture in the Events Suite this week. I've planned around it, so we will crack on with it as soon as we're required."

"That's great, Seth. We'll see you tomorrow." Perry smiled.

Turning to Lady Beatrice, Seth nodded and said, *"My lady,"* before leading his team out of the cafe.

She turned to Perry. "I'm looking forward to getting started in the Garden Room tomorrow."

"Me too. It feels like we're on the final straight now. The styling is totally my favourite bit." He clapped his hands together. "I can't wait to see the

Christian Lacroix *Jardin Des Reves* wallpaper up. It'll be a showstopper."

Loving Perry's enthusiasm, she smiled. "I hope my sister doesn't have a heart attack when she sees it. It's bolder than it looked on the mood board."

"She'll love it, don't worry." His eyes shining bright with excitement, he rose. "Shall we meet in the Breakfast Room at eight-thirty tomorrow morning? We're going to be rushed off our feet and I, for one, would like to tackle the day on a full stomach."

"Yes, of course. Daisy will be delighted. Other people's breakfast is her favourite meal, isn't it, Daisy-Doo?" Daisy looked up at her mistress, her tail wagging.

Taking a sip of her coffee, Lady Beatrice watched Perry stroll out of the cafe and smiled. She enjoyed their coffee catchups outside of the office. After their rocky start, these relaxed meetings had been vital in cementing their pleasant working relationship. And, even if she said so herself, they had done well so far. The rooms already completed looked amazing, and she was proud of what they had achieved.

I just hope these two remaining rooms go as smoothly.

8

8:30 AM, WEDNESDAY 7 APRIL

A small carriage clock sitting on a large wooden sideboard chimed as Lady Beatrice and Daisy walked across the black and white titled floor of the Painted Hall and exited through the south side door. Although the early morning sun had broken through the clouds, its rays didn't offer any warmth. Pulling her Burberry puffer jacket tightly around herself, she tucked her head into the collar and fought against the wind as she proceeded towards the grand glass doors of the Breakfast Room.

The cosy warmth of the indoors was welcome. Heading towards a table by a window in the far corner, she removed her coat.

She looked around. The Breakfast Room was nearly empty. Retail staff wouldn't be in until nine-thirty. The only inhabitants were Seth and Joe, who were sitting a few tables away. She waved at them, and they waved back as she took her seat. Catching the eye of Nicky, one of the servers, Lady Beatrice waited for her to come over.

"Good morning, Daisy." Nicky patted the little white terrier's head. Lady Beatrice smiled. All the staff greeted Daisy before her. "Good morning, my lady. What can I get you?" Nicky asked, taking her notepad out of her apron pocket.

"Good morning, Nicky. I'll have my usual large black coffee, please. Could I also have a cappuccino and—" She picked up her phone to check the message Perry had sent her a few minutes ago asking her to order breakfast for him. "Scrambled egg and smoked salmon on toast for Mr Juke, please."

"Of course, my lady. Thank you."

The main doors opened, and Pete Cowley entered. He looked around the room briefly before heading to where Seth and Joe were sitting. "Good morning, my lady," he said as he passed her. She smiled and returned his greeting.

Perry entered the room from the back door, which led to the kitchen, various offices, and the Events Suite. He waved to Seth, Joe, and Pete, calling *morning* as he made his way across the room to join Lady Beatrice. As soon as he was close enough, Daisy shuffled forward, her tail going like the clappers, and threw herself at his feet.

"Good morning, Daisy." He squatted down and rubbed her tummy. "How's my favourite girl?"

Raising his gaze from Daisy, he smiled at Lady Beatrice. "Good morning, my lady. All set for a busy day of styling and being fabulous?" he asked.

She nodded, grinning, as he sat down opposite her. Daisy settled down by his side. Not, Lady Beatrice noted, her side but his side. "Good morning, Perry. Yes, I'm looking forward to it. I've ordered your breakfast and coffee; it should be here shortly. How was your evening?"

Although at the start of this project she had taken part in 'the niceties' as a means to an end, now she was genuinely interested in his response.

"Well, Simon cooked an amazing chicken dish he's been experimenting with." He licked his lips. "I can safely say he's perfected it now." He grinned. "Then he went back to his writing, and I watched a show on television about people who want to buy houses on the coast in America for less than three-hundred-thousand dollars and still have a beach view." Perry was addicted to watching television reality shows. "How about you, my lady? Did you fit in a run on the beach before the wind became too strong?"

"Indeed. It was certainly blustery, but I managed about five kilometres before giving up. Then Daisy and I returned to the calm of the house, and I had a FaceTime call with Sam."

"And has he settled down okay?"

"Yes. He's happy to be back at school. He'd missed playing sports during the holidays. In fact, he's been training for an upcoming rugby match against a local school." She twisted her wedding ring around her finger. "He was so excited, but all I could think about were the various ways he could get hurt."

"You worry too much, Lady Beatrice. He'll be fine."

"Yes, I know. What matters is he's happy." She rolled her eyes at him and smiled. "But I'd rather he was happy without a broken nose."

Perry shook his head and laughed.

Nicky came over, delivering their drinks and Perry's food. Placing an extra plate on the table with two rashers of bacon on, she said, "This is for Daisy." She smiled down at the little dog, getting a tail wag in return.

"You are the most spoilt dog in the universe,

Daisy-Doo," Lady Beatrice said as she broke a rasher into small pieces and gave her one.

"It's just as well she goes for a run with you every day or she'd be the size of an elephant," Perry said as he smiled down at Daisy.

"Indeed."

"Oh, I forgot to say that Mrs C wasn't in her office, so I didn't pick up the keys for the Garden Room. We'll have to collect them on our way there after we're done here."

"That's fine." Looking around the room, she said, "I thought Sarah was meeting us for breakfast today?"

"Yes, me too. I popped my head around her door when I arrived first thing and she said she'd meet us here."

"Where is she then?" She stood up and looked out of the windows. There was no sign of her sister. She shrugged. "No doubt she'll turn up soon. So, tell me about this television show you watched last night. Did they find their dream home by the sea?"

They chatted for the next fifteen minutes while Perry ate, and Lady Beatrice fed tiny morsels of bacon to an appreciative Daisy. As she was about to suggest they started their work, her sister came in through the French doors. Strands of her long brown hair had escaped from its chignon and were hanging by the side of her flushed cheeks.

"Sorry I'm late. I was tied up in the office on a rather lengthy call," Lady Sarah explained as she unbuckled the belt on her Versace camel coat, removed it, and wrapped it around the back of her chair. She sat down, smoothing out her black Jil Sander wool dress and pushed the stray hairs back in place. "It's really windy out there." She looked around the room and waved at Nicky.

Lady Beatrice glanced at her phone. It was almost nine. "I'm sorry, sis, but we need to get on. We still have to mark up the contents before Alex and his team arrive at ten to remove what we don't want."

"Of course. I'll look in on you later and see how you're doing."

Nicky arrived at the table. "What would you like, Lady Sarah?" she asked as, once again, she bent down to pat Daisy's head. Daisy, who was now so full of bacon she was lying by Lady Bea's feet not moving, managed a feeble tail wag.

"Hello, Nicky. A large latte, two slices of toast with butter, and some of the lovely lime marmalade, if you have any, please."

"I think there's still some left, my lady. I'll check." With a smile, she headed for the kitchen.

As Lady Beatrice got to her feet, Daisy raised one eyebrow and stared at her, reluctant to move.

"You can leave her here with me if you'd like," her sister offered, looking down at Daisy. "I'll take her back to the office when I've finished here, and you can pick her up later. At least she won't be a distraction for the boys while they're moving heavy furniture around."

"That would be helpful, Sarah. Thank you." She turned to her little white terrier. "Daisy"—the dog raised her head off the floor and tilted it to one side —"stay with Aunty Sarah," Lady Beatrice told her as she crouched down and kissed the top of Daisy's head.

Moving away from the table, Lady Beatrice paused and looked back. Perry was staring at his empty coffee cup, a frown creasing his forehead. "Come on, Perry, we need to get on."

As if awoken from a trance, he jumped up, nodded to Lady Sarah, and followed Lady Beatrice out of the restaurant.

Lady Beatrice and Perry left the Breakfast Room through the back door. As they turned off the wooden panelled corridor and walked into Sophie

Crammond's office, they found the head house-keeper sitting at her desk, looking slightly flushed.

"Hello, Lady Rossex, Perry. I assume you're here to collect the key for the Garden Room. It's today you're clearing it out, isn't it?" When Perry nodded, she added, "Give me two seconds. I have it ready." She rose from her desk, extracted a set of keys from a bunch around her waist and unlocked a key safe on the wall behind her.

"Here you go," she said as she handed Perry the key and pushed the log in front of him to sign. "I hope it all goes well."

"Thank you, Mrs Crammond," Lady Beatrice replied, as Perry scribbled his signature. "We're hopefully nearing the end now."

They left her office and continued down the corridor. Turning left and passing the Smoking Room on their right, they arrived outside the grandiose, heavy doors of the Garden Room. Perry put the key in the lock, then turned to Lady Beatrice in confusion. He pushed the door open without turning the key.

"That's strange." He frowned, shaking his head. "The door is unlocked." Lady Beatrice shrugged, and they entered.

It was dim inside. The tarpaulin, still over the French doors, was blocking out the natural light.

Reaching over, Lady Beatrice switched on the main lights, and they stepped forward into the room. She walked the few steps to the sideboard and dropped her radio on the top before turning round abruptly when Perry made a noise like a mouse being strangled.

"Oh my giddy aunt!" Perry Juke slapped his hand up to his mouth, his face turning pale as he gawped at the body in front of them.

"Oh my giddy aunt, indeed." Lady Beatrice, the Countess of Rossex, replied.

There was a click as the flash on Perry's camera phone went off.

Dragging her gaze away from the spread-eagled form in front of her, she looked over at Perry and yelled, "What on earth are you doing?"

"I think Simon would appreciate some photos of a real dead body. You know, for a future book."

She stared at him, her mouth open in horror.

"Perry, behave please. We need to know if he's *actually* dead. Shouldn't we check for a pulse?"

"Go ahead, my lady," he replied as he took another couple of shots.

She cleared her throat. "Well, I don't know what

to do. There are always people around me who deal with situations like this." She coloured slightly and looked down at her boots.

"Always people around? Do you stumble across corpses on a daily basis, my lady? Or is it more like a weekly—"

"Perry."

"Okay." He grinned before the light in his eyes slowly died. Edging over to the body, he picked up the man's wrist. He stood there for a moment, staring into space before shaking his head. "He's definitely dead."

Lady Beatrice breathed out slowly, then reached behind her and picked up her radio, switching it to the security only channel. "Adrian, this is Lady Rossex, over."

The response from the other end was immediate. "My lady, this is Adrian Breen. Is something wrong, over?"

"Yes, Adrian. Please come to the Garden Room immediately, over."

"Roger that, my lady. I'm on my way now, over."

"Oh, and Adrian, you'd better call the police, out."

She put the radio down and looked at Perry, who was bending over the body, his arm reaching…

"Perry, don't touch anything!" she cried. He looked up at her, his head tilted to one side.

"Okay, Miss Marple."

She rolled her eyes in response. They both relaxed a little.

Her gaze darted back to the blood. What was that famous Shakespeare quote? '*Who would have thought the old man would have so much blood in him*' — *or something like that?* Looking at the side of his head and the rug, she had expected there to be more. She shook herself. How would she know? Thankfully, this was her first, and she hoped, her last 'in situ' dead body. They hadn't let her see James after his accident. She was grateful for that.

"Is it me or is it hot in here?" Perry asked, saving her from her thoughts. Unbuttoning the suit jacket of his maroon Burberry wool suit, he glanced at the radiator by the sideboard.

Lady Beatrice moved over and touched it. *Ouch.* "The heating is full on." She turned the controls down and moved slowly towards the body.

"Who do you think it is?" she asked.

He studied it for a bit. "Alex Sterling?"

She nodded.

They stood there for a few minutes in silence. A wave of sadness washed over her. She hadn't known Alex particularly well. In fact, she avoided him when she could, feeling awkward around him after his wife had died in her husband's car. Even so, it was tragic to see someone previously so full of life reduced to a bloody mess on a hundred-year-old rug.

Flash! Perry was taking more photos.

"Perry," she hissed, beckoning him over. He put his phone in his jacket pocket and joined her. She pointed at the table in front of the French doors. "Does that table look odd to you?"

He tilted his head to one side. "What do you mean by odd?"

She shook her head. "I'm not sure exactly. It just doesn't look right to me. Can you take a photo? And then we should lock up and leave."

He looked at her in surprise, then pulled his phone back out and took a couple more shots.

She grabbed his arm. "Come on, we need to go. Adrian and the police will be here soon."

"I need some air," Lady Beatrice said as she rushed down the corridor and hurried across the Salon, Perry following her. As they exited through the north side door, the refreshing breeze revived her after the stuffiness of the overheated Garden Room.

She leaned against the stone balustrade of the terrace steps and took a deep breath. Perry did the same.

Lady Beatrice smiled reassuringly at him before turning to look towards the main gate. She could see Adrian Breen and one of the other security guards running towards them. A rush of relief washed over her. She wanted to hand this problem over to someone else as soon as she could. *I need a large black coffee.*

Her eyes widened as a tractor towing a trailer came out of the clearing behind the trees, aiming for the two men. She gasped. *It's going to hit them! Oh no, not more dead bodies to deal with.* She wanted to close her eyes, but she was transfixed by the scene playing out before her. The driver slammed on his brakes at the same time as the two men swerved to avoid the obstacle. She let out a breath she didn't even realise she was holding. *Phew!* The men were still running in her direction. Shaking his head, the driver climbed out of the tractor and went to inspect the trailer. A mass of tree debris had fallen from the back when he had completed his emergency stop. He bent over and slowly scooped the pile back up onto the trailer.

9

JUST BEFORE 10 AM, WEDNESDAY 7 APRIL

Lady Beatrice unzipped her jacket and raised her face to the sun. The wind had calmed down now, and she closed her eyes, feeling the warmth spreading over her skin. *If it wasn't for the dead body, it would be a lovely day today.*

She opened her eyes and looked around her. On her far left, towards the Old Stable Block, she could see a figure organising a collection of second-hand books on a table outside the gift shop. Next door to that, outside the garden centre, one of the staff was arranging plants on a stand; herbs grown in Francis Court's kitchen garden were always popular with the public. Just by the side of the display, wooden tables and chairs were being laid out in front of the cafe. Above this, further over in the distance, smoke rose from a bonfire. *Probably someone burning branches.* The high winds had made a bit of a mess of the place these last few days.

That is the thing about death. Everyone not directly affected continues, business as usual. She remembered when James had died, how she'd wanted the world to stop. How she'd needed it to wait, so she had time to catch her breath. But it had carried on. Someone's death was nothing more than a sad hiccup on the path of everyone else's life.

She glanced over at Perry on the other side of the stone steps. He was leaning on the balustrade, talking on his phone. *Probably to Simon.* He was whispering his responses, as if death could hear him and would disapprove of the noise.

Ending the call, he walked over to stand beside her. "I was bringing Simon up to date," he explained, still talking in a hushed tone.

"What do you think happened, Perry?" she asked. "It all seems strange to me."

He frowned. "Well, I assume he had a heart attack or something caused him to fall. He then hit his head on the ugly marble table, which finished him off. What is it that's bothering you?"

She frowned and shook her head. "What you're suggesting makes perfect sense, but there's something about the room that seemed off to me. It was different to how it had looked the last time we were in there a few days ago, but I can't put my finger on what it is."

"Well, as far as I know, no one has moved or taken anything out of the room since." He snatched his radio from the step beside him. "I must let Seth and the boys know not to come over to move the furniture." He glanced at his watch. "I'm surprised they're not here yet. It's almost ten." Pressing the buttons on the radio, he said, "Seth, it's Perry, over."

While Perry filled them in, Lady Beatrice meandered down two stone steps. She looked towards the main entrance. *Where is Adrian Breen?* He'd said he was going to meet Fenshire CID when he'd passed her a few minutes ago on his way back from the Garden Room. The sun had gone behind the clouds. Shivering, she zipped up her coat. *I wish they would get a move on.*

She glanced up. In the distance a black Volvo came into view, creeping up the tarmac path, Adrian Breen trotting behind. He caught up as the car stopped and two men stepped out of the back. As the car carried on towards the car park, the trio made their way towards her.

Suddenly, she caught something out of the corner of her eye. Turning her head, she saw Alfie, her parents' five-year-old border terrier, running across from the Old Stable Block. *I bet he's seen a rabbit or a deer.* He dived into the clearing in front of the west wing and disappeared.

Returning her gaze to the three men approaching, she smiled. She thought she recognised the thickset grey-haired man talking to Adrian. He looked familiar to her.

"Lady Rossex, how nice to see you again." He stopped one step below her and offered her his hand. She took it and smiled back.

"Mike, what a pleasant surprise. Are you with CID now?" she asked.

Turning to Perry and Adrian, she explained, "Mike was the self-defence instructor on the kidnapping awareness course which Sarah and I attended a few years ago." Adrian nodded, but Perry still had a frown of confusion on his face.

"Mike, this is Perry Juke. He's been working with me on the Events Suite refurbishment."

Mike and Perry shook hands. "Detective Inspector Mike Ainsley, Fenshire CID. Watch out for this one." The inspector nodded in Lady Beatrice's direction. "She could lay you out in seconds."

Perry's head whipped round to stare at her in astonishment, while Adrian and Mike chuckled.

"So you've had a promotion then, Mike? Congratulations."

"Thank you, my lady. Yes, they offered me a chance to move to CID about a year ago."

"This is Detective Sergeant Eamon Hines." He gestured to the shorter, slighter man standing two steps below. DS Hines nodded at them in acknowledgment.

"I understand you and Mr Juke discovered the body, Lady Rossex?" Mike asked.

"Yes, we were due to move the contents of the Garden Room today as part of a refurbishment project we're undertaking."

"And do you recognise the body?"

Perry answered for her, "We think it's Alex Sterling. He's the estate manager here. But we can't be hundred percent sure."

"Thank you, Mr Juke," Mike responded. "Mr Breen has also expressed an opinion that it's Mr Sterling." He turned and looked back down the stairs. "Okay, well, we'd better go in and take a look, Hines." DS Hines climbed the stairs. "Breen, thanks for your help. I'll catch-up with you later." Adrian nodded and headed down the stairs.

As an ambulance made its way along the drive, Lady Beatrice asked, "What about us, inspector?

Do you need us anymore?" *I'm desperate for a coffee.*

"We'll need full statements from you and Mr Juke at some stage, but right now I want to see the scene of the accident. You're free to go. I'm sure we can find you when we need to."

As he followed Hines up the stairs, Lady Beatrice called after him. "Why are CID here, Mike? Does an accident really warrant this much attention?"

Halting, he turned back to face her. "You know how everyone at HQ gets jittery when anything happens here or at Fenn House. We have to be sure it's not a threat to your family, my lady."

"Of course. Thank you, Mike."

She looked over at Perry, about to suggest they go for a coffee. He was staring at her, his eyebrows raised, and his hands upturned in front of him. "A kidnapping course?" He demanded. "What on earth?"

She laughed, "Come on, Perry. I'll explain it all over a coffee."

Bea: *Perry & I in TBR having a coffee, sis. Bit of a*

dramatic morning, will tell you all about it when you arrive. xx

---

Gulping a mouthful of hot coffee, Lady Beatrice sighed. *I needed that.* Poor Alex, he'd never get to taste coffee again. But then maybe he'd been a tea man. She knew next to nothing about him. Had he been a cheerful or a sad man? She had no idea. So wrapped up in her own grief, she'd not given much thought to how Alex had coped with his wife's death. Had he been as shocked as her that his wife had been a passenger in her husband's car when the accident had happened? Had the press hounded him like they had her? *Should I have done more to check up on him?* She shook her head as she placed her cup back on the table.

"Are you okay?" Perry looked at her, concerned.

She smiled. "Yes, sorry, I was miles away. I was thinking about Alex. I didn't really know him. Did you know him well?"

"Not really," he responded. "From a work point of view, he was always cooperative whenever Sarah or I asked him to do something. He worked hard and took his job seriously. Outside of work, Simon and I bumped into him in the pub sometimes, but saying hello was the limit to our interaction. Alex was a man's man, so we had little in common."

Lady Beatrice scrutinised Perry. He still looked pristine in his maroon Burberry suit, black waistcoat, white shirt, onyx cufflinks, and polished black shoes. *Yes*, she thought, *I can imagine they were extremely different people.* She had only ever seen Alex in a T-shirt and combat trousers.

"What did other people here think of him?"

Perry raised his eyebrows. "Why do you ask?"

She hesitated. "I just wondered."

Perry looked as if he was about to press her further, but at that precise moment Lady Sarah rushed into the Breakfast Room followed by an excited Daisy.

Lady Beatrice bent down and ruffled the white fur on the top of her little dog's head. Daisy sat and closed her eyes, her tail sweeping the floor like a windscreen wiper. Straightening up, Lady Beatrice gave her full attention to her sister.

"What on earth is going on?" Lady Sarah demanded as she took a seat.

Lady Beatrice caught Nicky's eye and mouthed, "Large latte, please," pointing to her sister. Nicky nodded and headed off to the kitchen.

"Police are crawling all over the place and

there's an ambulance outside the front of the west wing." Lady Sarah peered at Perry.

"There's been an accident in the Garden Room," he told her.

"What sort of accident? There's an ambulance, for goodness' sake. Is someone badly hurt?" Lady Sarah cried, her eyes widening.

"It's all right." Lady Beatrice reached over and put her hand on her sister's forearm.

"Someone fell over and hit their head on the ugly marble side table," Perry interjected, whispering. "And do try to keep your voice down, Sarah, or it'll be all over Francis Court before you can say fatal accident."

"Fatal?" Lady Sarah's squeaked, her eyebrows shooting up. She whispered back, "Who?" while glancing from Perry to her sister and back.

"We think it's Alex Sterling." Perry informed her.

Before she could ask anything else, Nicky appeared with her latte and a plate of bite-size, colourful macarons. "Mr Hutton has been practicing his macarons to be ready for when afternoon teas resume on the first of May," she explained. "We're asking for feedback on the flavours. We have pineapple, cherry, kiwi, mocha, and Earl Grey."

"Thank you, Nicky. We'll try them and let you know," Lady Beatrice said as she took them from her.

Smiling, Nicky walked away. The three of them watched her until she had disappeared into the back.

"Why do you think it's him?" Lady Sarah blurted out.

"Well, there's the body of a man lying on his front with his face bashed in on one side and it kind of looks like him." Perry cringed.

The colour drained from Lady Sarah's face. Lady Beatrice pushed the plate of macarons across to her. "Have some sugar. It will help with the shock." Her sister took the yellow one, presumably pineapple, and consumed it in one mouthful.

"Mmm…delicious." She was still pale, but she looked calmer. "So tell me what happened," she whispered as she reached for another macaron, this time choosing a dark-red one. Cherry?

Lady Beatrice told her about finding the body earlier. "Oh, and you'll never guess who turned up from Fenshire CID?"

Lady Sarah shrugged; she still had a mouthful of food.

"Mike Ainsley!"

Lady Sarah frowned.

"He was the instructor when we did our kidnapping course. He taught self-defence."

Her face clearing, Lady Sarah smiled.

"He was a sergeant then," Lady Beatrice continued. "He's had a promotion and is now an inspector in CID."

"Yes, I remember Mike. He's a nice man. Didn't you knee him in the privates one time when he was showing you the split and kick manoeuvre?" She turned to Perry. "Poor guy couldn't walk for the rest of the afternoon." A strained laugh escaped her.

"It was an accident," Lady Beatrice mumbled as heat crept up her neck. "I got a bit carried away." She shrugged and took a sip of her coffee. She picked up the green macaron and popped it into her mouth. *Mmm... kiwi.*

"Did you say he's with CID? Why are CID here if it's a straightforward accident?" Lady Sarah asked them.

"Lady Beatrice asked the same question," Perry replied. "Apparently, it's because of you both being royal. They have to make sure there's no threat to you."

Sarah nodded. "Do you think a third one would be good for shock?" she asked as she took the brown macaron from the plate. "Mmm... mocha. God, these are good."

Her delighted expression morphed into a frown. "When you say fallen over, do you mean he tripped over something in the room? Are we going to be held liable?"

"No," Lady Beatrice quickly reassured her. "Perry means he fell to the ground and hit his head on the way down. It could've been a heart attack, or maybe he simply passed out."

Lady Sarah looked relieved, then her shoulders sagged again. "Poor Alex." She bowed her head. "We'll miss him. He's been a marvellous estate manager for all these years."

"Although he's quite young to have a heart attack, isn't he?" Perry probed.

"How old was he, do you know?" Lady Beatrice asked her sister.

"I don't know exactly." Lady Sarah frowned. "But considering he has worked at Francis Court for over fifteen years and before that he was at Drew Castle, he must be in his mid-forties. As far as I can remember, Gill was younger than him."

"I always felt sorry for him having to put up with her complaining all the time. She never looked happy—" Perry halted abruptly. Gasping, he put his hand up to his mouth. Lady Sarah looked at her sister with concern, but Lady Beatrice shrugged.

"I'm so sorry, Lady Beatrice." Perry looked mortified. "Me and my big mouth."

"Perry, it's fine," she reassured him. "Just because she and my husband died in a car together, it doesn't mean you can't mention her name."

He gave her a glimpse of a smile as Lady Sarah pushed the plate over to him. "Last one, Perry?"

He studied the grey-coloured macaron and shook his head. "I'm not sure the colour is doing it for me."

"So, what happens now?" Lady Sarah asked them.

"Mike said they would need to take statements from Perry and me, and then I imagine they will take the body away for someone to identify. I'm hoping if it's an accident, then they will be out of here soon, and we can get back to work."

"You said *if*, Bea?"

Did I?

Before Lady Beatrice could open her mouth, Perry piped up. "Well, Miss Marple here thinks someone interfered with the room layout, and now it doesn't look 'quite right'." He used his fingers as air quotes. Lady Sarah gasped, and Daisy moved to her side, looking up at her.

"For a start, please stop calling me Miss Marple." Lady Beatrice fixed her gaze on Perry, and he grinned back. She turned to her sister. "There are some things in the room that look odd, like they're not where they should be. Also, did you notice the lamp on the floor, Perry?"

"The one which had fallen off the table when it went over?"

"Yes. It's ceramic, and it landed on a wooden floor. Shouldn't it have broken?"

Perry and Lady Sarah glanced at each other.

"And another thing," she continued, "the table, ugly as it is, is also heavy and solid. How hard would Alex have had to hit it for it to fall over?"

"So, what are you saying?" Perry's wide gaze fixed on her. "Do you think it wasn't an accident?"

Sarah cut in. "Of course it was an accident. Why would it be anything else?" She rose. "I should see the police, and then I'd better break the news to Ma and Pa." She raised her hand to her mouth. "Oh God, I wonder who will tell Ellie?"

Oh no. Lady Beatrice had forgotten all about Alex's on-off girlfriend, Ellie Gunn. Remembering when her mother had broken the news to her of James's death, she knew Ellie wouldn't believe it at first, telling everyone that there must have been a mistake.

"Poor Ellie, it will devastate her," Perry said, shaking his head.

As Lady Sarah left, Nicky appeared at the table. "What did you think of the macarons?" she asked, looking at the almost empty plate.

"Oh, they were delicious, Nicky. Please let chef know." Lady Beatrice replied.

Staring at the grey macaron, Nicky shook her head. "I told him that colour would put people off the Earl Grey." She loaded the cups and plate onto her tray and left.

As Lady Beatrice stood up, Daisy moved slowly to her side.

"I need a run to clear my head, so I'm going to take Daisy to the beach," she said as they stood up from the table. "Go home and see Simon. We won't be able to do much more today. If they need to talk to either of us, then they'll no doubt be in contact."

Daisy had perked up at the word *beach* and was wagging her tail excitedly.

As Lady Beatrice moved away, Perry reached out and grabbed her arm. "Do you *really* think it's not an accident, my lady?" He looked more serious than she had seen him look all day.

She shrugged. "I don't know, Perry, but I'm sure the police are on it. We'll know soon enough."

10

EARLY AFTERNOON, THURSDAY 8 APRIL

Detective Chief Inspector Richard Fitzwilliam closed the tab of *The Society Page* online article. *Where do they get their information from?* The major press sites had been reporting the fatal accident at Francis Court since yesterday afternoon, all saying the victim was yet to be identified. Yet somehow *The Society Page*, a gossip mag mainly focused on the Astley family and not taken seriously by anyone at Protection and Investigation (Royal) Services, had correctly reported not only that the victim was Alex Sterling, but that Lady Rossex had found the body. He shook his head. *Is it time for me to suggest we commission an investigation into the source?*

The phone on his desk beeped and a button lit up green. He grabbed the handset. "Yes, Carol?"

"Chief inspector, I have Superintendent Blake on the phone. He said it's urgent."

Richard sighed. 'Urgent' from his boss meant extra work for him. If he was in luck, it would be something he could deal with quickly and get away as planned.

"OK Carol, please put him through."

The phone clicked, confirming the line had connected.

"Nigel, what can I do for you?"

"Richard, we have a problem at Francis Court."

Nigel Blake was not a man who bothered with pleasantries.

Fitzwilliam frowned. Because of his history with the place, he liked to keep an eye on what was going on at Francis Court, but yesterday's death there was an accident. He hadn't expected to be involved.

"I thought Mike Ainsley and his team had it all under control?"

"They do, but the autopsy results have come back. It looks like it wasn't an accident, after all."

Blast! That's my long weekend scuppered.

"So I need you to go to Fenshire and oversee the investigation. You know the score. We need to know no one in the royal family was the intended victim or is in any danger."

Fitzwilliam opened his mouth to refuse but had second thoughts; both men disliked whinging.

"I know you were due to be on holiday tomorrow, Richard, but I hear Francis Court is close to the beach. You can still pack your bucket and spade." Nigel Blake chuckled. Fitzwilliam didn't. He really wasn't looking forward to seeing Lady Rossex again.

"Look, I'm sorry, Richard, but with your knowledge of Francis Court and the Astley family, you are the only one I trust to deal with this. You can take DS Spicer with you. I understand she was born in the area, so she may be of some help with the locals."

Fitzwilliam sighed. "Of course, sir. I'll start to make the arrangements and we'll be there first thing in the morning."

"Good-o. I knew I could rely on you. Keep me posted."

The line went dead. Richard placed the receiver down and put his head in his hands.

Blast! Instead of a fun weekend in Devon with his nephews, he was off to Fenshire to deal with the snobbish Lady Rossex and her overprotective family.

He picked up the phone again. "Carol, please contact DS Spicer and tell her we're off to Fenshire in the morning and will stay there for a few days, maybe more. Then book us two rooms at The Waterfront Hotel in Fawstead. Thank you."

Picking up his mobile phone, he called his sister to cancel his plans of joining her and her family in Devon the next day.

Blast!

11

LATE EVENING, THURSDAY 8 APRIL

Snuggled up with Daisy on the teal velvet two-seater sofa in her sitting room, Lady Beatrice closed her laptop and placed it on the coffee table.

That was strange. Mike Ainsley had looked uncomfortable giving that statement to the press. *Something is wrong.* Picking up her phone, she texted Perry.

Lady B: *Did you watch Mike's press statement earlier? Seems like he was uncomfortable taking the questions...*

. . .

Pleased the police had refused to comment on the reports that she had found the body, Mike's response of, 'I cannot share any details with you while the case is ongoing', had shut them down, at least for the present. How on earth *The Society Page* knew it was she who had found the body, she didn't know.

Perry: *Simon said the same. He thinks they're hiding something, as they're now referring to it as an incident rather than an accident.*

Lady B: *Exactly! Something has changed, I am sure of it.*

Perry: *Okay Miss Marple! It's too late now, but first thing in the morning Simon is going to find out what is going on through his contacts.*

Lady B: *Good idea. See you tomorrow.*

. . .

Gazing out of the window, it was pitch black. She ought to close the curtains, but she didn't want to disturb Daisy, who was sound asleep beside her. She looked down at the sleeping dog, her head resting on Lady Beatrice's lap, her legs twitching as she dreamed. Sighing, Lady Beatrice looked out into the night; there was something mesmerising about the darkness.

She was uneasy. Something about Alex's death didn't feel right.

She recalled being interviewed by Mike yesterday. He had asked her to describe what she'd seen. Unnatural was the word that kept coming into her head. The room had looked *unnatural*. The scene had looked *unnatural*. When Mike had asked her to explain what she meant by *unnatural,* she'd been stuck, unable to put it into words. She'd told him it was like things weren't behaving in the way she would naturally expect them to. She wasn't satisfied with her response, but it was the best she could do. With interior design, it was hard to put a finger on just why some arrangements worked and others didn't. Styling was a combination of colour, proportions, and balance. Easy to see but hard to describe. She must look again at the photos Perry had taken yesterday and see if she could be more specific.

As she stroked the wiry fur on Daisy's back, her

mind went to a place she normally avoided — the accident involving her husband and the dead man's wife. Every time the press raked up the details of the accident, they hinted at a relationship between James and Gill. A relationship she'd always denied, preferring to believe there was a perfectly reasonable explanation for them being in the car together.

That was until five years ago when Fitzwilliam, that awful man from PaIRS, had shattered her illusions.

12

FIVE YEARS EARLIER...

Lady Beatrice paced the rug in the family drawing room, unable to imagine what Detective Sergeant Fitzwilliam wanted to discuss with her after all these years. She had hoped never to see or speak to him or anyone else involved in the investigation ever again.

Fitzwilliam's unexpected call last night had been vague. "There is something relating to your husband's death I need to talk to you about," was all he'd said.

Lady Beatrice could never forget DS Fitzwilliam. A tough and rugged looking northerner, he was the ex-military type — upright, disciplined and matter of fact. Although the investigation had been headed up by Detective Inspector Reed, as his sidekick, Fitzwilliam had accompanied him to most of their meetings. He had said little initially, but his stare had been disconcerting, as if he was judging her. And not in a good way.

Despite reeling from the shock of her husband's death, being ten weeks pregnant and with severe morning sickness, she'd been determined to talk to the authorities. But when Fitzwilliam had asked intrusive personal questions about her relationship with James, she'd thought him impertinent and had told him so in no uncertain terms. He, in return, had alleged he was only concerned for her safety, to which she'd responded, "I don't believe you." At this stage, the princess, who had wisely petitioned that she was in attendance with her daughter during the interview, had taken over. She explained to the PaIRS officers that her daughter was overwrought, and it would be best if they left. Within the hour, the princess had whisked Lady Beatrice away from her home at the Dower House to a suite of rooms on the second floor in the family wing of Francis Court, where she'd spent the next week in bed, debilitated by despair.

The rest of the investigation had not been pleasant either. She'd had the distinct impression Fitzwilliam didn't approve of her or her family's life of privilege. And if that was his attitude towards the royal family, she could only speculate what he was doing in PaIRS. Cringing, she remembered that in her fit of temper, she'd shared her thoughts with DI Reed, suggesting that maybe the detective sergeant was working from the inside to overthrow the monarchy. Twisting her rings on her finger, she hoped he wasn't coming here holding a grudge. *I didn't behave well,* she admitted. *I will try to create a better impression this time.*

Richard Fitzwilliam stalked into the room, followed ten seconds later by a red-faced Harris with a tea tray.

"Lady Rossex—" Fitzwilliam started.

Lady Beatrice's hackles were up immediately. *How rude!* Having ignored protocol by preceding the butler into the room and not being announced properly, he was now standing before her, radiating disapproval. Her earlier resolution to be civil went out of the window. She glared at him, her eyes narrowed, as looking over at the puffing butler, she cut him off.

"Harris?"

Harris pulled himself together and took a deep

breath. "Detective Inspector Fitzwilliam to see you, my lady."

"Thank you, Harris." She smiled at him, then looked over at Fitzwilliam. His jaw clenched, he glowered at her, looking like a man about to commit murder. *Mine!* She stared back.

Daisy, always more polite to strangers than her mistress, ran to greet him with her tail wagging. Breaking eye contact, Fitzwilliam bent down and stroked her head. Meanwhile, Harris, having deposited the tea tray on the coffee table, departed with as much dignity as he could muster.

"It's inspector now, is it?" Lady Beatrice asked in a clipped voice.

Still stony-faced, he replied equally tersely, "Yes, they promoted me a couple of years ago when they realised I wasn't trying to overthrow the royal family from the inside."

Her ears grew impossibly hot; she lifted her chin. "Indeed. Well, I'm pleased to hear it. Congratulations." She didn't smile at him.

"Thank you, Lady Rossex." He didn't smile back.

Fitzwilliam straightened up as Daisy returned to sit by Lady Beatrice's side.

"I'm here because a rather unusual situation has occurred at Fenshire CID," he informed her curtly.

Where is this going? She turned the rings on her finger and shifted her weight.

"Were you aware they had retrieved your husband's overnight bag from the apartment in Knightsbridge Court after the accident and sent it to forensics in Wynham?"

She gave a quick shrug. "I may have been, inspector. It was a long time ago."

"Well, they reviewed the contents and returned them to you a few weeks later."

She nodded.

"However, the overnight bag itself, for some reason no one can explain, was kept as evidence. Recently, while Fenshire CID were relocating their storage facilities, someone dropped the bag, and something fell out of the lining. It was a letter addressed to you."

No, no, no. I don't want to hear this.

She had a theory about the night of the accident. James had been coming back from London to surprise her. When he was almost home, he'd come across Gill in distress by the side of the road and offered her a lift somewhere local.

She didn't want there to be a letter. *A letter doesn't fit my theory.*

"Do you mind if I sit down?" she asked. She was either going to sit down now or fall down later.

"And please take a seat yourself, inspector," she added, indicating a chair on the other side of the Georgian coffee table. Sitting down opposite, she allowed Daisy to jump up on her lap. She scratched the back of the terrier's neck as Daisy circled once and settled down.

"Yes, of course, Lady Rossex." Fitzwilliam sat down, his eyes focused on her face.

What does he want from me? She shrugged her shoulders. "Please continue, inspector."

"I appreciate this is a shock for you, Lady Rossex. Would you like anything?" He glanced at the tea tray laid out on the table in front of them.

She sat up straight, pushing her shoulders back. "No, I'm fine, thank you. Please say what you need to say, inspector."

He put his hand in his pocket and retrieved an envelope. He laid it on the table in front of them. It displayed a single word on the front — Bea. She recognised James's handwriting and swallowed the lump at the back of her throat. She lifted her chin.

"The letter is unopened, Lady Rossex. A senior officer at Fenshire CID handed it straight to me. But here's the thing—"

She cringed, knowing what was coming next.

"I need to know the contents."

Taking a deep breath, she inspected the wedding ring on her right hand.

"I have to be sure that what's inside the letter has no impact on the inquest's verdict of accidental death. I'm sorry." He looked away, a slight pink hue appearing on his neck.

"Indeed." She didn't trust herself to say more. She could feel the tears trying to burst from her eyes. *I will not cry in front of this man.*

"First, can you confirm that it's your husband's handwriting on the envelope?" he asked, pointing to the envelope lying on the table. Lady Beatrice leaned forward slightly, tears clouding her eyes, and stared at it for a few seconds before nodding.

"Thank you, my lady. Would you like me to read it first?" he offered. "Then you can read it in your own time after I've left. If the contents have no material impact on the verdict, then I won't need to take any further action."

He appears to be trying to reassure me. How strange that he should care. She checked herself. Of course, it wasn't that. It was more likely he was embarrassed that the letter had been hidden for so long because of a procedural failure at their end. *He's probably hoping I won't sue them!*

She stood up. Daisy, unhappy about being displaced so soon after she'd got comfortable, huffed before following her mistress to the writing desk behind Fitzwilliam. Opening the drawer, Lady Beatrice withdrew a silver letter opener in the shape of a dagger.

As she moved to stand in front of Fitzwilliam, he involuntarily flinched, and his eyes narrowed before he cocked his head to one side. *Does he think I am going to stab him? Ha, ha, how tempting is that...*

She gave him a sinister smile as she handed it to him. "You may find this useful, inspector."

He took it from her outstretched hand, then sliced open the top of the white envelope.

"Please help yourself to some tea," she said as she moved away.

He leaned over and poured himself a cup. Daisy went to sit by the table. There were biscuits on a plate by the teapot and she was looking from him to them and back again, ever hopeful.

"Daisy, here." Lady Beatrice stopped and waited for her terrier to come to her side, then continued towards the large bay windows ahead of her.

Her heart was racing. She couldn't bear to watch Fitzwilliam's face as he read the letter.

Daisy jumped up on to a window seat in front of the middle set of windows and Lady Beatrice joined her, perching on the edge of the long blue cushion.

Looking sideways out onto the formal gardens, she inhaled and exhaled deeply.

She never tired of the view to the north of the estate. Beyond the gardens, over to the right, was the orangery in the distance, with the outline of the fifteenth century Church of St Francis nesting behind it. There were wedding preparations going on, and she watched as the staff set up the main room inside the orangery. Through the glass panels, they looked like a pack of industrious ants, moving things from one side of the room to the other.

A rustling sound came from Fitzwilliam's direction, followed by a discreet cough. She glanced back as he was putting his teacup down on the table. Standing up, he looked over at her, his face hard to read. Did she see a brief flash of sympathy? He turned away and laid the letter down, now returned to its envelope, on the side table.

He cleared his throat. "There's nothing in the letter I need to action," he said, not looking at her as he spoke. "I'll leave it here for you to read when you're ready." Glancing down at the letter, he then nodded and made his way towards her.

Don't say any more. I don't want your sympathy or pity.

She rose and started walking towards the door, Daisy trotting behind her. Fitzwilliam changed his direction, now also heading for the door. They met just to the side of it. Lady Beatrice reached out and pulled the bell.

Bracing herself, she knew she needed to say one last thing before he left. "I trust I can rely on your discretion, inspector? You can imagine the fuss the press will make if they know there is a letter." She needed to know she could rely on him not to share the contents of the letter with anyone. Searching his face, she fixed on his brown eyes and held her breath.

"Of course, Lady Rossex. I understand," he replied, meeting her gaze.

He looks sincere. She had no choice. She had to trust this disagreeable man, whether she liked it or not. "Thank you, inspector."

The door opened and Harris enquired, "Yes, my lady?"

"Please show Inspector Fitzwilliam out, Harris. Thank you."

The butler nodded. Putting his arm out, he steered Fitzwilliam through the door.

Lady Beatrice turned and sidled over to the table where the letter lay. It looked harmless enough. Picking it up, she looked at the front. *Bea.* The word did little to indicate the nature of the contents. It was neither the more formal *Lady Beatrice* nor the affectionate *Bubble Bea*, James's pet name for her since they were children. It simply said *Bea* — the shortened version her family used.

Standing there, letter in hand, it crossed her mind she could burn it right now and continue living in her happy bubble. She looked over at the fireplace. Even though it was early September and still quite warm, it was laid out, ready to be lit if needed. It would be so easy to pluck one of the giant matches from the black metal holder by the side of the grate, set fire to the mixture of newspaper and kindling, and throw the letter on top, watching it burn.

Daisy sniffed. She was sitting by the table, her nose only inches away from the selection of biscuits neatly arranged on the gold-rimmed plate. Smiling, Lady Beatrice put the letter down. She picked up a rich tea biscuit, Daisy's favourite, and the little dog sat to attention, shivering in anticipation. Lady Beatrice snapped the biscuit it in two and gave Daisy one half, then she shook her head.

I'm being an idiot. Even if she burned the letter, she couldn't forget it existed. The damage was already done. She stood up straight. *I'll have to face whatever it says and deal with it.*

Harris's footsteps echoed in the silence as he walked up the corridor outside. Snatching up the letter, she stuffed it in the back pocket of her jeans. Daisy instantly moved to her side, fully aware her mistress was holding the other half of the rich tea biscuit in her hand.

"Do you require anything else, my lady?" Harris asked as he entered the room.

"No, thank you, Harris. You can clear the tea things away. Come on, Daisy."

Richard Fitzwilliam stepped out of the north side door and took a deep breath. *Well, that was awkward.* He hadn't expected the letter to be so personal. If Lady Rossex wasn't so stuck up and condescending, he might have felt sorry for her. Well, he sighed, any hope that the letter would provide the key to James Wiltshire's death was now dashed. He'd better report in.

As he made his way along the path that ran parallel to the east wing terrace, he took his phone from his jacket pocket and tapped the number he wanted from his contacts list. He looked around to make sure he couldn't be overheard as the phone at the other end rang.

"Richard, how did it go?"

He gave the man a summary of the contents of the letter.

"Was the letter definitely from him?"

"Lady Rossex confirmed it was his writing on the envelope and I did all the visual checks the handwriting guys had told me to do. The Es, As and Ts were consistent with the sample I studied of his writing, sir."

"I sense a *but,* Fitzwilliam."

"I don't know, sir. It just doesn't *sound* like the man I got to know during the investigation, or the man you've described to me. He didn't come across as a whiner, but in the letter, he does. In fact, if I'm being totally honest, he comes across as a bit wet, sir."

"You're right. It doesn't sound like the man we knew. But then, who ever really knows what goes on behind a public face?"

"That's true, sir."

"And how was Lady Rossex?" A lightness entered the man's voice.

"Much as she was nine years ago, sir — entitled, reluctant to co-operate and dismissive."

The man at the other end chortled. "I knew you would enjoy seeing each other again."

Fitzwilliam bit his tongue and made no response.

The voice at the other end returned to its earlier seriousness. "So no sign that she was expecting a letter?"

"No, sir, just the opposite. She looked as if she wanted it to disappear."

"Right, well, that supports my theory that she doesn't know more than she'd previously told us. So I think that wraps it up."

Fitzwilliam opened his mouth to say more, then changed his mind. "Yes, sir." It was best left alone now.

"Thanks for the call, Richard." The line disconnected.

My sweet Bea,

There is no easy way to tell you this. I'm sorry, but I'm leaving.

I know it will sound like a cliché, but please believe me when I say it's not you, it's me.

I will always love you, Bea. You have been my smart, beautiful, and funny best friend ever since we were children. But I'm not in love with you and I'm not sure I ever have been. And if you're honest with yourself, I think you'll realise that you have never been in love with me either.

Since we were adults, we've always focused our relationship on our public life — that string of activities and duties to perform has come first. You accept your life of duty. You accept the responsibility that comes with privilege. And even though you hate being the centre of attention, you put on a smile and face the press when you know it's required. But I'm not like you, Bea.

Deep down, I have always wanted more. The last twenty-five years of doing what everyone expected of me has meant there is almost no me left any more. The right school, the right university, the right job, the right wife - I have tried to live up to the mantle of the future Earl of Durrland. But time and time again I have fallen short and now I'm exhausted. I can no longer see what value I have to you, the royal family, or my parents. No one asks my advice or wants my contribution, no one needs me, Bea. Not even you.

On top of feeling like a spare part, the constant attention from the press every time we step out of Francis Court has become unbearable for me. I've said nothing until now because I didn't want you to think I wasn't able to stick out my stiff upper lip and suck it up, like you do. But the truth is, I can't.

I don't know how long I could have carried like

this, but four months ago, something happened that changed everything for me — I met Gill Sterling.

We were just friends to start, meeting up for coffee and walking in the grounds together, two 'extras' at Francis Court, blending into the background while all eyes were on the major stars. We talked about our lives and how we both felt trapped and unhappy. It was such a relief to talk to someone who understood. Before I was aware of what was happening, I fell in love. It was earth-shattering, all-consuming love. Something I had accepted I would never experience.

Although reluctant at first, she eventually told me Alex had been abusing her for years. Recently, it had become more physical. I have seen the marks on her face, her wrists and her legs. She was at her wits' end. She was frightened if she said anything that Alex would punish her. Since then, all I have wanted to do is take Gill somewhere safe, away from the husband who hurts her. It's taken a while to persuade her to trust me, but Alex has been getting more and more controlling recently and she has finally agreed to let me help. We are off to Mexico and then who knows? We will find the right place for us to settle down. Somewhere we can be our true selves.

I'm so sorry, Bea, but I can't face telling you in

person. I expect the press will go crazy about this and I will do anything I can to help mitigate the inevitable scrutiny, so you have my permission to tell them whatever you need to. The family will know how to handle it. Let me know what is going to be said and I will issue a statement of confirmation. Of course, I must eventually tell my parents I have left. They will be enormously disappointed in me, but then what's new?

Gill will tell Alex she's going back to live with her family in Ireland, and she wants a divorce. She will warn him if he tries to find her, she will go to the press. I doubt Alex will say anything in the circumstances.

No one need know we are going away together. I leave tomorrow morning and she is flying to join me a few days later. There is no reason why anyone will make the connection.

I hope one day you will forgive me. For once in my life, I must do what is right for me.

Your loving,

James x

13

LATE EVENING, THURSDAY 8 APRIL

Lost in the past, Daisy interrupted Lady Beatrice by shoving her whole body underneath her mistress's arm. A little pink tongue darted out from the white furry face and landed on her cheek. She laughed. "Thank you, Daisy," she said, as she moved the still wriggling terrier away from her. Standing, she plodded over to the windows. She stood there for a few minutes, breathing deeply and evenly.

The darkness was so complete it seemed as if she was being sucked into a black hole. She'd tried hard not to think about James's letter over the last five years, keeping it buried as best she could. But Alex's death had stirred it all up, bringing those memories and feelings back up to the surface. And, of course, now, once the press found out about Alex's death, it would all get raked up yet again. *Won't they ever let it drop and leave me alone?*

She shook her head to clear her blurred vision and closed the curtains.

14

MID-MORNING, FRIDAY 9 APRIL

"Would it look better if we moved the sideboard over here, and then the lamp could go here on the floor?" Lady Beatrice asked as she pointed at the screen showing the virtual layout of the Smoking Room. Mike had told them they wouldn't be finished with the Garden Room for a while, so they'd started designing the only other room not yet completed.

Death or no death, they had to be ready for the grand reopening on the first of May.

"Yes, I like that," Perry responded. "We can then move the tray onto the sideboard." He moved it with his mouse. "And use this vase for some height." She nodded. "Great. I'll ring the supplier this afternoon and chase up the lamp." He made a note on his pad and Lady Beatrice took a sip of her coffee.

Daisy, curled up on the Joules bed Perry had bought for her a few weeks ago, made a woofing sound in her sleep as her legs twitched.

"Deer," Perry whispered, nodding at Daisy. "On the beach, back of the estate. The deer heads off into the dunes, but Daisy can't stop in time and crashes into the sea."

Lady Beatrice grinned.

Daisy whimpered, and her front legs made tiny jerky movements.

"Running along a field in Aintree." Lady Beatrice was going big this time. "She accidentally takes a left and finds herself taking part in the Grand National. She wins by a nose!"

They creased up as they watched the little dog in her bed, now motionless and snoring.

Perry's mobile phone rang, making them both jump. He picked it up and mouthed to her, "It's Simon."

Sitting up, she adjusted her green Gucci T-shirt, tucking it into the back of her black jeans. This could be the call they'd been waiting for.

Simon had been in the Fenshire Police for fourteen years, ten of those in CID, before he'd left five years ago to write crime novels. He still had great contacts in Fenshire CID, and this morning he'd been making calls to see what he could find out about Alex's accident. Lady Beatrice had met Simon twice over the last ten weeks and had warmed to him instantly.

"*Murder!*" Perry's exclamation made her start. She jumped up. "Love, I'm going to put you on speaker before Lady Beatrice grabs the phone from me." She rolled her eyes at him and rushed to close his office door.

"Right, can you repeat what you just said for her benefit, love?"

"Okay, Lady Beatrice?" Simon's voice was deep and steady, with a barely perceptible Fenshire accent.

"Hello Simon, did you say murder?"

"That seems to be their thinking," he confirmed. "I spoke to my friend Roisin in Wynham—"

"Forensics are based there," Perry jumped in.

Simon continued, "She said the autopsy report states the injuries to his head are inconsistent with falling on the table. The doctor who examined him onsite had concerns that the wound was too wide and too deep. The post-mortem looked at the wound site and, in their view, it's more consistent with him being hit *with* the table. Oh, and they checked his vital organs and there was nothing to suggest why he fell. His heart was fine, and there were no blood clots. They've sent a sample of his blood away, but the results will take a few weeks to come back."

Lady Beatrice peered over at Perry. His eyes were bright with excitement.

"Well done, love," Perry said.

"I have more. I then spoke to a mate, Steve, in CID. They've confirmed the dead man is Alex Sterling, but they're having trouble contacting his younger brother, who is his next of kin. He's in the Army and on exercise somewhere remote. So Ellie Gunn formally identified Alex yesterday afternoon."

"Poor Ellie," Perry cut in. "I know they had broken up recently, but after fifteen years together, she will be devastated."

Fifteen years? Lady Beatrice frowned. *But Alex's wife Gill only died fourteen years ago.* That was interesting. If true, it means Alex was having an affair with Ellie while his wife was alive.

"And you'll like this, my lady. Even before the autopsy report came back, Mike had them looking at why the lamp didn't break when it fell from the overturned table. They concluded that it should have broken when it hit the wooden floor. Oh, and they sent the table to forensics."

Lady Beatrice smiled at Perry. *With any luck, it would never come back.*

"They've been trying to work out if it could've fallen over when a person of Alex's size fell on it. Mike must have taken your concerns seriously."

"That's great inside information, Simon. When do you think Mike will tell us officially?" she asked.

"Steve said they will send the forensics boys back today. They'll need to do a more thorough sweep of the room now it's a crime scene. From my experience, they will need to re-interview everyone to decide who the suspects are."

"How exciting!" Perry exclaimed.

"Thanks, Simon." Frowning, she shook her head. She wasn't so sure she shared Perry's excitement.

"Thanks, love, I'll talk to you later." Ending the call, Perry looked at her expectantly. "Well, what do you think of that?"

"I don't like it," she replied. "Because of the time of day he died and the fact that whoever killed him had access to the Garden Room, it has to be someone here at Francis Court." She paused and cleared her throat. "One of us is a murderer, Perry. I don't like that at all."

———

Perry and Lady Beatrice strolled back from the Breakfast Room with Daisy trotting between them. The sun shone overhead; the heat broken by the cool breeze. They were turning the corner on the southwest side of the house when Perry's radio crackled into life, startling them both.

"Mr Juke, this is Mike Ainsley, over." They looked at each other in confusion. When had Mike got a Francis Court radio?

"Mike, this is Perry Juke. What can I do for you, over?"

"Can you and Lady Rossex come over to our temporary offices next to the cafe, please? I need a chat, over."

"Sure Mike, we'll be there in five minutes, out."

"They must have set up quick," Lady Beatrice said, frowning. "I didn't notice anyone in that area of the Old Stable Block when we left for coffee, did you?"

Perry shook his head. "No, but I suppose now it's a murder enquiry, they need resources and space to do it properly. We'll have to get used to them being here for a while, I imagine."

A thought flitted across her mind. "I wonder if this means they will keep us closed to the public while they do their investigation. Mother will *not* be happy."

"The princess will have no choice. They can't have the public trampling over potential evidence," Perry pointed out.

After entering the courtyard at the rear of the Old Stable Block, they made their way across the other side to the back of the retail units. She could see movement in an office to the right of the cafe's back door; she pointed it out to Perry, and they headed in that direction.

When they walked in, Mike was talking to a man and a woman, both of whom were facing away from the door. Lady Beatrice stopped with a start. *There is something familiar about that man.* He was just over six feet and well-built. As she inched closer, she could see he had short brown hair flecked with grey.

Oh, no. Please. No. Her muscles tensed. Her mouth went dry.

"Lady Rossex, Mr Juke, may I introduce Detective Sergeant Tina Spicer and Detective Chief Inspector Richard Fitzwilliam from PaIRS? They will oversee the investigation." Mike smiled as the couple turned around to face them.

Fitzwilliam had a smirk on his face as he held out his hand to Lady Beatrice. She scowled at him as she refused to take it. "Is that Dick for short?"

15

ALMOST LUNCHTIME, FRIDAY 9 APRIL

"A pleasure to see you again, Lady Rossex." Fitzwilliam's voice dripped with sarcasm as he dropped his arm to his side.

Daisy, traitor that she was, ran up to him, her tail wagging. He bent down to stroke her head. "It's Daisy, isn't it? Hello, young lady." She was all over him like a rash.

I'll have to have words with her later about her poor taste in men.

"Another promotion, *chief* inspector?" *They must value his particular brand of judgemental impertinence*, Lady Beatrice thought dryly.

"Well, the higher I rise in the organisation, the easier it will be for me to overthrow the royal family, my lady." He smirked.

Horrid man.

Mike, Perry, and DS Spicer looked back and forth between the two of them, their brows furrowed. Fitzwilliam and Lady Beatrice continued glaring at one another.

Breaking the tension, Mike said, "Lady Rossex, Mr Juke, we can confirm the victim of yesterday's incident is Alex Sterling. We also have reason to believe his death wasn't an accident. As this is now a murder enquiry, PaIRS has asked DCI Fitzwilliam to oversee the investigation."

"Why?" Lady Beatrice asked, still staring at Fitzwilliam.

"When members of the royal family involved up in an incident like this, I have to be assured they're neither a potential victim"—Fitzwilliam smiled at her like a spider at a fly—"nor a suspect."

"A suspect?" She huffed. "Are you suggesting I or a member of my family murdered our estate manager, chief inspector?" She glared at him. *How dare he suggest such a thing!*

"We can't rule anyone out at this early stage, Lady Rossex." He was still sneering at her. Her blood boiling, she wanted to wipe that smile off his face.

DS Spicer moved in front of her boss. "Lady Rossex, I'm sure no one is seriously implying a member of the royal family is a murderer." Turning back to Fitzwilliam, she gave him what Perry often described as a Paddington stare. "It's our job to make sure neither you nor your family are in any danger." She smiled and Lady Beatrice took a deep breath.

She seems nice and much more reasonable than her boss.

"Well, we wouldn't want you to be murdered in your bed now, would we, Lady Rossex?" Fitzwilliam quipped, grinning from over the top of Spicer's head. He continued, "Anyway, there is no need for you to worry your royal head about it. We will keep out of your way and have this investigation wrapped up as soon as we can."

How arrogant! She took a deep breath. *But I will not rise to it and give him the satisfaction.* Ignoring Fitzwilliam, she smiled at Spicer. "Thank you, sergeant. I appreciate your concern."

Lady Beatrice turned to Mike. "Mike, can we still have access to the corridor leading to the Smoking Room tomorrow? We need to start on that room, if possible. We're on a tight deadline."

Before Mike had time to reply, Fitzwilliam jumped in. "I'll need to review the crime scene, Lady Rossex, before anyone can decide about access. This is a murder enquiry now and, unfortunately, it will take as long as it takes."

God, he's so smug!

"Oh, and we'll need to re-interview you and Mr Juke about your discovery of the body," he added.

Oh great! "Of course, chief inspector," Lady Beatrice said, moving towards the door. She needed to be as far away from this annoying man as possible. She turned to Mike. "You know how to contact us, Mike. Come on, Perry, I need another coffee. Daisy, here." Smiling at DI Ainsley, and without acknowledging Fitzwilliam, she sashayed out of the door, followed by a bemused Perry and a reluctant Daisy.

16

LUNCHTIME, FRIDAY 9 APRIL

"Hateful man!" Lady Beatrice thundered as soon as they were out of earshot. "I can't believe he has the audacity to turn up here and start telling me what I can and can't do in my own home." She snorted and threw her arms up in the air.

Perry was silent beside her. Stopping, she turned to look at him. He stopped too, his gaze fixed on her as if she had developed a second head.

"What?" she barked at him.

"Oh my giddy aunt," he cried. "What on earth was *that* all about?"

She exhaled loudly. "I'm sorry, Perry, but DCI Fitzwilliam and I have history, and it's not a particularly pleasant one at that."

"You don't say." He bit his lip, his eyes

sparkling. "You called him a dick!" He could hold it in no longer and burst out laughing. Laughing too, all Lady Beatrice's anger dissipated.

As they carried on strolling around the side of the house towards the Breakfast Room, she told Perry that Fitzwilliam had been the DS investigating James's accident and they had butted heads on more than one occasion.

"Simon was also involved in the investigation," Perry told her. "Did you know that?"

"Really? I don't recognise him from then, but it was all a blur at the time. Sorry." She shrugged.

"Don't worry. He was only a junior detective then, recently assigned to CID. He will remember the team from PaIRS though, so he may know some gossip about your DCI Fitzwilliam." Perry had a sparkle in his eyes.

She raised her voice. "*My* DCI Fitzwilliam? There's nothing *my* about that man. If I never see him again in my life, it will be too soon."

"I think the lady doth protest too much." Perry ran up the stone steps to the terrace, Daisy close on his heels. They disappeared inside the Breakfast Room before Lady Beatrice could respond.

Scowling, she scurried after them. By the time she entered, Perry was heading over to their usual table by the window on the far side. Daisy trotted beside him, then sat down by his side, ready for whatever food he would inevitably share with her. When Lady Beatrice took the seat opposite him, he looked up and broke into a huge grin.

"You're becoming impertinent, Mr Juke," she said, trying to suppress a smile.

"I'm only teasing you, Lady Bea." He shrugged. "It's what friends do." Still smiling, he placed his order with Nicky as she came over. Two coffees and two omelettes - one cheese and mushroom and the other ham and cheese.

"Oh, also a large black coffee for Lady Rossex and a chicken Caesar salad." He looked at Lady Beatrice to make sure he'd got her order right. She nodded.

Nicky patted Daisy's head and whispered, "Good girl, Daisy. I'll see what I can find for you." Pocketing her notebook, she headed off towards the kitchen.

Perry went back to his phone, and Lady Beatrice contemplated what he'd said.

Friends? It had been ages since she'd spent time with anyone outside of her family. She'd forgotten what it was like to meet new people, let alone make friends. But she liked Perry and was more comfortable in his presence with every day they spent together. And they laughed. A lot. *Is that friendship?*

She smiled to herself. She liked that he had called her *Lady Bea. My lady* had sounded stilted to her. *Lady Bea* was a significant improvement.

Hold on, two omelettes? "Are we expecting company, Perry?"

"Yes, I've asked DCI Fitzwilliam to join us for lunch. I think you and he need to get to know each other in a less formal setting."

What!

Perry sniggered. "Your face is a picture!" He continued quickly, "No, I've asked Simon to join us. Is that okay?"

She rolled her eyes. "I'm going to clobber you if you carry on like this." She tried to sound stern at the same time as trying not to dissolve into laughter. "Of course, that's a great idea. We can discuss the murder with him face to face."

Returning with their drinks, Nicky also laid a side plate with half a chicken breast cut into cubes on the table. "This is for Daisy." She patted the dog's head and left.

"They spoil her rotten in here," Lady Beatrice complained to Perry as he picked up a morsel of chicken and gave it to Daisy. She shook her head. "I don't know why I'm telling you; you're just as bad."

"Oh, come on, I see you sneaking her bits of food, too. It's those big brown eyes, no one can resist them." Grinning, he gave Daisy another bit of chicken. Lady Beatrice gave up.

As he straightened, he looked towards the door. His eyes lit up and his face softened. She looked around. Simon was striding towards their table.

Tilting her head to one side, she sighed wistfully. *How amazing to have someone you love so much that your eyes light up when you see them.* She remembered that whenever James had entered a room, his gaze would seek her out. When he found her, he would give her a barely perceptible nod of his head and a brief smile. The thoughtful gesture of checking in, that moment when their eyes had met, had made her feel cared for. *But that isn't the same, is it?*

"Okay, Lady Beatrice?" Simon smiled at her. At five eleven and stocky, with short light brown hair and a well-trimmed beard, he was classically handsome. He was wearing a loose-fitting white T-shirt, blue jeans and brown leather boots — the epitome of cowboy casual. Perry, in contrast, had today dressed his six-foot-one lean frame in an ultra-trendy grey Kenneth Cole suit, with a fitted black T-shirt underneath, light grey socks, and black slip-ons. He looked like he'd stepped out of *Vogue*.

And yet somehow, they look right together.

She smiled back. "Hello, Simon, you're just in time to eat," she said as Nicky arrived with their food. They ate for a little while in comfortable silence. Perry, now and then, dropping a piece of chicken into Daisy's mouth.

"So—" Perry started, as he put his knife and fork down on his plate and pushed it away from him. He turned to Simon. "You missed some fun this morning, love." Looking at Lady Beatrice, he smirked. "Lady Bea here was truly fearless against a rude adversary. She was so sarcastic and witty, she could almost be gay!"

Lady Beatrice choked on a mouthful of chicken. Perry was still grinning, but there was also a look of something else on his face. *Like he is proud of me.*

"What happened?" Simon asked as he lay down his fork and looked between the two of them. Lady Beatrice sipped some water, trying to compose herself.

Perry carried on. "Do you remember Richard Fitzwilliam from PaIRS? He's tall and ruggedly handsome in a gruff, serious sort of way. He was part of the team who oversaw the investigation into James Wiltshire's death?"

Ruggedly handsome? Lady Beatrice snorted, then quickly covered it up with a cough.

Simon nodded. "He was a detective sergeant then, I think?" he looked at Lady Beatrice and she nodded in response.

"Well, he was insulting to Lady Bea during that investigation, and now he's back here overseeing the murder investigation into Alex's death, and he's still being unpleasant to her," he finished with a flourish, winking at his partner.

Swallowing down another snort, Lady Beatrice said, "He's a boorish and disrespectful blockhead who thinks he's better than everyone else."

Simon smiled wryly. "I remember him being quite brusque with our team back then."

She smiled. "And he's insolent." Lifting her chin, she added. "But I will not let him intimidate me."

"Although, to be fair," Simon continued, "he's well respected within Fenshire CID. He sees things through to the end and doesn't give up easily."

Her eyes narrowed. *No doubt he's perfectly capable.* He wouldn't be a chief inspector at his age (she estimated he was only seven or eight years older than her) if he had not impressed those around him. She shrugged. *Well, he hasn't impressed me.*

"Lady Bea called him a dick to his face!" Perry blurted out.

Heat rushed up her neck. "That's not quite true, Perry. His name is Richard, after all." She shrugged again, then burst out laughing. Simon and Perry laughed too.

And he told me not to worry my pretty little head over it. How dare he dismiss me like that!

"In fact, I have a good mind to play him at his own game."

"What do you mean by that?" Simon asked.

"I thought that with your contacts and our knowledge of Francis Court and the people who work here, we could solve this murder ourselves."

Perry's eyes danced. "Great idea! We'll need something to do given that they won't let us into the rooms we have to finish. We could interview the staff, work out where everyone was, and come up with a list of suspects."

Simon frowned. "Whoa there, Cagney and Lacey. Slow down. It's not that simple. This is a murder investigation. You can't just go barging in, talking to witnesses, and looking for clues. That's the job of the police."

"Killjoy!" Perry pouted at his partner.

"I'm sorry, but I know how dangerous it can be when civilians get involved with an investigation. I saw it firsthand when I was in CID. You can accidentally lead witnesses or mess with evidence. I'm sure it won't be done maliciously, but often it's enough to destroy a police case and allow the perpetrator to get away with it. You wouldn't want that, would you?"

Perry and Lady Beatrice shook their heads, looking rather sheepish.

"So what can we do?" Lady Beatrice asked. "I feel we should do something."

Simon hesitated.

"Oh, come on, love. It wasn't too bad when this"—he placed his hand on his chest—"gorgeous civilian got involved in an investigation, was it?" He smiled coyly. Simon shook his head, a grin twitching at his lips. "And I bet you would love to get involved in hunting down a killer. It might even be great research for your book." Perry leaned in, his eyes shining. "You know you want to…"

Resting his chin on one hand, Simon looked between them both. Then, shaking his head, he sighed. "Okay. Well, for a start, you're not to do anything without running it past me first. Is that clear?" They both nodded enthusiastically. "Next, you cannot speak to anyone unless the police have already interviewed them." Again, they both nodded. "And finally, if any of us find out anything new, we tell the police immediately. Agreed?"

They both answered, "Yes."

He grinned at them. "All right. I may live to regret this, but I suppose it can't do any harm to make a list of potential suspects."

Perry clapped his hands together. "Great, we can start now."

Simon looked at his watch and stood up. "Sorry, but I have a video call with my editor in twenty minutes. Why don't we meet you in the pub tonight, Lady Beatrice, say seven?"

"The pub?" She twisted the rings on her finger.

"The Ship and Seal, on the green in the village."

She shook her head.

"Have you ever been to the pub in the village?" Perry asked.

"Um, no," she replied. "I've driven past it a few times, but I've never been in. Won't it be full of press?" She bit her bottom lip. Facing the public was one thing. Entering a pub full of press was more than even her newly confident self could cope with.

"It's okay," Simon replied in a reassuring voice. "The landlord, Dylan, won't allow press into the pub. It hacks off the locals."

She raised her chin. "All right, I'll give it a go."

Smiling, Simon patted Daisy on the head. "It's a dog friendly pub too."

He rose from his seat and left.

"Don't worry," Perry said, reaching over and patting Lady Beatrice's arm. "You'll be fine. It's mainly locals and the odd tourist. It's quiet this time of year. Simon and I will be there with you."

He winked at her. "Just promise me you won't get steaming drunk and cause a fight."

17

LATE AFTERNOON, FRIDAY 9 APRIL

Lady Beatrice planned on walking to the pub. Using the lane from the north side gate to the village, it would only take ten minutes.

But at five she received a call from DS Spicer asking if she could speak to her face to face.

Not wanting to take the risk of encountering Fitzwilliam, Lady Beatrice suggested they meet in Perry's office. Leaving Daisy curled up with Alfie on the sofa in her sitting room, Lady Beatrice arrived at the same time as Spicer. Taking a seat in a chair around the office table in the far corner, she gestured for Spicer to take the one opposite.

As she sat down, Spicer's phone vibrated. "Sorry, my lady. I won't be a minute," she said as she answered.

Lady Beatrice picked up her own mobile phone. Lifting it up so it partially covered her face, she took the opportunity to surreptitiously study the woman opposite her. Spicer was about thirty, Lady Beatrice estimated, and she was fresh-faced and pretty. Her pale skin suited her oval-shaped face. Her red lips stood out, making her look a little pouty. She wore next to no makeup, although Lady Beatrice could detect a smidgen of mascara emphasising her sharp blue eyes. Her blonde shoulder-length hair, cut into a fashionable long bob, suited her slim frame. She was probably a 'petite' in dress terms. Today she looked business-like in black trousers and a black jacket. *The light pink T-shirt is a nice touch*, Lady Beatrice thought. It added a softness to the look. Overall, she looked like a woman you would happily hand your dog over to for them to walk, knowing they would bring them back safe and sound.

Spicer put her phone down and smiled. "Lady Rossex, thank you for meeting me. I need to talk to you about your personal security."

Putting her phone down, Lady Beatrice frowned.

"While this investigation is ongoing, we need to make sure we keep you safe." Spicer smiled again and raised her hand. "Don't worry. While you're on the estate, nothing needs to change. It's when you are outside the grounds we have to consider. So can we discuss what happens when you go off site on your own?"

Lady Beatrice shifted in her seat. *Well, this is embarrassing.* Apart from when she went on a run with Daisy, she didn't go off site on her own. In fact, she rarely went off site at all. *I'm glad I'm not having this conversation with Fitzwilliam.*

"I run on the beach three or four evenings a week with my dog," she informed Spicer

"Great. Do you drive to the beach and then run?"

"No, you can get to the beach from the south-east corner of the estate. It's about a mile there. I run through the dunes and along the beach, turn back on myself and return the same way. I do around ten kilometres in total." *Does that sound like a humble brag?*

"Okay, so we need to figure out a way to make you safe. Are you able to vary your run times, so you're not running at the same time every day?"

"Is it really necessary?"

Spicer nodded. "I'm afraid so, Lady Rossex. We need to take precautions while we investigate this murder. I also need someone to escort you. DCI

Fitzwilliam runs regularly; would you object to him running with you?"

Yes, I would — violently! "How about if I stick to running round the estate while the investigation is on? Would that work?" Lady Beatrice offered.

"Yes." Spicer nodded. "But please, if you want to run somewhere outside of the estate, then let me know and I'll find someone to run with you." She looked at Lady Beatrice and smiled. "It doesn't have to be the chief inspector."

"Indeed. Thank you."

"Do you go off site to meet with friends?"

About to say no and admit she was persona non grata outside of her family, Lady Beatrice remembered she was going to the pub tonight. *Thank goodness for Simon and Perry.* She told Spicer of her plans and the sergeant agreed to make arrangements for Lady Beatrice to be taken and dropped off with the least amount of fuss.

"Can I ask that if you decide to go anywhere, please let me or Adrian Breen know? We'll then make sure there's someone to get you there and back safely. Thank you, Lady Rossex. I appreciate your co-operation."

Watching Spicer leave the office, Lady Beatrice slowly stood. Not convinced that all this was truly necessary, she left the office and exited through the

Old Stable Block side door. As she rounded the corner, she was aware of the bright lights radiating from just outside the main gates. The press were still there, and it looked as if they were setting up camp for the night. Maybe the extra security wasn't such a silly idea after all.

Arriving at the north side gate at about six-fifty, she had expected to see a car waiting for her across the road on the other side. She was curious when Jeff Beesley, the lead officer for this evening's night shift, asked her to follow him.

"Hop in, Lady Rossex," he told her in a cheery voice as he pointed to a security buggy. "I'll have you and your little dog at the pub in five minutes and the press won't even know you've left the estate."

She held on tight to Daisy as the vehicle rounded the corner coming out of the lane. Flying over the tarmac pathway at what felt like an alarming speed, the buggy jumped when the surface changed to grass. With her clinging to the outside frame, they hurtled towards the pub on the other side of the green.

Too late now, she thought. *I must go through*

with this. How bad could it be? She'd have Perry, Simon, and Daisy with her. *You'll be fine,* she told herself as they skidded to a halt.

As Lady Beatrice unfurled herself from the buggy, legs shaking, Jeff handed her a card with a mobile phone number on it. "Ring or text me when you want picking up, my lady."

She hesitated, glancing over at the supercharged golf cart. *In that? It'll be freezing.*

Jeff chuckled, and with a brief nod, drove off.

Lady Beatrice entered the pub with Daisy and looked around for Perry and Simon. Daisy headed left towards the back of the pub. Not waiting for her mistress, she darted through an archway and into an annex off the main bar area.

Lady Beatrice followed, and soon she could see Perry and Simon sitting at a booth in the far corner. As she advanced towards them, they waved. By the time she arrived, Daisy was already on her back at Perry's feet, having a tummy rub.

"Would you like a drink?" Simon asked as he jumped to his feet.

"A gin and tonic would be lovely, thank you."

He nodded before making his way to the bar.

"So this is your first time in The Ship and Seal, what do you think?" Perry asked as he moved along the seat and Lady Beatrice slid in beside him. Daisy jumped up on the seat Simon had vacated opposite and lay down.

Lady Beatrice scanned around the pub and was pleasantly surprised. Although it was an older building, the inside looked contemporary and inviting. The sage green walls worked well with the dark-grey carpets. The combination of leather sofas and mustard tub chairs in front of low, chunky wooden coffee tables gave it a cosy feel. Along the perimeter were booths with built-in seats on either side of wooden tables. The surroundings were spacious but remained intimate at the same time.

"I like it. It's much bigger than it looks from the outside," she replied. "I was expecting cramped dark rooms with wooden floors, brass horseshoes, lots of Toby jugs, and bar stools," she admitted.

"Well, this is the posh bit." He beamed. "Dylan Milton and his wife Janey, who own this place, had it done up a few years ago to appeal to visitors and day trippers. They planned to do the whole place, but the locals weren't keen, so they agreed to keep the bar area as was. It's the one on the right as you first come in. There are no brass horseshoes, but it has a wooden floor, bar stools, and a selection of real ales. It keeps everyone happy."

Simon returned with her drink and copies of the menu. He shifted Daisy along the bench as he sat down and she rearranged herself, resting her head on his lap. Opening a menu, Lady Beatrice was impressed by all the options. Not sure what to pick, she asked them what they'd recommend.

"If you want something light, then the sea bass dish is great. If not, you can't beat the pork belly with apple," Simon replied.

"And the triple cooked chips are to die for," Perry added.

She opted for the sea bass. Simon chose the pork belly and Perry the mushroom risotto. Simon headed off to the bar with their order, and Lady Beatrice told Perry about her rather unusual mode of transport to the pub. He was still chuckling when Simon returned.

While they waited for their food to arrive, Simon took out his laptop.

"Right. I got as much information from Steve as I could earlier, and I've written it down. You can then add to it if you know anything more. Steve said they've narrowed the time of death to between eight twenty-three and five past nine."

"How did they do that?" Perry asked.

Simon consulted his notes.

"Well, Seth Padgett and Joe Fox saw Alex just before they went into breakfast, so that's the last time anyone saw him alive, as far as they know.

And you two found the body shortly after nine. Does that sound about right?"

Frowning, Lady Beatrice rubbed her forehead. "I arrived at the Breakfast Room at around… eight-thirty, I think. Seth and Joe were already there, and Pete arrived as I sat down." Nodding, she remembered checking her phone. She added more strongly, "We left just after nine. Sarah arrived five minutes before."

Simon's fingers sailed across his keyboard. "Next, I have a list of everyone who the police interviewed who were onsite that morning before you discovered the body. The police have excluded anyone who was working, like the serving staff, the kitchen staff and those who work or live in the main house. They were with others the whole time, so they have alibis. We don't need to worry about them."

Lady Beatrice and Perry nodded in agreement.

Looking up from his laptop, Simon said, "So, the list is, you two, Ellie Gunn, the catering manager, Sophie Crammond, the head housekeeper, Joe Fox, the apprentice gardener, Pete Cowley, another gardener, and Seth Padgett, the head gardener. Does that sound like everyone?"

"What about Lady Sarah? She was around that

morning. Did the police interview her?" Perry asked.

Simon checked on his laptop. "No, they didn't. I'll add her to the list."

"So, what happens now?" Lady Beatrice queried.

"Well, now that we know the approximate time of death, we can establish the time frame and work out where everyone was. That will crystallise the list of suspects who don't have a confirmed alibi."

Lady Beatrice nodded. "Where did Seth and Joe see Alex?"

"They had left the south gardens and were heading towards the Breakfast Room. They saw him coming from the direction of his cottage and going towards the Old Stable Block."

Closing his laptop as their food arrived, Simon put it back in its case and shoved it under the table. They ate in silence. The food was too delicious to stop eating to talk. Lady Beatrice was amazed that food of this quality was being served in the village pub.

As they were coming to the end of their meal, shouts erupted from the bar. Tables and chairs screeched across the floor. Putting his knife and fork down, Simon stood up and headed towards the noise. Lady Beatrice stared after him, a slight chill running up her spine.

"What's going on do you think?" she asked Perry, her eyes wide, one hand on her phone.

"Nothing to worry about. Simon will sort it out," he replied reassuringly.

"Daisy, no!" Her faithful companion was about to help herself to the remaining pork belly on Simon's plate. Stopping immediately, Daisy looked at Lady Beatrice as if to say *I wasn't doing anything.* "Lie down, Daisy." Lady Beatrice commanded, and the little dog settled back on the seat with a sigh.

Simon returned and took his seat next to Daisy. "It's all fine. Just a couple of press trying their luck. Dylan stopped them before they ordered a drink. He asked them to leave immediately."

Lady Beatrice looked over at the archway where she had come in earlier, her hand still gripping her phone.

"Don't worry, my lady. I saw them out myself and watched them drive off," Simon reassured her.

She smiled and thanked him, relaxing back in her chair. It was good to know he had her back.

"Right, let's make a plan," Simon said, bending down to retrieve his laptop and moving his plate out of the way. "So, taking our list, what we need to do next is work out each person's movements between the period eight-twenty and nine-fifteen. Who did you see, other than each other, and Seth, Joe, and Pete?" He looked across at Perry.

"Well, I know Mrs Crammond wasn't in her office when I went to pick up the key from her a few minutes before eight-thirty," Perry said.

"What about Ellie Gunn? Did either of you see her?" They both said no.

"Great, so that just leaves Lady Sarah," he replied.

"Wait," Lady Beatrice interrupted. "Surely my sister is not a suspect? She told us she was in her office taking calls." She twisted the rings on her right hand.

Simon replied, "Of course not. But I suggest we talk to her and find out if she saw anyone."

Lady Beatrice let out a breath and smiled at him. *I overreacted. Of course, they aren't suggesting my sister's a suspect.* But then, who is? Ellie Gunn seemed the most obvious — the bitter ex-girlfriend. *But I like Ellie.* How about Mrs Crammond? She hadn't been there when Perry had gone to get the keys. So where had she been? But then, why would she kill Alex? Why would any of them?

Shaking her head, she finished the last of her gin and tonic and picked up her phone. "I think I'll make a move if you don't mind." She texted Jeff. "I'll talk to Sarah tomorrow. I'll also try to get a few more details from Seth, Joe, and Pete about what they saw. Is that all right?"

"Great," Simon replied. "Perry, will you talk to Ellie Gunn and Mrs Crammond?" Perry nodded. "And I will have a chat with Adrian Breen. We worked together at Fenshire Police. I'll see if I can confirm who was onsite and what time they arrived."

Lady Beatrice's phone beeped.

Jeff: *Your carriage awaits outside, my lady. I have a blanket ready.*

Simon Lattimore watched Lady Beatrice leave. Her long red hair hung loosely around the shoulders of her brown suede jacket. Her biker boots made a *clunk, clunk* on the stone floor as she hurried towards the door. Simon thought she looked much younger than her thirty-five years.

She scanned nervously around her as she left the security of the booth. *No doubt searching for press*, Simon thought. As she disappeared through the door, he turned to Perry.

"Will she be okay getting home, do you think? Did they send a car for her?" he asked.

Perry laughed and told him about the security buggy.

Relaxing, Simon said, "Actually, that's a great idea. A car going in and out of Francis Court through the main entrance will attract press attention, but it's unlikely they're watching the north side gate as it's for pedestrians only."

When Perry suddenly frowned, his laughter dying away, Simon tensed up again. "What's up?"

"Do you think we should disregard Lady Sarah as a suspect because of who she is?"

Simon's eyes widened, then narrowed. "No, of course not. Why do you ask?"

"I popped my head round her office door to say good morning when I arrived on Wednesday. It was about eight. We chatted for a few minutes about our plans for the day and when I told her I was meeting Lady Bea at eight-thirty for breakfast, she said she'd join us." Perry paused.

"Go on," Simon said, encouraging him.

"Just before eight twenty-five, I left my office and thought I may as well pick her up on the way. But when I got to her office, she wasn't there. Neither was her coat and mobile, so I assumed she'd already left to go to breakfast. As I was slightly early, I went the front way so I could pick up the keys from Mrs Crammond on the way to the Breakfast Room and save us some time later."

He put his hand up to his chest. "Oh my giddy aunt, Simon. Alex could have already been dead in the Garden Room when I went past." His hand moved to his mouth. "Or even worse, he could have been in there dying and crying out for help as he heard me go past." The colour drained from his face.

Simon reached across the table and covered Perry's other hand with his own. "Perry, even if someone killed him that early, from what Roisin told me, he would have died immediately. So you don't need to worry about it. Carry on. You were going to get the keys."

Perry squeezed Simon's hand, took a deep breath, and continued, "When I arrived at Mrs Crammond's office, she wasn't there, so I went along the corridor and into the Breakfast Room. Lady Bea was already at our table, but Lady Sarah wasn't there. She didn't arrive until almost nine."

"Did she say where she'd been?"

"That's the thing, love. She said she'd been in her office on a long call."

Simon's eyebrows raised slightly.

"I didn't press it then because I assumed it was a personal matter, but she was not in her office and her coat and phone were gone."

Perry looked at Simon, waiting for his comment.

"Okay, well, that's certainly interesting. But before we get too carried away, I suggest you talk to her and see what she says. There is probably a perfectly reasonable explanation."

Perry smiled. "Yes, of course, you must be right. And that's why I love you so much. You put things in perspective for me. Now, should we finish up our drinks, go home and watch the rest of *Top Chef Masters*?"

18

EARLY MORNING, SATURDAY 10 APRIL

The Society Page online article:

Investigation Into Fatality at Francis Court in Fenshire is Now a Murder Enquiry

As we reported yesterday, the victim of the fatal incident which took place at Francis Court in Fenshire on Wednesday, has been confirmed as estate manager, Alex Sterling (44).

Francis Court issued the following statement last night, 'It is with deep sadness that we confirm the death of our estate manager, Alex Sterling, yesterday. Alex had worked for the Duke and Duchess of Arnwall for fifteen years and during that time was a valued member of staff. He will be greatly missed by the Astley family and his colleagues at

Francis Court. The circumstances of his death are being investigated by Fenshire CID and a team from the Protection and Investigation (Royal) Services (PaIRS). Our thoughts are with his family and friends at this difficult time.'

Heading up the PaIRS team is Detective Chief Inspector Richard Fitzwilliam. DCI Fitzwilliam was also part of the team who investigated the death of the Earl of Rossex, James Wiltshire, and Alex Sterling's wife, Gill, fourteen years ago.

A little dickie bird tells us DCI Fitzwilliam and Lady Beatrice, the Countess of Rossex, did not hit it off well while he was investigating her husband's death. Although not confirmed by the police, a source at Francis Court tells us Lady Beatrice discovered the body, so it will be interesting to see what happens now they have been thrown together again.

Walking across the Old Stable Block courtyard with Daisy by her side, Lady Beatrice glanced over to see if Sarah was in her office. It was empty. She had hoped to ask her sister if she had seen anyone on the morning of the murder and, in particular, if she'd seen Alex. Given he had been heading to the

Old Stable Block and Lady Sarah had been in her office, there was a high probability she'd seen him as he'd arrived. Lady Sarah could hopefully tell them where he had gone next. *I'll have to catch her later.*

She paused in front of the massive green sliding door of the gardening shed; it was open. *Now would be a good time to talk to Seth, Joe, and Pete.*

Once her eyes had adjusted to the lack of light inside the voluminous barn, she saw a figure at the far end of the building. As she moved closer, she identified Joe Fox, the young apprentice gardener. She looked around, but he appeared to be on his own.

"Hello Joe," she said, as she stopped in front of him. Daisy trotted up to him, tail wagging, to say hello.

He immediately finished what he was doing and bent down to scratch Daisy under the chin. "Hello, beautiful," he said to her. She licked his hand in return. He turned and stood before Lady Beatrice, fidgeting. "Your Ladyship," he responded in a shaky voice, giving her an awkward bow. Daisy had made herself comfortable at his feet.

"Joe, sorry to trouble you. I'd like to ask you a few questions about the morning of Alex Sterling's death, if I may?"

Joe looked furtively around the barn. "Am I in trouble?"

"No, of course not, Joe. I didn't mean to alarm you."

"It's just that I've already spoken to the police, Lady Rossex. I couldn't tell them much. My mum gave me the third degree when I got home, but I didn't do anything. I hardly knew the dead man."

His wide eyes staring into her face, Lady Beatrice tried to reassure him. "It's okay, Joe. No one is suggesting you had anything to do with Mr Sterling's death. I just have a couple of questions about what you all did that day. Just so I can get things straight in my head." She smiled at him. "Can you help me?"

He nodded.

Phew. I see what Simon meant about not barging in and upsetting witnesses.

"Thank you. So, what time did you start on Wednesday?"

"I arrived at about six-fifty, my lady. I like to get here early."

She nodded at him in what she hoped was an encouraging way. "And what did you do then?"

"Um, well, we always have a cup of tea together here before we start on the day's jobs. Seth tells us what he wants us to do. That morning he wanted me to work in the rose garden, so I took the buggy and went over to the south gardens."

"The rose garden is my favourite part of the grounds," Lady Beatrice told him. "It always looks well-tended. Now I know it's you I have to thank for that." Grinning, he relaxed. "So then what happened?"

"Nothing, my lady. I worked there until Seth came to pick me up for breakfast. Then we went to the Breakfast Room together."

"Is that when you saw Alex Sterling?" she asked. Joe was looking over her shoulder towards the door. Daisy jumped up, her tail wagging. Lady Beatrice turned to see Seth Padgett edging into the dim light. She coughed, and Joe looked back at her.

"Yes, we were over by the front of the rose garden, and he was on our left walking towards the Old Stable Block."

"Which way was he coming from?" she asked, trying to visualise the scene in her head.

"From the southwest of the estate, my lady."

Seth had now joined them. "Is everything okay, Lady Rossex?" he enquired as he bent down to stroke Daisy's head.

"Yes, thank you, Seth. I was asking Joe about seeing Alex on the morning of his death."

"Ah. Well, I was with Joe when we saw him,

my lady. He was coming from the direction of his cottage and appeared to be heading over to the Old Stable Block."

"He has—sorry, I mean had, an office here, I understand?"

"Yes, my lady. He was wearing overalls, wasn't he, Joe?" When Joe nodded, he continued, "So I just assumed he was ready for the move we were due to do for you and Mr Juke at ten. Maybe he was getting an early start, my lady?"

"That's possible. Did he normally go to breakfast with everyone else?"

"Not always, my lady. I guess with his house being so close, he sometimes ate there before he left."

"And what time was it you saw him?" Joe looked at Seth.

"It was a few minutes after I picked Joe up. We walked to the Breakfast Room and not long after we sat down, you and your dog arrived, my lady."

"Yes," she confirmed. "I remember seeing you both. Pete Cowley came in shortly after me and joined you. Do you know where he'd been?"

"He was up at the compost clearing area, my lady. Then he came and joined us for breakfast at eight-thirty," Seth replied.

"Thanks, Seth. Did he say if he saw Alex on the way?"

"Can't say I've asked him, my lady, but you can ask him yourself." He looked at his watch. "He'll be here any minute to clean up. We finish at noon on Saturdays."

As if on cue, Pete entered the barn and made his way towards them. Daisy ran over to meet him. Stopping, he bent to fuss her then carried on towards them on with Daisy by his side.

"Lady Rossex." He nodded at Lady Beatrice before heading over to stand beside Joe and Seth. He glanced at Seth and raised his eyebrows.

"Ah, Pete, just the man," Seth said. "We're talking to Lady Rossex about the morning Alex Sterling died. She asked if you saw him on your way to the Breakfast Room?" They all looked at Pete expectantly.

"No, I didn't." He shook his head, then hesitated. "Which is strange, now that I think about it, as he and I must have been heading in the same direction."

"Ah, but from where you were the trees would have obscured your view," Seth said.

Pete went silent for a moment and then murmured, "I suppose so."

Seth looked at his watch again and Lady Beatrice glanced at her phone, confirming it was just after twelve.

She smiled at the three men. "Many thanks for your help, gentlemen. I'll let you get on and enjoy the rest of your weekend. Come on, Daisy."

The Breakfast Room was busier than usual when Lady Beatrice and Daisy entered a few minutes later. The grounds were open to the public again, and there were a handful of tourists scattered around the restaurant, along with some retail staff taking an early lunch. According to Lady Sarah, their mother got into a stand-up row with Fitzwilliam, threatening to sue PaIRS for loss of earnings if he refused to let her re-open. *I wish I'd been there.* Lady Beatrice smiled to herself. He must have capitulated eventually as they had opened the gates at ten this morning, as usual. Daisy ran over to where Perry and Simon were sitting to say hello. There was already a large black coffee waiting for Lady Beatrice.

"Sorry I'm late. I managed to catch Seth, Joe, and Pete before they left for the weekend."

"No problem," Simon replied. "We haven't ordered food yet."

A server appeared and took their orders. As soon as she left, Simon asked, "So how did it go with the gardening boys?"

She told them what they had said, then Perry reported on his conversation with Mrs Crammond.

"She told me she'd arrived onsite at eight and went straight to her office, where she stayed all morning. She also told me Ellie Gunn arrived about ten minutes later and popped her head around the door to say good morning. When I queried why she hadn't been in her office when I went to pick up the key just before eight-thirty, she said, 'Oh yes, I had a headache and went out into the fresh air for a little while.' She was vague and seemed touchy."

"Do you think she was lying?" Simon asked.

Perry paused and then shrugged. "I don't know." He frowned. "But she definitely didn't want to talk about it anymore. She stood up and said, 'Oh, is that the time? I should be leaving.' So, I took the hint and left."

"What about Ellie Gunn? Did you see her too?" Lady Beatrice asked.

"No, it's her day off. I'll have to catch-up with her on Monday. Oh, and that reminds me, Mrs C said Cass was in early too that day. She came in with Ellie."

"Who's Cass?" Lady Beatrice asked

"Ellie's daughter. She works here in the garden centre and lives with her dad in Fawstead Town. Sometimes she stays with her mum overnight in the village if she's opening up the next morning."

The server returned with their food, and they stopped talking while she placed it on the table.

As they ate, Simon reported Adrian Breen had given him access to the security log, which recorded all comings and goings at Francis Court.

"I took photos of the list of people who'd entered the estate, both through the side gates and the main entrance, on the day of the murder." He showed her his screen. "We need to add them to the suspects spreadsheet so we can cross reference them. Then we can check we've talked to everyone who was onsite during the critical period." He settled back in his seat and folded his arms.

"That sounds great, Simon. It feels like we're getting somewhere," Lady Beatrice said, sliding his phone back across the table.

As she stood to leave, the two men grinned at each other, then Simon nodded to Perry.

What are they up to?

"Do you have anything planned tonight?" Perry asked.

Sitting down again, she replied, "I have nothing

on for the rest of today except taking Daisy for a run around the estate. Why do you ask?"

"Well, we wondered if you'd like to come over to the cottage tonight and eat with us?"

She hadn't been expecting that. Meeting them in the pub last night had been fun. But it had been an evening with a purpose. *This is different.* This was going to their home. A social invitation; more personal than going to the pub. *What will we talk about?* She studied them. They were both leaning forward. Perry was rubbing his hands together while Simon was smiling at her. *Do they really want me to say yes?*

"I'd love to," she replied.

They beamed at her.

"Brilliant!" Perry clapped. "Simon is cooking, and I'll be pouring the wine."

"And getting in the way," Simon added. They both laughed.

"Oh, and you can bring Daisy, of course," Perry added.

"We'll look forward to it," she told them. "What time do you want us?"

"About seven?" Simon replied.

"How will you be arriving, my lady?" Perry grinned. "By security buggy or car?"

"I've no idea." She giggled. "It'll be a surprise.

And thank you so much for asking me." She shocked herself by adding, "I can't remember the last time I went out on a Saturday night."

Her cheeks heated. *Did I just admit to them I have no social life?*

Jumping up, not meeting their gaze, she said, "Come on Daisy," then fled out of the door.

19

LUNCHTIME, SATURDAY 10 APRIL

Perry said goodbye to Simon at the entrance to the Old Stable Block courtyard and walked across the cobbles to his office. There was movement in Lady Sarah's, and he quickened his pace, wanting to catch her before she left. He knew he would feel so much better if he could clear up the discrepancies in her story. Entering her office, he found Lady Sarah packing up her laptop.

"Hi, Sarah."

She looked up and smiled. "Perry, I thought you'd already left for the weekend?"

"No, I was having an early lunch with Lady Beatrice and Simon in the Breakfast Room. I've come back to pack up my office before I go." She nodded.

"So have the police interviewed you yet?" he asked, quickly adding, "Mine is on Monday first thing, and I wondered what it'll be like." He rubbed his forehead.

"Yes, Mike and a young sergeant interviewed me this morning. It went fine, but then I had little to tell them."

"So you didn't see anyone that morning before you met us for breakfast?"

She shook her head. "I was in my office with my head down, writing the final copy for the marketing brochure. I didn't see or talk to anyone." Not meeting his eyes, she patted her bun and smoothed down her dress.

What about the long phone call she had mentioned at breakfast? He frowned. *Do I challenge her or accept her statement even though I'm sure it's not true?* Their excellent working relationship was important to him, but then so was the truth. He remembered what Simon had said about there being a reasonable explanation. *Here goes.*

"I came by at eight-thirty, but your office was empty."

Shrugging, she gazed over his shoulder. "Oh, did you? Well, it must have been when I popped out to the loo."

With your coat? Perry was now sure she was hiding something, but he didn't want to push too far before he spoke to Simon. He nodded.

She reached for her camel cashmere coat and put it on, pulling the belt tight. Picking up her phone, laptop, and car keys, she said, "Sorry, Perry, I need to go. Have a fabulous weekend, and I hope your interview goes well on Monday."

And with that, she disappeared, leaving Perry to return to his own office deep in thought.

"Have a good evening, my lady. Let me know when you need picking up." Jeff doffed his cap as Lady Beatrice stepped out of the security buggy. She was getting used to being driven around in this unusual mode of transport. Daisy was enjoying it too, having spent most of the journey on Lady Beatrice's lap with her head stuck out of the side, her ears flapping.

Lady Beatrice opened the sage green gate and ambled up the pathway to Rose Cottage. She inhaled deeply; the scent of rosemary filled her senses. *Mmm... I love that smell.* Continuing up the path, the symmetrical white stone building ahead of her looked larger than she had expected from the road. Clutching the bottle of malbec Harris had selected for her from the Francis Court wine cellar, she rang the bell.

Perry swept open the door and stood before her, grinning. "Welcome to Rose Cottage," he announced, his arms stretched out in the manner of a ringmaster. Daisy barked, wagging her tail, and running around his feet. He laughed as she skidded to a halt in front of him, ready for a fuss. He bent down and stroked her head. "You smell lovely Daisy," he said as he sniffed his hand. "I love rosemary. It makes me think of home."

They entered the hallway as Daisy ran ahead through the open door towards the back of the house. Following Perry into a spacious open-plan kitchen and dining area, she found Simon standing by a sizeable stove, saying hello to Daisy.

"It smells fabulous in here," Lady Beatrice said as she handed the bottle of wine to Perry.

"I take no credit for that," Perry responded. "It's all that man over there." He nodded in Simon's direction.

"Okay, Lady Bea?" Simon smiled as he placed a mighty earthenware pot on the marble island. "You two sit down. I won't be long."

He gestured to the large wooden table and chairs over on the other side of the room. The black trimmed double bi-fold windows behind them overlooked the garden and as Lady Beatrice sat down, the evening light cast jumping shadows on the table. At the end of the long cottage-style garden, she could see what looked like a summerhouse.

"How's the latest book going, Simon?" she asked as he walked over to the table and placed a plate of tomato and olive focaccia in the middle.

"In fits and starts. I'm still in the planning stage, so it's slow going some days."

Disappearing back to the kitchen area, he returned a few minutes later with the oversized casserole dish. Daisy followed him, or more accurately, followed the food. As he lifted the lid off, the aroma was so intoxicating, Lady Beatrice salivated. She and Perry peered inside. There were three lobster tails surrounded by a stew. She could see mushrooms, pine nuts, and chunks of fish.

"It looks and smells amazing, Simon. What is it?" she asked.

"It's my take on an Italian fish stew called *Buridda*. It's a traditional dish made with the cheaper cuts and offcuts of fish, but I thought lobster would elevate it. Right, let's dig in."

Happy to oblige, she held out her plate and accepted a slice of focaccia. When Simon had served Lady Beatrice and Perry, he took a bowl and filled it with some of the fish.

"I haven't forgotten you, little girl," he said as he placed it in front of Daisy.

"Simon, this is incredible," Lady Beatrice exclaimed as she took a second mouthful. It was, indeed, as delicious as it had smelled. "I had no idea you could cook this well. You should be a chef."

Perry and Simon exchanged confused looks.

She fidgeted in her seat. *Have I said something wrong?*

"Do you watch *Elitechef* on the television?" Perry asked.

She shook her head. "No, sorry, what is it?"

They grinned at each other. "It's a well-known and popular cooking show. Amateur cooks compete over various rounds, and after each round someone gets eliminated until there are only two left. The final two cook off against each other in the finale and one of them wins the title of *Elitechef.*" Simon explained.

Perry carried on. "They also do a celebrity version. Simon was in it last year, and he won!"

"Well, I'm not surprised," Lady Beatrice responded. "This is scrumptious."

"And he wrote a cookbook afterwards," Perry chipped in. He jumped up and hurried over to a shelf near the fridge. He came back with a cookbook and handed it to her.

On the cover was a picture of Simon standing in front of a table of colourful vegetables and fresh pastas. *Simon Cooks* was beautifully typeset at the top.

"How did I not know this?" she asked. "I'm so sorry. You must think I'm completely out of touch."

"It's fine," Perry reassured her. "If you've never seen the show, then you wouldn't know Simon is now a famous chef and cookbook author, as well as a crime writer." Smiling, he laid his hand on Simon's arm and squeezed it.

Simon blushed and cleared his throat. "I'm hardly a chef and that was my one, and possibly only, cookbook. I love cooking and I was lucky." He shrugged.

"You are too modest, love." Perry patted his hand.

"I agree," Lady Beatrice added. "This is as good as anything I've had in a Michelin starred restaurant. Better, in fact."

"I'd still rather be a writer, but thank you for the compliments." He smiled at them both and picked up a piece of focaccia.

They finished the stew, and Simon retrieved a plate of cheese and biscuits from the kitchen.

Lady Beatrice sighed. "I don't think I have any room left," she said, holding her stomach.

"I'll leave it here in case you change your mind," he said with a wink.

Looking away from the tempting display of cheese in front of her, she reached for her bag lying under the table. She took out a folder and handed them each a sheet of paper.

"I've made a list of suspects and their known movements from the information we have gathered so far. I thought it might help us."

They looked at her in astonishment.

She shrugged. "All right, I admit it. I had nothing better to do this afternoon." They all laughed.

"So we still need to talk to Ellie Gunn," she said. "Perry, you're doing that on Monday, aren't you?" When Perry nodded, she continued, "And we mustn't forget her daughter, Cass. I can't imagine she is our murderer, but she may have seen something that will help us."

"I wouldn't be so quick to dismiss her," Simon responded. Perry and Lady Beatrice looked at him in bewilderment.

"She's only nineteen years old," Perry countered.

"I know, but the rumours are she didn't approve of the relationship between her mother and Alex. She blamed him for her parents' split."

"How do you know this?" Perry quizzed him.

"I overheard Mrs Cutter talking about it to Peter in Tappin's Teas a few weeks ago."

Lady Beatrice frowned. *Who are these people?* She looked at Perry, hoping for enlightenment.

"Mrs Cutter was one of my neighbours when I lived at Daffodil Cottage before I moved in with Simon. I rent the cottage out to Ellie Gunn now. Oh, and Tappin's Teas is in the village, on the road that leads to the beach."

"Peter Tappin is the owner, a huge gossip and still in the closet," Simon added.

"Simon!" Perry dramatically slapped his hand to his chest and shook his head. "Poor Peter just hasn't met the right woman yet." They both dissolved into a fit of laughter.

"Sorry," Simon apologised to her. "It's a standing joke with us. We're convinced he's gay, but he seems to be in total denial. He acted shocked and disgusted when Perry moved in with me three years ago. Even now, when we go into his tearoom together, he is ever so disapproving."

"I like to go in there sometimes just to see his face." Perry giggled. "He tuts and huffs like the ancient women he likes to gossip with. He particularly dislikes me. I'm sure he had a crush on Simon and hasn't forgiven me for stealing him away."

Simon shook his head. "Perry, I love you dearly, but you do talk nonsense sometimes." He smiled at his partner, and Perry playfully stuck his tongue out in return.

"As I was saying," Simon continued, "Mrs Cutter told Peter that Alex had called at Daffodil Cottage when Ellie was out. Cass, who stayed that night, opened the door to him and they had an argument on the doorstep. Mrs Cutter heard it all from her sitting room where she happened to have the window open."

Perry rolled his eyes and shook his head. "More like she saw Alex arrive and opened the window to eavesdrop on the conversation, the old bat."

Simon continued, "She heard Cass tell him to go away and leave her mum alone. Alex responded that he just wanted to talk to Ellie. Cass lost her temper and shouted at him, accusing him of breaking her parents up. She told him if he didn't leave her mum alone, he would be sorry. Mrs Cutter was shocked. She told Peter that Cass was normally such a nice, quiet girl."

"Well, that *is* interesting," Perry remarked.

"Indeed," Lady Beatrice agreed.

"It certainly gives Cass a motive," Simon pointed out.

"I'll try to see her on Monday," Perry informed them.

20

MID-MORNING, MONDAY 10 APRIL

The Society Page online article:

Heavy Security Presence at Wilton College and Francis Court as Killer Still on the Loose.

Yesterday, Lady Beatrice (35), the Countess of Rossex, arrived at Wilton College accompanied by a team of close protection officers. Her son, Samuel (13) has been a boarder at Wilton since January, following in the footsteps of both his father, James Wiltshire, and his paternal grandfather, William Wiltshire, who are Wilton alumni.

Lady Beatrice was there to support her son who was playing in his first cricket match for the school. James Wiltshire, who was killed in a car accident fourteen years ago, was a previous captain of the

Wilton College cricket team. Lady Beatrice must be proud to see her son following in his father's footsteps. Wilton College beat neighbouring school, Milton Academy, by twenty runs.

Meanwhile back at Francis Court, the popular press, camped out nearby, continue to speculate if the Astley family who live there, and the public who visit the house and grounds, are safe and ask if enough is being done to catch Alex Sterling's killer.

"Good morning, Perry." Lady Beatrice entered Perry's office and moved straight to the coffeepot sitting on the machine on top of his bookcase. She poured herself a mugful, while Daisy licked Perry's hand and then wandered over and settled in her bed.

"So, how did—" she asked.

"I spoke to Ellie this—" Perry began.

They both laughed.

"You first," Lady Beatrice told him.

"Thanks," he replied. "So I spoke to Ellie. She confirmed that on the morning of the murder, she walked here from the village with Cass. They left at eight, so that's consistent with them being logged in at the north side gate at seven minutes past eight.

She said she parted with Cass, who was going to the garden centre, shortly after they arrived. She continued to her office, going via the north side door. Then she went to say hello to Mrs C before going to her own office, where she was until about nine-fifteen when she had a meeting scheduled."

"Can anyone confirm that?"

He shook his head. "Not that I know of. I asked her if she saw anyone, but she said no, she was busy doing some costings."

Lady Beatrice huffed. "Well, that doesn't help us much, does it?"

"No, not much. Cass isn't back in work until Thursday, so I can't do anything further on that front either."

She leaned back in the chair and crossed her arms. *So, what now?* Her phone burst into *Bring Me Sunshine*. Picking it up, she switched the alarm off. "I have to go for my interview. How did yours go?"

Perry shrugged. "It was with Mike and the pretty female DS from PaIRS. It was straightforward. I went through finding the body again and they asked a few extra questions about when I arrived onsite and who I met."

She nodded. That was a relief. At least she wouldn't have to deal with Fitzwilliam. "That sounds fine. I'll ask Mike when we can have the Garden Room back. We need access soon, now that we've almost finished the Smoking Room. Come on, Daisy."

DS Spicer smiled at Lady Beatrice as she and Daisy entered the PaIRS office. Lady Beatrice's smile turned to a scowl. *Blast! What's he doing here?* DCI Fitzwilliam was leaning on the outside edge of an office desk, his arms crossed. *Maybe he's just leaving?*

"Good afternoon, Lady Rossex. Thank you for coming," Spicer said, sounding like she was welcoming Lady Beatrice to a drinks party rather than a police interview.

Daisy sniffed at Spicer's hand and received a pat on the head. She then headed over to Fitzwilliam, tail wagging. He bent down to fuss her. Lady Beatrice frantically looked around, but couldn't see Mike Ainsley in the cramped office. "Are we waiting for Mike?" she asked Spicer.

"No," Fitzwilliam butted in. "Sorry, but it's just us. Mike was called away, but I assured him we could manage you all on our own."

Sarcastic numpty!

He was still fussing Daisy. Lady Beatrice wished Daisy didn't like him so much.

"Would you like to sit down, Lady Rossex?" Spicer gestured towards a round table with four chairs in the corner of the office. Sitting down next to Spicer, Lady Beatrice frowned as Daisy trotted behind Fitzwilliam, then curled up by his feet when he took the chair opposite her. *Daisy, you traitor!*

"Before we start—" Lady Beatrice turned to Fitzwilliam. "Can you confirm when we can have the Garden Room back, please, chief inspector? We've already lost five days and my deadline to complete this project is non-negotiable."

"Well, I am sorry this murder has disrupted your schedule, Lady Rossex. How inconvenient for you," he jeered.

That's not what I mean, and you know it.

"But unfortunately, it takes the forensics boys time to go through the room with a fine-tooth comb when someone has been bludgeoned to death." He crossed his arms, and placing his elbows on the table, leaned forward.

She sighed. "I understand *that,* chief inspector, but as far as I'm aware, the forensics team left on Saturday morning. Are they coming back?"

"You should be able to have the room back by

two," Spicer replied for him, clearly wanting to move on. She sent a warning look to her boss.

"Thank you." Lady Beatrice gave her a grateful smile.

"So, Lady Rossex, can we go through the morning Alex Sterling died, please?" Fitzwilliam asked, taking a notebook from his jacket pocket. She opened her mouth, but he ignored her and carried on talking. "Your maid, Naomi, told us she woke you up at eight, brought you a coffee and left to take Daisy out. Is that correct?"

His disapproval of the misconception that she had someone to wake her up, bring her a coffee, and take her dog out to the loo for her every day, was written all over his face. Lady Beatrice wanted to shout at him *I don't!* Instead, she sat back in her chair and crossed her arms. It wasn't normal for Naomi to bring her coffee or take Daisy out. Lady Beatrice had known nothing about it until Naomi had knocked on her door that morning. *Why am I feeling so defensive?* She wished it didn't bother her so much; but he was just so judgemental. *Get a grip, Bea, and don't rise to it.*

"To be more accurate, chief inspector, Naomi is my mother's maid. But yes, that's correct," she disclosed.

"She said she returned about fifteen minutes

later with Daisy and you'd showered and were in your dressing room getting ready?"

Really? Did he need to confirm all these personal details about her morning routine? *Let it go, Bea.* She shifted in her chair and nodded.

"Then she cleared up your bathroom and made your bed while you were in your sitting room drinking your coffee?"

This is ridiculous! *He's definitely doing this to embarrass me. Well, I will not make excuses. I don't care what he thinks. I won't let him get to me.* Lady Beatrice nodded again.

"Is there anything you'd like to add, Lady Rossex?" He asked nonchalantly.

Well, he did ask... two can play at this game. I'll show him unnecessary details.

Lady Beatrice took a deep breath. "I finished my coffee. I have it black, so it had been a little too hot for me to drink earlier. Obviously, I left the cup for someone to clear up later. I put Daisy's harness on her; I managed to do that all by myself." She looked at him and smiled sweetly. DS Spicer appeared to be stifling a snort of laughter.

"I left the room with Naomi and Daisy. When we reached the end of the corridor, I realised I'd not picked up my mobile phone. I asked Naomi what the time was. She looked at her watch but said it still showed eight, so it must have stopped working. She said it had been running slow and probably needed a new battery. I decided I had time to go back to my sitting room and retrieve my phone, so I told her to carry on without me. When I returned to my apartment and retrieved my phone, it said eight twenty-six." She took another deep breath, planning to continue, but Fitzwilliam interrupted her.

"Don't you wear a watch, Lady Rossex?" He'd made it sound like an accusation.

"No, chief inspector. I live in a vast house which is chock-full of clocks. At least one in every room. So unless I'm in a corridor with none, as I was in this instance, I only need to look around to know what the time is." She smirked and recommenced her narrative.

"So having collected my phone, Daisy and I turned right out of my rooms and down the corridor. We took the west wing stairs at the bottom of the corridor to the ground floor. There we entered the Painted Hall. There are lots of clocks in the Painted Hall, chief inspector, and I'm sure I heard one of them chime, so it must have been eight-thirty."

Spicer, sitting next to her, appeared to be shaking.

"We then proceeded through the side door of the main entrance, turned right, and followed the front of the house along until we reached the front doors to the Breakfast Room. We walked into the restaurant and seated ourselves at a table on the right-hand side of the room, near the window over-looking the terrace. Seth Padgett, the head gardener, and Joe Fox, the apprentice gardener, were already there at that point. I ordered coffee and food from Nicky, the server. Pete Cowley, another gardener, arrived a few minutes later. Perry Juke arrived shortly after Pete, but from the back entrance of the room." She paused and asked him in her best inno-cent voice, "Would you like to hear what I had for breakfast, chief inspector?"

She could hear Spicer taking a slow breath in, as if to calm herself. She was looking down so Lady Beatrice couldn't see her face, but she ap-peared to wipe her eyes as she picked up her pen, ready to take more notes.

"That won't be necessary, Lady Rossex," Fitzwilliam replied. He leaned back in his chair, his arms hugging his chest, his face pinched. "Let's skip to when you found the body, please." Unravelling his arms, he picked up a piece of white A4 paper. "I have the statement you and Mr Juke gave to DI Ainsley here, and I'm going to ask you some supplementary questions. So to start with, I understand from Mr Juke that the two of you collected the keys from Mrs Crammond, the head housekeeper, at ten past nine. Is that correct?"

Lady Beatrice nodded.

"So then what happened?"

She made to open her mouth, but he jumped in. "And Lady Rossex, please keep it brief. I'm only interested in what you saw relating to the crime scene, not how you moved across the room."

Insufferable man!

"Of course, chief inspector. I'm sure we both have better things to do than waste time on unnecessary details."

Spicer put her hand up to her mouth and coughed while Fitzwilliam cast Lady Beatrice an angry glare. *If looks could kill...*

She continued, "When Mr Juke went to unlock the door, we discovered it was already unlocked. It was dark inside, so I switched on the main lights. And that's when we saw the body."

"Then what did you do?"

"Mr Juke checked for a pulse, and I radioed Adrian Breen, our head of security."

"And did you touch anything in the room, Lady Rossex?" he asked, still staring blackly at her.

"No."

"Are you sure?"

Of course I'm sure you frightful man! She nodded.

"So you didn't touch the radiator then, my lady?" Fitzwilliam gave her an unblinking glower.

Lady Beatrice sighed. *Rats!* "Yes, sorry, I forgot. Perry, sorry, Mr Juke, commented on how hot it was in the room. I went over to the radiator, and it was on full. I turned it down."

"So you did touch something, then?"

She slowly nodded, barely managing to stifle a wince.

"Thus wiping off any fingerprints that the murderer may have left." He pierced her with an accusatory stare.

Oh for goodness' sake! I didn't know it was a murder scene, did I?

"Unintentionally, I suppose that's possible. But surely a murderer would have worn gloves?" she said, returning his stone-cold stare with one of her own.

He looked down at the paper. "Did you touch anything else, Lady Rossex?"

"No!" she replied, trying hard not to shout.

Fitzwilliam raised an eyebrow. "Then what did you do next?"

"We locked up the room and waited outside for Mr Breen and the police to arrive."

"Did you leave immediately after you called him?"

"Yes."

"Are you sure, Lady Rossex?"

Oh no, what else did I do? She couldn't think of anything. She nodded.

"You told DI Ainsley that the room looked"—he referred to the statements—"*unnatural*. What does that mean exactly, Lady Rossex?"

I don't know! She sighed. What could she say that wouldn't make her look like an idiot?

"The layout of the room just looked odd to me, chief inspector. It wasn't how I remembered it being when we were in there two days earlier."

"Was something missing?" he asked.

She shook her head. "No, I don't think so."

He wrinkled his nose. "It just looked *odd*?"

She'd had enough now. "Yes, chief inspector. I can't put my finger on why. It just did." Rising from the chair, she continued, "Is that all? I'm extremely busy and I'd like to get on, if you don't mind." She glared down at him, mirroring his grim look. He unfurled himself from his chair and stood up, towering over her.

"That is all… for *now*."

She wanted to scream. Instead, she smiled insincerely at him, then turned to catch Spicer's eye.

"Are you any further forward now that you have interviewed everyone?" she asked her. Spicer rose from her chair and glanced over at Fitzwilliam.

He responded before she could. "Our enquiries are ongoing, Lady Rossex."

Not helpful. Stomping towards the door, she signalled for Daisy to follow her. She turned to Fitzwilliam and grimaced. "Well, let's hope your enquiries come to something soon before we are all murdered in our beds, chief inspector."

Lady Beatrice entered the back door of the cafe. *Was I childish with my parting remark?* That man irritated her beyond belief. She couldn't help herself.

She waited at the counter behind two other people and texted Perry.

Lady B: *That man really lives up to his name! On the plus side, we can have access to TGR at 2. Can you organise the gardening boys to be there at 3, please? I will meet you there at 2 as I want to take a few measurements and mark up items before they take things away. Is that all right?*

. . .

She reached the front of the queue and ordered a tuna sandwich and a large black coffee to go.

Perry: *OMGA! What did you do? No, don't tell me now. You can tell me all about it later when I see you. Boys booked for 3. Will see you there at 2.*

21

2:05 PM, MONDAY 12 APRIL

"Nice one!" Perry Juke exclaimed, grinning at her, clearly impressed with her parting shot at DCI Fitzwilliam.

"Do you think it was childish of me?" She was still concerned she'd behaved dreadfully.

"No. You were retaliating. That's not childish. Promise me I can come with you the next time you talk to him. I can stand at the back and have fits of the giggles with the pretty DS."

Lady Beatrice wrinkled her nose at him. Picking up the tape measure, she headed over to the walnut cocktail cabinet along the wall on the far-left side of the room. Natural light poured in through the French doors and the room looked so much brighter now that the tarpaulin was down. She heaved a sigh; something was still nagging her about the room's setup.

"Let's measure up the drinks cabinet and see if it will fit in the Salon as you've suggested," she said.

Daisy followed them across the room and crouched down in front of the cabinet, her nose pressed to the bottom. They moved the unit a fraction away from the edge of the wall so Lady Beatrice could fit the tape measure up against the back.

"The width is seventy-five centimetres," she relayed to Perry, and he made a note on his phone.

"Daisy, what are you doing? Get out of the way," Perry cried as she darted between his legs, nearly knocking him over. Trying to reach underneath the cabinet, she was pawing at the front, sniffing.

"What is it, Daisy?" Lady Beatrice asked her. "When she acts like this, it normally means her ball has gone under a piece of furniture," she told Perry. "Is there something underneath there, Daisy?"

As Daisy tried to squeeze herself under the cabinet, they moved the piece further away from the wall, lifting it as they went. Daisy was now pawing at the back of the cabinet from the side.

"Daisy, leave!" Lady Beatrice cried.

Daisy stopped and plopped herself down, her

tail still wagging. They pulled the cabinet further away from the wall. Lady Beatrice looked behind it and could see something round and shiny, about the size of a fifty-pence piece, against the back leg.

"Stop!" she shouted at Perry, putting her end down. "There's something behind there."

Turning on her phone's flashlight, she angled it at the back of the drinks cabinet to take a better look. The object was about five centimetres in diameter and dark-blue or dark-grey.

Lady Beatrice let out an involuntary gasp. "It's a button," she said as she straightened up. Then she frowned. "I suppose it might be nothing to do with the murder."

"You could be right." Perry's eyes widened. "But this room and the Smoking Room had a complete spring clean only ten days ago. They would've moved all the furniture, so it can't have been there long."

"But if forensics already examined this room, how on earth could they have missed it?" Perry shrugged. "I think we need to call the police."

Perry nodded and gently placed his end of the cabinet back on the wooden floor. He picked up his radio. "DI Ainsley, this is Perry Juke, over."

Lady Beatrice moved Daisy away from the cabinet and squatted down to give her a big hug.

"Good girl, Daisy," she said as the terrier wagged her tail and licked Lady Beatrice's ear.

"Mr Juke, this is DS Spicer. DI Ainsley is off site. Can I help, over?"

Perry looked at Lady Beatrice, and she nodded. She would rather have dealt with Mike, but right now, they didn't appear to have a choice.

"DS Spicer, we've found something in the Garden Room you need to see, over."

"Mr Juke, we're on our way, out."

We? Lady Beatrice looked at Perry. "Did she say *we*?" He nodded.

No! Not Fitzwilliam again so soon. She couldn't bear to face him again after his earlier interrogation of her. Would he now accuse her of tampering with evidence? *Is it too late to run and hide?*

It was at that moment DCI Fitzwilliam strode into the room, DS Spicer following closely behind.

"So, what's this about, Mr Juke?" Fitzwilliam demanded.

Lady Beatrice looked over at Perry, who was on his phone texting. She answered for him. "Chief inspector, Daisy has found something behind the leg of the drinks cabinet. We thought it best to call you before we moved anything in case it's important evidence. It's a button."

There was an immediate change in

Fitzwilliam's demeanour. He beckoned to Spicer, and they walked over to the drinks cabinet. "Which leg?"

"The left one at the rear." Lady Beatrice pointed.

Fitzwilliam took out his phone, and using the flashlight, he peered behind the cabinet. Spicer looked over his shoulder. They stood up and he nodded to her. "Take a photo and bag it up, then call Mike and ask him to send the forensics team back and tell them to do a proper job this time."

"Is it—" Spicer began, but he cut her off.

"Looks like it."

Fitzwilliam turned to Lady Beatrice, a smirk on his lips. "I'm afraid we're going to need the room back for a while." His tone was sharp, his voice unapologetic.

She was not being removed from this room again without a fight. "But chief inspector, we need to get on. Is it *that* important?"

"Lady Rossex," he barked back, his jaw clenching. "As I've already explained to you once today, this is a murder enquiry and therefore has precedence over your room makeover. Do I make myself clear?"

How boorish! "Crystal," she snapped back.

"Come on Daisy, Perry. Let's leave the police to do their job… again."

Daisy, who was sitting next to Fitzwilliam, looked up at him. He bent down and patted the top of her head, saying, "Well done, Daisy, you clever girl."

Leave my dog alone! Lady Beatrice glared at him. How dare he speak to her like a child *and* thank Daisy, but not them? "Daisy, here."

Daisy padded over and followed Lady Beatrice and Perry as they moved towards the door. Reaching for the handle, Lady Beatrice turned and regarded him, her head held up high. Before she could stop herself, she opened her mouth. "Just as well your forensics boys went through the room with 'a fine-tooth comb'"—she air quoted—"because we know how important it is when someone has been bludgeoned to death, don't we, chief inspector? If you need to borrow my dog again, just give me a shout."

As they left the room, she was sure she heard a snort of laughter from the corner where DS Spicer was putting the evidence into a bag.

Lady Beatrice was still spitting feathers by the time she, Perry, and Daisy had reached the Old Stable Block Cafe. She had stormed out of the Garden Room, down the corridor and out via the north side door, Perry scampering behind her.

Why did I do that? I'm behaving as badly as he is. All those years of not showing my emotions in public for fear of it getting into the press, and here I am losing my cool in front of PaIRS officers. For all she knew, DS Spicer was making a note of all these juicy exchanges and would sell her story to the press when this case was over. Shaking her head, she turned to a pink-faced Perry as she paused outside the door to the cafe. "I'm so sorry, Perry. That *was* childish. But that man just brings out the worst in me."

Perry stopped by her side and caught his breath. "You were magnificent, Lady Bea. He was so insulting to you; he deserved that remark. I tell you, there are a bunch of gay queens out there who could learn a lot from you!" He grinned as he opened the door for her.

She didn't know what he was talking about, but he was laughing, so she assumed it was a compliment of sorts.

Simon was already in the cafe when they entered, his laptop open in front of him. The cafe was empty — no surprise, as it was due to close for the day soon. Running over to Simon, Daisy jumped onto his lap and tried to lick his face. He chuckled, and picking her up, gently returned her to the floor. Lady Beatrice plonked herself in the chair opposite him as Perry went to the counter to order drinks.

"You look flustered, Lady Bea. Are you okay?" Simon asked.

"Oh Simon, I just *can't* control my mouth when I'm around that man!" she wailed.

He looked slightly startled, but gave her a reassuring smile. "I'm sure it's not that bad. Tell me what happened. What man are you referring to?"

But before she could answer, Perry, who was back with their drinks, jumped in. "DCI Fitzwilliam, who else?" He winked at his partner. "He was really rude to us, and Lady Bea gave him such a bitch-slap you wouldn't believe."

What? "But I didn't lay a finger on him." She raised her nose. She would never stoop that low.

Simon laughed. "He means a putdown."

"And not just a regular putdown," Perry added. "But one worthy of Joan Rivers." He turned back to Simon, his eyes shining.

Lady Beatrice shook her head, still confused. She took a sip of her black coffee as Perry informed Simon about the button. "I had the impression they knew where it came from, didn't you?" he asked Lady Beatrice once he'd finished.

"Indeed. DS Spicer was going to say more before Fitzwilliam cut her off."

After a silent moment of contemplation, Simon said, "I'll give Steve a call later and see what I can find out. Maybe he can throw some light on it."

Lady Beatrice looked at her phone. *Crikey, is that the time?* Shooting up from her chair, she said, "I'm really sorry, but I have to go. Sarah and I are off to a charity dinner tonight in London, organised by my brother. I need to get ready. Can we discuss this more tomorrow?"

"We're off tomorrow," Perry reminded her. "Simon and I are going to a food festival in Mells-next-the-Sea. Simon is doing a demonstration."

She nodded. "Of course. Sorry, I'd forgotten. Have a lovely time, you two, and I'll see you on Wednesday."

She stood up and called Daisy. "Oh, and I'll talk to Sarah tonight and ask her if she saw anyone on the morning of Alex's murder," she told them.

They exchanged a look.

What is that about?

She was about to ask when Simon nodded. "Yes, that would be helpful. Thank you."

22

EARLY EVENING, MONDAY 12 APRIL

In the back of the Daimler, Lady Sarah Rosdale sat bolt upright as she stared out of the window. She had not spoken a word since they'd left Francis Court thirty minutes earlier.

The silence was making Lady Beatrice uncomfortable, so to lighten the mood she told her sister that she, Perry, and Simon were working on a list of suspects for Alex's murder.

Lady Sarah turned to face her younger sister, head on, eyes blazing. "What in the hell are you doing, Bea?"

Lady Beatrice instinctively shifted away from her.

"Since when did you become the police?" Lady

Sarah hissed. "Because I thought you were an interior designer working on my events suite."

Lady Beatrice opened her mouth to respond, but Lady Sarah continued in haste, "Do I need to remind you the grand opening is in two weeks, and we have two rooms not yet completed? Forgive me if I am struggling to find amusement in the little games you and Perry are playing. Surely you have more important things to do than question my staff about a murder that is none of your business?"

Lady Beatrice winced, tears starting to build up behind her eyes. Sarah had never talked to her like this before. She was at a loss for words.

Returning to stare out of the window, Lady Sarah's chest rose and fell rapidly.

What have I done? Lady Beatrice's mouth was dry. "I'm so sorry, Sarah," she whispered. "We'll have it completed on time, I promise."

Lady Sarah exhaled loudly and, still not looking at her, replied, "Just leave the investigating to the police, Bea, and concentrate on your job... please."

Lady Beatrice's chest tightened. "Of course," she replied. She hated that she'd let her sister down.

They spent the rest of the journey in silence. As the car pulled up at the National Army Museum, Lady Sarah grabbed Lady Beatrice's hand. "I am sorry, little sis," she said with a heavy sigh. Her fingers trembling, she squeezed her sister's hand and smiled. "It's a special night for the first-born favourite, so come on, let's do our thing."

Releasing hands, they stepped out of the car into the flashing lights of the press photographers.

23

EARLY MORNING, TUESDAY 13 APRIL

The Society Page online article

The Astley Siblings Support Care for Heroes at Charity Dinner in Chelsea

Last night Lady Beatrice (35), the Countess of Rossex, and Lady Sarah Rosdale (38) joined their brother, Frederick Astley (38), Earl of Tilling, at the National Army Museum in Chelsea for a charity dinner in aid of Care for Heroes. Lady Sarah looked elegant in a Safiyaa ruffled sleeve gown in peach with royal blue Chanel sandals and a matching clutch bag. Lady Beatrice appeared more edgy in a black Zuhair Murad lace passiflora gown with Valentino pumps, also in black. Frederick Astley looked dapper in his black-tie dinner suit.

The dinner for two hundred and fifty, held in

the Atrium of the NAM, was to launch the cam-paign, Rehab for Heroes. This will fund the con-struction of a purpose-built recovery complex for military personnel requiring rehabilitation and those needing support following an injury. The site will comprise of easy-access chalets built around three lakes with communal rehab facilities onsite. The Astley family has already donated the land, a 900-acre site in Fenshire just outside Fawstead. The campaign hopes to raise £20,000,000 to build the complex and operate it for two years.

Frederick Astley, an ex-Lieutenant Colonel in the Intelligence Corps, is a patron of the charity and is spearheading the Rehab for Heroes cam-paign. He delivered an impassioned speech about the importance of looking after our injured military heroes and how the Fenshire facility will meet the medical, psychological, and welfare needs of hun-dreds of service personnel.

After the dinner, Lady Beatrice and Lady Sarah returned to Francis Court, where the recent murder of a member of staff, Alex Sterling, remains un-solved. It is rumoured DCI Richard Fitzwilliam from PaIRS, who is overseeing the investigation by Fenshire CID, is coming under increasing pressure from his superiors to make an arrest while the press continues to question if members of the royal family are in danger.

Finishing her coffee, Lady Beatrice checked the time on her phone - seven. *Can I go back to bed for a few hours?*

Heading towards the bedroom, she jumped when it vibrated in her hand.

Ma: *Darling, are you up? Do you have 5 mins to pop along and see me? I am dying to know how it went last night and Sarah says she is too busy to talk. I have pain au chocolat... xx*

Lady Beatrice sighed. She could have a snooze later.

Bea: *Morning. Yes I am up. Give me 15 mins to have a shower and I'll be with you. xx*

Leaving her parents' apartment, she opened the door to let Naomi out with the tea tray. Naomi placed it on the trolley, standing ready outside the door.

"Thank you, my lady." She gave a quick curtsy, then pushed the trolley down the corridor towards the service lift.

As she walked away, Lady Beatrice remembered Sarah had expressed her concern last night about the impact the investigation was having on the staff. "Naomi," she called after her. When Naomi stopped and turned around, Lady Beatrice moved towards her. "How is the staff coping with the police being onsite and asking questions?"

"I think most are doing okay, my lady. It's unsettling to have the police around, but most of us just want them to find the murderer, and then we'll feel safe again."

"Indeed, Naomi. I can imagine it's making everyone feel a little uneasy."

"Yes, a little. Although I have to say that inspector chap who interviewed me was very kind and patient."

She couldn't be talking about Fitzwilliam, she thought. *He's uncivil and accusatory.* It must have been Mike who interviewed her. Lady Beatrice nodded, encouraging her to continue.

"There's been gossip among the staff, my lady." She paused, looking uncertain.

"Has there?" Lady Beatrice gave her the green light.

Taking her hands off the trolley, Naomi crossed her arms. "Well, my lady, as you probably know, Alex Sterling and Ellie Gunn have been on and off for years. Even before his stuck-up wife died." She hesitated and uncrossed her arms, resting them back on the trolley.

"I've heard his wife wasn't popular," Lady Beatrice responded, hoping she would continue.

Huffing, Naomi crossed her arms again. "All she did was complain about how awful Fenshire was compared to her beloved Scotland. She was fed up with Alex never having time to spend with her because he was always working. At first, I think a few people felt some sympathy for her, but after a while, when she made no effort to settle in here, even they lost interest in her."

Lady Beatrice smiled and nodded.

"Sophie Crammond and Ellie tried to make friends with her when she and Alex first arrived. They even invited her for coffee and lunch and to some staff events, but she wasn't interested in mixing with the likes of us. She was such a cold fish; it's no wonder her husband looked elsewhere."

Naomi nodded her head twice, her folded arms still squashing her ample bosom.

"Of course, he called it off with Ellie when his wife died, my lady," she reported, approvingly.

Is there an etiquette for these things?

"But they reunited after Ellie left that idiot Ross Gunn and moved into Mr Juke's cottage." She sniffed. "I don't think it was plain sailing, though. They were always arguing. I think she wanted to move in with him and make it all official like, but he wanted to keep it quiet. He still wouldn't acknowledge they were together, even though we all knew." She took a breath before continuing. "Not everyone was happy about them being together, mind you. Cass Gunn, who's a real daddy's girl, thought if they broke up, then her mum would go back to her dad.

"Not that it would have happened, I can tell you. That man is too soft for Ellie. She'd be a fool to go back to him." Naomi paused again. Uncrossing her arms, she brushed down her apron as if she had been baking and it was covered in flour. Then she was off again.

"And Sophie Crammond didn't approve. She thought Ellie would be better off without Alex mucking her around. Of course, she always had to pick up the pieces when they had a row. In fact—"

She looked around the corridor and then whispered, "I overheard her having a right go at him a few weeks ago. She didn't see me, of course. I was in the office next door, picking something up for your mother."

She paused. After a few seconds, Lady Beatrice pushed, "What did she say?"

"Well, she told him if he didn't want to be in a proper relationship with Ellie, then he should leave her alone. She said Ellie was too good for him and didn't deserve to be treated so poorly. She was almost shouting." Naomi shook her head and frowned. "I'm not sure I have ever heard her so cross. She is normally calm and collected, is Mrs C."

"And what did he say?"

"He said he'd tried to end it, but she wouldn't let him go. Mrs C was even more animated. She told him it wasn't Ellie's fault, and it was wicked of him to blame her. She told him if he didn't sort it out, she would sort it out for him. They had moved outside her office by then so I could see his face. He looked right flabbergasted, I can tell you. She was proper telling him off, pointing at him and shouting."

That was interesting. "What do you think she meant by that?"

"I don't know, my lady, but he scuttled off looking sheepish." Grinning, Naomi glanced at her watch and then at her trolley.

"I'm so sorry, Naomi," Lady Beatrice said. "I've kept you from your work. Thank you for the chat. I'm glad you're all coping with the situation. If there is anything I can do to help, please let me know."

"Thank you, my lady." Curtsying, Naomi hurried off.

Pacing the floor in her sitting room, Lady Beatrice unzipped her hoodie and threw it over the nearest chair. *Is it me, or is it hot in here?*

She headed over to the sofa where Daisy was still curled up like a small deer, exactly where she'd left her an hour ago. Staring at the sleeping terrier, she rubbed the back of her head. *Get a grip, Bea! Am I going to do this or not?*

She sighed heavily. She hadn't read the letter from James since that day, five years ago, when she had sobbed her way through it. Barely registering the details, her sole focus had been on finding out that her husband wanted to be with someone else. But some of it must have stuck in her mind, because now she couldn't reconcile the impression James had given in the letter of Gill as a sweet, downtrodden wife abused by her husband, and the moaning, unfriendly, faultfinder as described by Perry and Naomi.

Had she mis-remembered what James had written?

There is only one way to find out.

The writing desk was on the adjacent wall. Swallowing down the bile rising in her throat, she slowly walked over to it, her legs trembling, and pulled out the captain's chair. She sat down and opened the top right-hand drawer of the desk. When the drawer was out as far as it would go, she reached to the back and released a catch, revealing a small, thin, extra drawer. Taking out the envelope with *Bea* on the front, she removed the letter inside. She stared at it, her heart pounding. *Come on Bea, you can do this.*

Moving back to the sofa, she sat down next to Daisy and carefully unfolding the white paper, took a deep breath and read…

A tear had travelled down Lady Beatrice's cheek and was now tickling her top lip. She brushed it away and sniffed. She buried her hand in Daisy's white fur, the gentle rhythm of the little dog's breathing offering some small comfort.

Her heart was heavy in her chest. *Oh James, I didn't know you were so unhappy. How did I miss that?* It must have been awful for him to feel so trapped in his life. *How did I not realise he was struggling?* James was naturally quiet, more of an observer than a talker. But although he was a deep thinker, that hadn't stopped him from opening up to her in the past. *Why didn't he tell me how he was feeling?* It was unlike the James she knew.

But re-reading the letter now, she wasn't sure she'd ever really known him.

She cast her mind back to the months before the accident. Admittedly, he'd been a bit distracted around the end of that year, but when she'd asked, he'd told her nothing was wrong. She frowned. There was a vague recollection in her mind that he had been worried about not being able to find some notes he had made on a recent trip to the USA. But apart from that, he was the James she had always known — supportive and steady. Could it be that what she thought was a mild distraction because of lost papers was, in fact, him wrestling with the decision to leave her? She wiped another tear from her face and hung her head. *Was I so self absorbed that I couldn't see what he was going through?*

Would it have made any difference if James had known she was pregnant? Would a son have given him a new purpose in life? *Now I'll never know.* She rubbed her hands over her face. There was no point torturing herself with these questions. *It's in the past.*

She took in a deep breath and slowly let it out. Twisting her wedding ring around on her third finger, she turned over in her mind what the letter had said about Gill and Alex, but she still had the same dilemma. *I'm not sure it's clarified anything.* Perry had said he felt sorry for Alex, having to put up with Gill, but that wasn't the picture painted by James. Was Alex the bully Gill told James about? Or the husband putting up with an unhappy, complaining wife who Naomi described?

And is any of it connected to Alex's death?

Perry: *Simon's just had a text from CID Steve. The button was from the overalls Alex was wearing when he died. There was one missing. Hope your event went well last night and you had a nice long lie in this morning. I've eaten so much I feel sick. See you tomorrow.*

24

EARLY MORNING, WEDNESDAY
14 APRIL

Walking past the Garden Room with Daisy, Lady Beatrice saw Perry was already inside. Daisy ran over to the French doors and pressed her nose against the glass, her tail wagging, eager to reach her favourite person. Daisy had missed Perry yesterday. Lady Beatrice was shocked to find she had missed him, too.

A huge grin spread across Perry's face. Waving, he strode over to unlock the French doors. "How's my favourite girl?" Perry asked as Daisy threw herself at his feet, her tail wagging so fast she was in danger of falling over. He bent down to fuss her.

"I'm great, thanks," Lady Beatrice declared as she entered the room.

Perry laughed and whispered loudly to Daisy,

"You know I meant you, right?" She looked up at him with adoring eyes, still wagging her tail at a hundred miles an hour. "But we'll let mummy think we meant her, shall we?"

Lady Beatrice grinned. "How was the food festival?" she asked him as she picked up a handful of neon yellow stickers from the French Louis XVI mahogany sideboard. Perry had written on them already — *keep in this room, move into storage, sell/donate, move to…* and *get rid.*

He picked up two takeaway cups and handed one to Lady Beatrice. She put the stickers back on the marble top and thanked him as she took it.

"It was great," Perry said enthusiastically. "The weather was lovely — sunny and warm — and there were lots of people there. Simon's demonstration went down a storm — so well, in fact, they've asked him to do another one next month."

"Indeed, it sounds like it was a great success."

"You must come with me to the next one. You'll love it." He looked down. "And Daisy, you will love it too. There's lots of food." Daisy wagged her tail in agreement.

"I'd like to come, but it may cause too much trouble. You know, with security and so on — I'm a liability at public events, I'm afraid." She sighed.

"Nonsense. We'll dress you up in disguise. No

one will ever know." She laughed, but he looked deadly serious. "Honestly, Lady Bea, you deserve to have fun too, you know. We can figure out a way to make it work *if* you want to."

He was right. *How many times have I made excuses not to go somewhere because of the fuss and effort required?* She would love to go to a food festival with Perry and Simon. "I would love to," she said, a big grin spreading across her face.

"Well, there's another one next month. We'll talk to Simon and make a plan." He clapped his hands together and grinned back.

Lying down, Daisy settled herself on the rug by their feet.

"So how was your brother's charity do on Monday night?"

She told him all about the dinner and how proud she was of Fred and his ambitious plans for injured veterans. They agreed they would offer their interior design services for the chalets and communal areas when he reached that stage in the project.

Lady Beatrice took a sip of her coffee. "I've been thinking about the button we found. If we assume from Spicer's reaction that it came from the overalls Alex was wearing, then how on earth did it end up under the drinks cabinet all the way over by the French doors? It's not even in a direct line from where the body was lying, so it couldn't have rolled there."

Perry looked over towards the French doors and nodded. "I know. I can't figure that out either. It's a bit of a mystery."

After taking another sip of coffee, Lady Beatrice placed the cup down on the sideboard next to the stickers. "Perry, can I ask you something, please?" She twirled the rings on her finger and waited for him to respond.

"Of course, what's up?"

"You've worked with my sister for a long time. Is she snappy and anxious when she's stressed about an event?"

"No." Shaking his head, he said, "If things get down to the wire, she becomes nervous and talks too much, but she's never snapped or been impatient with me. She's calm and collected, at least on the surface, anyway." He frowned. "Why do you ask?"

She told him about her exchange with Sarah in the car on their way to London.

When she'd finished, Perry looked thoughtful for a few moments. "I don't think it has anything to do with us not meeting the opening deadline. I think there's something else."

"What do you mean?" Lady Beatrice asked. He

rubbed his nose and looked down. *What does he know that he's not told me?*

"Okay. I said nothing to you before because..." He was still avoiding her gaze. "Well, you were so adamant Sarah couldn't be a suspect I didn't think you would listen." Lady Beatrice opened her mouth, but he ignored her and carried on. "I think she's hiding something that happened on the morning of Alex's murder."

A wave of nausea washed over Lady Beatrice. "What do you mean, hiding something?" she whispered.

"I don't know for sure." His face flushed. "But I called for her on my way to meet you for breakfast and she wasn't in her office. Her coat and phone weren't there, so I assumed she'd already left." He held up his hand as she opened her mouth. "Please let me finish. There's more."

She waited.

"You remember when she did eventually join us for breakfast, and she said she'd been on a long call?" Lady Beatrice nodded. "Well, when I asked her on Saturday why she was late, she said she'd been working on the marketing brochure and had lost track of time. When I told her I had called in to pick her up to go to breakfast at eight-twenty-five, she was flustered and said she must have popped to the bathroom."

Lady Beatrice jumped in. "Well, that could be true."

Perry shook his head. "But why would she take her coat to the loo when it's indoors and only a stone's throw from her office?"

I'm stumped. Why was Sarah lying about where she was? Her stomach churned.

Perry continued, "According to CID Steve, Lady Sarah said she was in her office from when she arrived onsite until just before nine, when she left to meet us for breakfast. But Pete Cowley, who went back to the gardening shed to change before going to breakfast, used the toilets just as the cleaner was leaving. He told the police that the offices were empty. So they know she was lying to them."

Lady Beatrice gasped. "Oh my gosh, Perry. Why did she lie? Do they think she's a suspect?"

He nodded. "They've been trying to arrange another interview with her, but she's being elusive."

"I can't believe she's involved with Alex's murder, can you?" she asked him, her voice trembling. She held her breath.

"Gosh, no!"

She exhaled in a rush.

"I think she was somewhere else and doesn't want anyone to know, but I don't think she's a killer," he clarified.

"Is that why *you* didn't tell the police she wasn't in her office when they interviewed you?" Lady Beatrice asked.

"They didn't specifically ask me if I had seen her, so I didn't lie." He grinned, looking abashed. She wanted to hug him.

"What do we do now?" she asked.

"Let's ask Simon later. He may have a suggestion."

As Lady Beatrice slapped a *get rid* sticker on a nasty looking red and yellow vase with a chip on the rim, she was deep in thought. *What is Sarah up to?* Her sister was one of the most straightforward people she knew. Maybe a little over-protective sometimes, but you always knew where you were with her. *It is so unlike her to lie.* She rubbed the back of her neck, trying to work out the knots on either side.

"Hello?" She jerked her head round. Standing by the French doors, his hands on his hips, Perry stared at her. "I said, what about this table? Do you want to keep it in this room or put it in storage?"

She walked over to the antique French oak side table standing in front of the doors. One of the two drawers at the front was ajar. She frowned. This was the table that had looked odd to her on the morning they'd found Alex's body. *Was it the slightly opened drawer that had caught her attention?* She shrugged; it could have been.

There was an art deco black and white tray on top of the table. Something about the way the objects were arranged made it appear unbalanced. *The heights are all wrong.* She shook her head and stepped back to study it in full. *And the table's not straight.*

That's it! That was what had looked odd. *The table isn't in the middle of the French doors.*

"Perry, do you still have the photos you took a few days before the murder on your phone? It would've been Saturday morning, on the fifth."

He picked up his phone and started scrolling through his photos. "Yes, I have them here."

Moving over to him, she peered over his shoulder.

"Look for one that shows this table in front of the windows," she said, pointing at the side table.

He stopped scrolling. "This one?"

"Yes!" she cried. "The table. See where it is?" She pointed to the table in the photo. "It's dead centre in the middle windowpane of the French doors, see?" He studied the phone and nodded. "Now look where it is now." He raised his head. "It's not in the centre anymore. It's just off to the right."

"So someone has moved it." He shrugged. "With forensics here, they have probably moved it half a dozen times since I took the photo."

Lady Beatrice shook her head. "Indeed. However, remember how I said the room looked odd when we found Alex's body, but I couldn't put my finger on what was wrong?" He nodded. "I think it was the table and the tray on it. Look at the photo again — see how that miniature vase, pot plant, and candle are arranged, with the vase in the middle? Well, look at it now. The vase is on the right-hand side, making it look off balance." He still looked confused. She pointed to his phone. "Go to the photos you took while we were waiting for the police to arrive. You took some of the room, remember?"

He scrolled on and then stopped. "Gosh, Miss Marple, you're right," he confirmed, realisation dawning on his face. "So it was moved between

Monday afternoon and Wednesday first thing when we found the body?"

Lady Beatrice's heart was racing. "Yes! And we know from Mrs C that no one accessed the room during that period—"

"Except the murderer." Perry finished for her.

There was a discreet cough from the open French doors that startled them both. Daisy ran over to sniff the newcomers.

"Excuse me, Mr Juke, Lady Rossex. We were passing by and saw you through the open doors. Do you want us to move things for you now?" Seth Padgett asked, standing in the door frame. Pete Cowley and Joe Fox stood next to him, staring curiously into the room.

"Thanks Seth, but we're still marking up and it will take us a little while. In fact, the police haven't officially handed the room back to us yet, so we can't move anything until tomorrow." Perry responded. "But thank you for asking." He smiled dismissively, then turned back to Lady Beatrice. They moved over to where they'd found Alex's body, trying to see the scene in full.

"But why would the murderer need to shift the table that was standing by the window?" he asked her.

She shrugged. She had so many questions swirling around in her head. "As far as we know, they came in through the unlocked front door. What about Alex? Did he move it? But why would he? Why would either of them be over by the French doors?" She shook her head from side to side, trying to make sense of it all.

"I don't know." He fiddled with his phone.

"Look!" he cried, and she peered over his shoulder.

"I've screen-shotted the two photos so we can flick from one to the other," he explained. "See here? The ugly marble table is also in a different place. Even that sofa"—he pointed to the green leather Chesterfield—"has moved a few inches to the left."

"But why?" Lady Beatrice asked.

She turned away from the Chesterfield, towards the French doors and was surprised to see Seth, Pete, and Joe were still on the terrace, fussing Daisy.

"Daisy, leave the poor men alone." Approaching, she smiled at them. "I do apologise, gentlemen.

She never knows when enough is enough. Perry will let you know when we need you. Thank you."

The men stood up. Seth bowed his head, and they left.

"Really, Daisy," Lady Beatrice scolded her. "People have things to do rather than fuss you all the time." Daisy sat in front of her, her tail wagging. Lady Beatrice turned back as Perry made a squeaking sound.

"Call me Hercule Poirot because I think I have the answer." He was staring at the photos, his eyes bright. She rushed over.

"I think someone moved all these things to create a path to where we found Alex's body here." Lady Beatrice looked at where he was pointing in the photos.

"It's possible, but why?" Then it dawned on her. "Unless the murderer came in through the French doors. Remember the tarpaulin was over them on the day of the murder? Someone could've come in that way without being seen."

"But why would they have to move the furniture to get to where Alex was?" Perry asked, his cheeks flushed. "Oh, oh. What if the murderer had to move the body?" His eyes shone. "Or what if the murderer killed him somewhere else and brought the dead body in through the French doors?"

"Brilliant! That would also explain why no one from the offices saw anyone in the room's vicinity at the time of the murder." Lady Beatrice agreed excitedly.

Perry clapped his hands together. Lady Beatrice walked through the room, following a path to the French doors and back to where they had found the body.

"Well, Poirot, I think you have it." She patted him on the shoulder. "It would explain how the button from Alex's overalls ended up on that side of the room. Maybe it got caught on something as the body was being moved." She was as excited as him.

"We should tell the police." Perry picked up his radio.

"Call for Mike," Lady Beatrice said as he pressed the button on the side.

"This is Perry Juke for Mike Ainsley, over."

They stared at each other, willing Mike to pick up on the other end.

"Mr Juke, this is DCI Fitzwilliam. What can we do for you, over?"

Blast!

"Can someone come to the Garden Room please, over."

"Is it urgent, Mr Juke, over?"

He really is the rudest man ever.

Before Perry had time to respond, the radio crackled back into life. "Mr Juke, this is DS Spicer. We'll be there shortly, out."

25

MID-MORNING, WEDNESDAY 14 APRIL

Not wanting to touch anything else in case the forensics team had to be brought back a third time, Lady Beatrice and Perry Juke locked all the doors and moved into the Smoking Room next door to wait for DS Spicer and her boss.

Lady Beatrice perched on a sofa by the French doors, Daisy curled up next to her, while Perry stood texting Simon. Peering outside, she saw DCI Fitzwilliam striding along the terrace, followed by DS Spicer, who was practically jogging to keep up with him. As they approached, Lady Beatrice stood up and unlocked the doors with the bunch of keys Perry had fetched while she had been locking up the Garden Room. Sliding open the French doors, she stepped out on to the terrace, smiling at Spicer. "Come in this way. It will save you having to go around through the side door."

Spicer nodded. "Thank you, my lady."

As she and Fitzwilliam entered, Daisy jumped off the sofa to welcome them, and Perry put his phone in his pocket.

Fitzwilliam bent down to Daisy. "Please don't tell me you've discovered another clue forensics has missed Daisy or I'll have to sack the lot of them." She wagged her tail at him in response. Straightening up, he looked over at Perry. "What can we do for you, Mr Juke?" he asked in a detached voice, looking around the room.

How crass! Lady Beatrice rolled her eyes and moved over to stand by Perry's side.

When Perry explained how she had raised concerns about things being in the wrong place in the Garden Room on the morning they'd discovered the body, Fitzwilliam looked at Lady Beatrice sceptically.

He sighed. "Haven't we been here before, Lady Rossex? You throw out these comments of *unnatural* and *wrong place,* but you can't provide any specific details."

She took a deep breath to quell the indignation rising in her. "Well, now I can be specific, chief inspector." She then tried to explain to him about the interior design principles of space and proportion, but after a few minutes when he tried (not very hard) to suppress a yawn, it was clear he wasn't interested.

He soon interrupted her. "Please don't tell me you have called us here because a few things have moved in a room that has had dozens of people in and out of it over the last week."

Lady Beatrice sighed in exasperation. "Maybe it'll be easier if we show you?" she suggested to Spicer, who nodded in return.

When they entered the Garden Room, Lady Beatrice led Spicer to the patio doors. Fitzwilliam had stopped short and was in the middle of the room, leaning on the back of the Chesterfield, his arms crossed.

"This table"—Lady Beatrice pointed to the French oak table—"wasn't in this position two days before the murder. Also, the items on this tray are in a different order." She continued to ignore Fitzwilliam, concentrating on explaining their theory to Spicer. As she walked the sergeant through the route to where they had found Alex's body, she pointed out where someone had moved other items along the way.

"This is all vaguely interesting, Lady Rossex,

but the forensics guys would have moved them during their search." He smirked.

Lady Beatrice took a deep breath and turned to glare at him. *You cannot hit a police officer. Think what the press would say.* "Be that as it may, chief inspector, I noticed things had moved on the morning we found the body. We also have photos of the scene before the murder." She pursed her lips. "I'm sure that someone with your intelligence can see that a simple comparison of photos will confirm this."

Lady Beatrice fixed her gaze on Fitzwilliam. Perry stifled a snort, while Spicer turned her head away and coughed.

Come on, Mr-I-have-all-the-answers. Shoot that one down!

"And why would a murderer need to move, ever so slightly, a whole lot of furniture that was nowhere near where you found the body?" He returned her piercing stare.

Lady Beatrice gave him a sly smile. *Nice try, chief inspector. Wait until you hear this.*

Perry, clearly wanting to be in on the reveal, jumped in and explained their theory about Alex being killed elsewhere. Fitzwilliam's smirk faded the longer he talked until a scowl replaced it.

"How do you know a button came off the deceased's overalls?" he barked.

Seeing the panic on Perry's face, Lady Beatrice interjected. "We don't know for sure, chief inspector. But Alex was wearing overalls and the button we found looked like it came from the same overalls. Also, the way you and DS Spicer behaved when we found it, we guessed you knew where it had come from. Are we wrong?" She turned to DS Spicer. The sergeant shook her head before Fitzwilliam could reply.

"Your little investigation has been most diverting, Lady Rossex, but your theory makes no sense. The patio doors were locked. Why lock them after the fact when the main doors weren't?" Shaking his head as if he was talking to a child, he started advancing towards the door. "And why would a killer go to so much trouble when they could simply lure the victim into the room on some pretext or other, kill him here and leave via the unlocked door?"

How dare he dismiss our theory without even considering it! "So, how do you explain the movement of objects and furniture along a path from the windows to where we found the body, chief inspector?" Lady Beatrice burst out, failing to contain the frustration bubbling up inside her.

"I don't believe it's relevant, Lady Rossex."

Of course it's relevant, you stubborn man! They might have got a few things wrong, and he'd brought up some good questions, but that didn't mean he should dismiss out of hand their theory that someone had moved the furniture.

"But anyway, thank you for letting us know, Mr Juke. Please email DS Spicer the photos you took in the days preceding the murder." He nodded to them, then marched out. DS Spicer smiled apologetically behind his back as she followed.

Lady Beatrice opened her mouth to tell Perry just what she thought of Detective Chief Inspector Richard Fitzwilliam and what he could do with the photos, when Daisy sprung up and ran towards the doorway.

DS Spicer reappeared, looking embarrassed. She leaned down and patted Daisy on the head and then rose to address them. "I'm sorry about the chief inspector. He's under a lot of pressure from above to wrap this up as soon as possible, but progress is slow, and we're waiting on results." She shrugged. *She looks tired*, Lady Beatrice observed.

"So please leave it with me," she continued, "There may be something in your suggestions, so I'll look at those photos, Mr Juke, and see if they can help us." She handed Perry her card.

"Yes, of course. I'll go back to my office and email them to you now," Perry replied as he took the card.

Spicer expressed her thanks and left the room.

"How embarrassing when you have to go back and apologise for your boss's behaviour." Perry grinned.

"I expect she has to do it a lot." Lady Beatrice returned his grin. "Right, we need to return to the office so you can email those photos, and then we need to catch up with Simon, don't you think?"

Walking into Rose Cottage, the comforting smell of baking bread engulfed Perry Juke and Lady Beatrice. Without hesitating, Daisy ran ahead into the kitchen to find Simon, and they followed.

"It smells amazing in here, love." Perry gave Simon a peck on the cheek before moving around the kitchen island to look at what was on offer. "What are we eating?"

"I've made rolls, which are in the oven and will be out in a minute, and I've made some cauliflower cheese soup from the produce left over from the demo yesterday. Can you set the table while I finish, Perry? Lady Bea, please take a seat. It won't be long."

While Perry went to the lofty wooden dresser in the corner of the kitchen and started taking out bowls and cutlery, Daisy made herself at home in the plush dark-green velvet armchair that looked out over the garden. Lady Beatrice joined her, shifting her over so there was space for them both to fit. Turning sideways, she peered into the room.

Perry had almost finished getting the table ready and Simon was taking rolls out of the oven. They were a well-oiled machine, working together, each doing the thing they were best at. She heaved a sigh.

Were we ever like that? Sometimes it had felt as if we were two people playing a role. One it turns out neither of us wanted. James had stood back and let me shine, reducing himself to the support act.

But I never wanted to shine on my own. I wanted someone by my side, not behind me. Someone supporting me, not following me. I wanted to be part of a team, stronger together, like Perry and Simon. James had been right. We did what they expected of us, never questioning if it was what we wanted or what we needed.

She brushed a tear away from her eye.

Perry and Simon arranged things on the table;

they were exchanging looks and laughing about something one of them had said. There was an ache in her chest. *Will I ever have that for myself?* She sighed again. Simon looked up, gave her a huge smile, and beckoned her over. Standing, she smiled back. *I am so grateful to have these two remarkable men in my life now. They make me feel part of something intimate and heart-warming.*

The soup was delicious, and the rolls were soft and still warm. As they ate, Perry told Simon about the moving furniture in the Garden Room and their theory about the dead body being brought in through the French doors. He showed Simon the photos, but Simon pointed out that forensics could tell if someone moved Alex's body after he died.

"How so?" Lady Beatrice asked, a heat flushing up her neck. *Please don't say I've made a fool of myself in front of Fitzwilliam again.* She would have to leave the country.

"There are various techniques. For example, they will look at liver mortis. That's the final stage of rigor mortis, and it shows where the blood pools once the heart stops beating. From that, they can tell if the victim died on their back, front, or side," he explained.

"So if a person died on their back, but then someone moved the body and left it face down, they could tell because the blood would have stayed in the victim's back?" Perry clarified. Simon nodded.

Rats! It sounds like that's their theory scuppered. *Oh, no!* Fitzwilliam would have known all of this. No wonder he was so resistant to the idea. *I've done it again! He must think I'm such an idiot.* She put her chin in her hands and sighed. Hang on though. Someone had definitely moved the furniture. That must be relevant, whatever Fitzwilliam said.

As if reading her thoughts, Simon said, "However, I think the furniture being moved is important."

"Well, Fitzwilliam didn't think it was," Perry whined.

"Yes. He basically dismissed everything we said and told us we were wasting his time!" Lady Beatrice huffed.

"He has a lot on his plate, I should imagine. Steve tells me Fitzwilliam and Ainsley are being battered daily by the palace and the higher-ups at PaIRS. They are desperate to reassure the press that the Astley family is safe, but they can only do that once they can announce they have arrested someone. Right now, it seems they have no credible suspects."

Lady Beatrice told Simon about the conversation she'd had with her sister on Monday evening and asked him what he thought they should do.

"Someone"—he tilted his head in her direction —"needs to persuade Lady Sarah to talk to the police. She must tell them the truth; she may have vital evidence and not be aware of it."

Lady Beatrice nodded and looked at Perry hopefully. "She might take more notice of you than her little sister."

He shook his head. "Nice try, but no, she won't. I'm an employee at the end of the day. I'm sorry, but it has to be you, my lady."

Simon nodded in agreement, and Lady Beatrice resigned herself to accepting the task. "All right, but don't hold your breath."

"Next," Simon continued, "we need to figure out the conundrum around the keys. I think it's central to what happened. We know someone unlocked the front door, but we don't know who had a key. According to Steve, Mrs Crammond told the police the only key was on her or in a locked safe. Did Alex have a key? Could someone have got hold of a copy? And now we need to consider access via the French doors. Where are those keys?"

"If I remember rightly, they're usually on the same key ring as the front door key," Perry responded, then frowned. "But now I think about it, they were missing when we picked up the keys from Mrs C that morning. It was just the one key on the key ring."

"That's definitely odd," Simon said. "It could be important, as whoever had the French door keys could be our murderer."

"I can talk to Mrs Crammond when I get back," Lady Beatrice offered. "I want to ask her about an argument she had with Alex a few weeks before the murder."

She told them about her conversation with Naomi.

"Perry, could you find out about the key cutting process?" she asked. "I know Ward oversees things like that and has a key cutting machine in his workshop. He should be able to help you."

"Isn't he your driver?" Perry looked confused.

"Yes, he's the family driver, but he's also in charge of the maintenance works and any external contractors. Quite a few of the staff who work for our family have dual roles," she said. "For example, Harris is my father's valet, but also the butler when required."

"Okay, I'll find Ward when we get back."

"And I'll give Steve a ring and see if there is anything new from a CID point of view. I fancy the pub tonight. Let's reconvene there later," Simon said.

"What about motive?" Lady Beatrice asked. "At what point do we consider why someone killed Alex?"

"That's a good question," Simon replied. "Normally, once you prove someone had the means and opportunity, then you consider motive. Right now, we're still focussing on who does and doesn't have an alibi, as in opportunity, and who had means. That's why the keys are so important. At the beginning, investigations are a simple process of elimination."

Her shoulders slumped. She huffed. *This is much harder than I thought it would be.*

Simon smiled. "Don't get too disheartened. It's a bit of a slog, but eventually we'll get there."

She nodded and smiled back. "Come on Daisy, we need to go." Daisy opened one eye, sighed, and closed it again; clearly, she had no desire to move from her spot in the sun.

Simon grinned. "Leave her here with me, and we'll meet you in the pub later."

As Lady Beatrice approached the head housekeeper's office, the door was open. Mrs Crammond was at her desk. "Hello, Mrs Crammond. Can I have a word?" she asked, smiling.

"Yes, my lady, please sit down." She gestured towards the office chair on the other side of her wooden desk.

Lady Beatrice sat down. "Mrs Crammond, can you help us solve a puzzle, please?"

"I'll do my best, my lady."

"Thank you. We're confused about what happened on the day of Alex's death regarding the keys. We're trying to find out if someone could have entered the Garden Room via the French doors."

"I thought the front door was unlocked. Why would anyone need to use the French doors to access the room?"

Mrs Crammond had made the connection much faster than Lady Beatrice expected. *Have I underestimated Sophie Crammond?*

"The police are now looking at the possibility that whoever killed Alex did so elsewhere and brought his body in via the French doors." Lady Beatrice replied. *Technically, I am not lying*, she told herself. DS Spicer *did* say she would have a look at their theory, even if Fitzwilliam had dismissed it out of hand.

"Who has a key to the Garden Room French doors?"

"They're on the key ring with the other keys for the room. I keep all keys in the key lock box here in my office." Mrs Crammond pointed behind her. Lady Beatrice looked at the lockbox on the wall behind the desk. It was grey, about the size of a regular cushion, and had a number pad on the front.

"Is there a code to access it?"

"Yes, my lady."

Lady Beatrice could sense she was less keen to cooperate with her than she had been earlier. "And who has the code?" She smiled to encourage Mrs Crammond to share, but the head housekeeper looked away from her.

"Just me, Lady Rossex. I hold the master keys on me at all times." Showing her the bunch of keys hanging off the belt around her waist, she said, "I'm the only person who has the access code."

She was still avoiding Lady Beatrice's gaze.

What is she hiding? "And what happens if you're not here, Mrs Crammond?"

"Well, Lady Sarah has the code as well. I also believe they lock a copy of the codes for all the safes and key boxes in his lordship's study in the case of an emergency."

Sarah? Of course! Why didn't I think of that before? Her sister managed the Events Suite so she would need access to the keys out of hours. *Blast!*

"Mr Juke seems to think the French door keys weren't on the set you gave him when we collected the key from you on the morning of Alex's death?"

Mrs Crammond nodded. "Yes, that's correct. Lady Sarah had taken them the weekend before. She was looking after the builders while they worked on the windows."

"When did she hand them back?" Sweat trickled down her back. She couldn't face the implications of this if the police were to find out.

Mrs Crammond swivelled her chair around and punched a code into the access pad on the key safe. Opening it, she took out a piece of paper. It looked like a log of some sort. Using her finger, she looked down at the sheet.

"She signed them back in on Thursday, my lady."

Dismayed, Lady Beatrice thanked her. As Mrs Crammond turned back to return the keys and the sheet to the safe, Lady Beatrice raised her hand.

"As you have the sheet in front of you, Mrs Crammond, can you tell me who else signed out keys for the Garden Room in the days before and after Alex's death, please?"

For a moment, Lady Beatrice thought she was going to refuse, but then the other woman sighed and looked at the sheet in front of her.

"No one else, my lady, except you, who took them out on Monday, and Mr Juke, who signed them back in later that day. Mr Juke also signed them out on the morning of the murder and the police have been back and forth for them since then," she said, showing the sheet to her. Lady Beatrice studied the list and could see no other entries except herself, Sarah, Perry, Mike Ainsley, and DS Spicer.

She nodded. "Thank you, Mrs Crammond."

Mrs Crammond returned the sheet to the safe. It clunked shut.

"We've been wondering who could have unlocked the front door to the Garden Room. Mr Juke is worrying he left it unlocked by accident on the Monday when we finished in there." Lady Beatrice shook her head. *Poor Perry, tortured by guilt.* She must be a better actress than she thought because Mrs Crammond was quick to reassure her.

"Perry doesn't need to worry, my lady. It was locked when I checked it late afternoon on the Tuesday. I check the doors of all rooms in the west wing before I leave each night." She tilted her head and added, "Even the French doors."

"He will be relieved." Lady Beatrice smiled. "Is it possible someone came into your office while you were out early on the morning of the murder?"

"No, Lady Rossex. I was in my office all morning."

"Sorry, forgive me, but I understood you weren't here when Mr Juke came to pick up the keys a few minutes before eight-thirty?"

She coloured. "Oh yes, sorry, I forgot. I had a headache, so I took some paracetamol and popped out to clear my head. I was only gone for a short while." She crossed her arms, her elbows resting on the arms of her chair.

"Did you see anyone while you were out?"

"No. I meandered around the south gardens while the tablets took effect and then came back."

"Indeed." Lady Beatrice smiled. "The south gardens are my favourite place to unwind."

Mrs Crammond uncrossed her arms and, leaning forward, smiled back.

"What did you think of Alex Sterling, Mrs Crammond?" Mrs Crammond started at the change of direction, but she responded straight away.

"Well, I don't like to talk ill of the dead but, to be honest, I didn't really like him much." She shook her head. Lady Beatrice nodded encouragingly. She continued, "I felt sorry for him being stuck with such a sourpuss of a wife. We all did. And then she died, and we felt sorry for him being on his own. But he wanted everyone to do things his way, and that's not how we do things here."

She ran her hands over the skirt of her navy-blue dress before threading her fingers together and resting them on her knees.

Lady Beatrice couldn't help herself. She had to ask. "And what about his wife?"

"I get on with everyone, Lady Rossex. Ask anyone here. But I think he should have left her in Scotland." She shook her head. "Ellie and I frequently invited her to have coffee or lunch with us when they first arrived, but she wasn't interested in making friends. She moaned about how boring Francis Court was compared to Drew Castle, and she kicked up a fuss about how much time Alex spent working. No one wants to listen to that all the time, so eventually we gave up." She shrugged and looked defiantly at Lady Beatrice.

Lady Beatrice nodded sympathetically. "There is only so much you can do to help someone who doesn't want to help themselves, isn't there?"

Mrs Crammond smiled at her. "Yes, my lady, that's exactly it." Seeing Mrs C had warmed to the subject, she wondered if she should use this opportunity to find out more about Alex and Gill's relationship. *Maybe she can help shed some light on the situation.*

"Would you have described Alex Sterling as a bully, Mrs Crammond?"

The head housekeeper tilted her head to one side and said nothing for a few seconds. "No." She shook her head. "I'm the first to admit I didn't like him much, but I wouldn't have called him a bully. He was passionate about Francis Court and his job here — I'll give him that. And he worked hard too, I know. He was a stickler for the rules, but I never heard him disrespected by anyone. He told you to do something rather than ask you." It was clear from her face that she'd disapproved of his management style. "But I never saw him aggressive towards anyone or shout or anything of that nature."

"I heard a rumour he abused his wife."

Mrs Crammond looked perplexed.

Lady Beatrice's heart skipped a beat. *Have I gone too far?*

"I wouldn't have thought so, my lady." She paused, as if considering the accusation, before shaking her head. "I saw no sign Gill was frightened or wary of him. She appeared aggravated by him more than anything else." She looked at Lady

Beatrice curiously. "Can I ask where you heard that, Lady Rossex?"

Oh, no, now what do I say? "Um, I can't remember. It was such a long time ago."

It sounded pathetic even to her own ears, but Mrs Crammond nodded. "I'll tell you this, my lady: it wouldn't surprise me if she started it herself. She came across as someone who liked to play the victim. She was always looking for sympathy and attention."

She appeared satisfied with her conclusion.

Lady Beatrice changed the subject. "So, you had no problem with your friend Ellie having an affair with Alex then?"

Mrs Crammond raised her eyebrows.

"It's the worse kept secret at Francis Court, Mrs Crammond." Lady Beatrice reassured her.

"Well, I won't say I approved, but I understood. Ellie's husband, Ross, was a bit of a wet blanket and wrapped up in his work most of the time. She was feeling neglected and so was Alex. It's no surprise they turned to each other. Ellie is so full of life — she's positive, attractive, and fun." Her face lit up when talking about her friend. "So different from Gill Sterling. And Alex was a man's man, you know? Strong, decisive, in charge — all the things Ross wasn't."

"It sounds like they were a good match. But I've heard recently they were arguing a lot?"

"Yes, well, Ellie wanted to make things official between them. She wanted them to live together. She was even going to start divorce proceedings against Ross." Looking troubled, she shook her head. "But it turned out Alex didn't want that. He wanted things to stay as they were. Ellie was heartbroken."

"Indeed, I can imagine."

"A few months ago, she gave him an ultimatum. If he didn't want to move forward with their relationship, then they were through. He wasn't happy, of course, and tried to persuade her to change her mind. But she was adamant it was over this time."

Her face pink, she glared at Lady Beatrice. "All he needed to do was stop messing her around and leave her alone, but he wouldn't listen." Her face was now deep purple. She clenched her jaw.

I wouldn't want to meet her in a dark alley at night, Lady Beatrice thought, a slight shiver running up her spine. Clearly, now wasn't the time to ask her about the argument Naomi had overheard between her and Alex.

As quickly as the anger had overtaken Mrs Crammond, it dissipated. Her shoulders sagged. The fight had left her. Looking embarrassed, she glanced at her watch and blurted out, "Excuse me, my lady, but I have to check on some supplies due to be delivered any minute."

Rising, she hurried to the door.

Lady Beatrice let out her breath. Well, that was unexpected. Picking up her phone, she texted Perry.

Lady B: *How did it go with Ward? I have had an interesting conversation with Mrs C. Do you have time for coffee in TOSB cafe?*

26

LATE AFTERNOON, WEDNESDAY 14 APRIL

Lady Beatrice stood at the serving counter in the Old Stable Block Cafe and ordered a black coffee and a large latte. She surveyed the cafe. It was quiet and empty, save for one table occupied by two middle-aged women eating scones and sipping tea. As she moved past them to a table in the corner, she heard them whispering.

"Oh, Cathy, look, I think that's Lady Beatrice."

"I think you're right. She's taller in real life, isn't she? I just love her long red hair. Do you think she has a special shampoo made just for her?"

"Probably. She is royalty, after all."

Do people really think things like that about me? Her mother's voice came into her head. *If you don't give them an insight into who you are, they'll simply make it up*. Did she need to open up a bit more and let people see the real her? As much as she hated to admit it, her mother was normally right.

A warmth spread through her body as she sat down and faced them. Giving them a beaming smile, she mouthed, "Hello." *Maybe I'll share with them the make of the shampoo I use.*

Eyes wide in disbelief, they bowed their heads awkwardly and returned to their afternoon tea.

Or maybe not.

A few minutes later, Perry entered the room at the same time as a server came over with their drinks. "Thanks, Jasmine," he said, as she placed their order in front of them. He pulled the milky coffee towards him and added sugar from a long thin sachet. Picking up his spoon, he stirred. "That was perfect timing." He smiled at Lady Beatrice as he sipped his drink. "So, you had an interesting chat with Mrs C, did you?"

"Before I tell you about that, tell me how it went with Ward."

"Well, you were right. He's in charge of the key cutting machine, which is locked when not in use. He's the only one who uses it and, unless he goes on holiday, the only one who has a key for it. I asked what happens if he's not there when someone wants a key cut, and he said whoever it was would have to come back when he was."

Lady Beatrice laughed. That sounded like Ward. He lived in a black and white world.

Perry continued, "I had to tell him you had particularly asked me to come and talk to him before he would answer any of my questions."

"He's been with the family since he was eighteen-years-old, so he's protective of us all."

"Anyway, he said that to have a key cut you need a permission slip signed by the key holder. It gets logged in a book — where the key is for, who requested it, and who gave permission. He keeps the permission slips and files them by date. I had a look at the log and in the last six months, no one had keys cut for the Garden Room." He sighed. "So, I think that rules out the idea that someone had a key cut for either the French doors or the front door, don't you?"

"Indeed. It must be someone who already had a set of keys or access to them, at least."

"Well, that's only Mrs C then."

"Well, not quite." She grimaced. "Sarah also has access to the key safe in Mrs C's office. She provides cover for when Mrs C is off."

Perry frowned. "That's not good."

"It gets worse. Sarah signed out the French door

keys to the Garden Room on the Saturday before the murder and didn't return them until Thursday. She told Mrs C that she needed them for something to do with the builders."

Perry nodded. "Yes, she was liaising with Charles about the windows. But even so, that's not great timing." Silence descended as the implication sunk in.

"It's just as well that the police think little of our theory about the French doors," Perry said, rubbing his fingers against his forehead. "Maybe they won't find out."

"Actually, that wasn't the interesting bit."

He cocked his head to the side. "Tell me more."

"I talked to Mrs C about Ellie and Alex and their relationship. She told me a similar story to the one Naomi told. Ellie gave Alex an ultimatum about a month ago. When he refused to take their relationship forward, she broke it off with him."

Perry rolled his eyes. "Those two were always breaking up and getting back together, so it's no big deal."

"Mrs C said this time Ellie meant it, but Alex was trying to persuade her to change her mind. Here's the bit that's interesting." Perry leaned in. "Mrs C became very agitated when she was talking about Alex." She screwed her eyes as she tried to recall Mrs C's exact words. "She said all he needed to do was stop messing Ellie around and leave her alone, but he wouldn't listen. What do you think of that?"

"Do you think she killed him?" he whispered, leaning forward.

"I don't know," she whispered back. "What do you think?"

"I like Mrs C and don't want to believe she did this. But she seems to be the most likely suspect at the moment."

He leaned back, crossed his legs, and picked up his coffee. Taking a sip, he appeared to be contemplating her question further. When he'd finished, he placed his cup back on the table and looked around the cafe. The two ladies were motioning to leave. They stole a quick glance at Lady Beatrice and Perry as they rose. Lady Beatrice smiled at them, and they scurried away. Perry waited until they had left, and the cafe was empty.

"Well, Miss Marple, you know what detectives always look for — means, motive, and opportunity." She nodded in agreement. "So let's consider each one and see if Mrs C has all three," he suggested. She nodded. "Okay," he continued, "we know she had the means. In fact, she's the only person, except Sarah, who had access to the keys to the Garden Room."

Lady Beatrice crossed her arms.

"And of course, we don't believe Sarah is involved," he added quickly, shaking his head. "Mrs C has a complete set of all the keys on her and is the only person who has access to the key safe. Tick." He mimed ticking an item off a list. "So next we need to consider motive."

"Motive is based on one of two things — love or money," Lady Beatrice chimed in. Perry raised an eyebrow, and she shrugged. "I read that somewhere."

"Okay, well, if that's the case, unless Alex left her a pile of money in his will that we don't know about, it has to be love." He looked at Lady Beatrice. She shrugged. "Well, let's park that for the moment and look at opportunity. She lied when she said she was in her office between eight twenty-five and five past nine. Her office was empty when I went to pick up the keys before breakfast. When I challenged her about it, she was vague about where she had been, saying she had a headache and went for a walk."

"She said the same to me when I spoke to her earlier. She told me she was in her office, but when

I questioned that, she said she'd been for a walk in the south gardens."

"She has no alibi for the time of death." Perry did an exaggerated tick off his imaginary list. "Next we need to think about if she could physically have done it." He looked at Lady Beatrice. She shrugged again. "Well, she isn't a massive woman, but she's sturdy and is probably stronger than she looks," Perry said. "So let's say that it's not impossible that she could have killed him. Tick." He gave a slightly less emphatic air tick this time.

"I would've disagreed with you until I saw how furious she was when she was talking about Alex and the way he treated Ellie. She was scary, Perry."

"Ah, that could be it!" he exclaimed. Lady Beatrice frowned and looked at him for clarity. "Love!" he cried. "Mrs C loves Ellie Gunn. That's what makes her so protective of her and why she would kill Alex to stop him from hounding Ellie. Tick"

He did his final air tick and looked triumphantly at Lady Beatrice.

"Do you mean you think she's in love with her romantically or loves her in an older sister way?" she asked, still frowning.

"The latter," he replied, then paused. "Actually, I wouldn't rule out the first option either. I've not known Mrs C to have a romantic relationship in all the years she's been here, so maybe she's secretly in love with Ellie."

Lady Beatrice raised her eyebrows. "Well, I suppose that's an excellent motive, if it's true."

"It's a crime of passion!" Perry cried with a flourish.

He could be right, Lady Beatrice acknowledged. She didn't know Sophie Crammond or Ellie Gunn well enough to have an opinion.

Leaning forward, he put his elbows on the table. "I hate to say it, but we now have means, motive, and opportunity. Mrs C is our murderer!"

As Lady Beatrice sauntered towards the temporary police offices, she hoped they had gone home for the day. She wanted more time to consider their theory. Perry was convinced that Mrs C was the only probable killer. She agreed with him that Mrs C had means, motive, and opportunity. And crucially, she was the only person who had all the keys to the Garden Room. *I suppose she must be the murderer.* Lady Beatrice had expected to feel more elated when they discovered who had killed Alex. It surprised her to feel more sad than delighted.

All the lights were off in the office used by CID as Lady Beatrice approached, but there were people moving about in the PaIRS office next door. *Blast!* She would have to go through with it now. Standing outside the door, she crossed her fingers, hoping DS Spicer was in there and not Fitzwilliam.

She'd not wanted to do this on her own, but a delivery issue had called Perry away and he was currently driving to King's Town station to collect a pair of black and white imperial Italian candlesticks that were the centrepiece of their styling for the Garden Room. She had reluctantly agreed to talk through their theory with DI Ainsley or Spicer while he was gone.

She twisted the rings on her finger; she was now regretting letting Perry go. *Come on Bea, you can do this.* She took a deep breath and knocked on the door. "Hello?" she asked, as she opened the door and entered.

She was relieved to see the friendly face of DS Spicer smiling back at her. A quick glance around the room showed her that Spicer was alone. Her muscles relaxing, she smiled back.

Spicer sat at a desk opposite the door, her laptop open in front of her. She rose and walked towards Lady Beatrice.

"Hello, Lady Rossex. What can I do for you?"

Lady Beatrice was about to open her mouth when she sensed a movement behind her. She turned her head. *Oh, no!* DCI Fitzwilliam had entered the office. She stiffened.

Moving to her side, he forced her to turn all the way towards him. He folded his arms. "Ah, Lady Rossex, this is a pleasant surprise." He looked like a fox entering a chicken house. "Have you another theory to share with us?" he sneered.

This man is insufferably offensive! She raised her chin. "Actually, chief inspector, we've worked out who the murderer is. I thought it might interest you, as you seem to have struggled to work it out yourselves." *Well, that worked. He looks flabbergasted.* Lady Beatrice looked over at Spicer, expecting her to look back encouragingly. Spicer was frowning. There was a heaviness in her stomach. *Oh no, me and my big mouth.*

"Really, my lady?" Fitzwilliam moved over to where Spicer stood in front of her desk. He turned towards Lady Beatrice, perched on the edge of the desk, crossed his ankles, and folded his arms. "Do tell."

They were both staring at her, their heads tilted to one side. Ready and waiting.

Why did I say that? She had been intending to discuss their theory with someone, not present it as a fait accompli. Bile rose in the back of her throat. She swallowed it down. *I'm going to have to brazen it out now.* "We've looked at who had means, motive, and opportunity, and it's our belief that Mrs Crammond killed Alex Sterling," she blurted out.

DS Spicer looked at Fitzwilliam, her eyes wide. He shook his head at her and returned to stare at Lady Beatrice, giving nothing away. "Continue," he instructed.

"Mrs Crammond is the only person who has keys to the Garden Room, and she has no alibi for the time of death. She lied about being in her office at the time that someone killed Alex." She paused. Spicer was looking at a spot over Lady Beatrice's shoulder, a blush creeping up her neck. Fitzwilliam was still gazing at her, his eyes sparkling and his lips clamped together.

Keep going Bea. It will be over soon. "We think she's in love with Ellie Gunn and it enraged her, the way Alex was treating Ellie." She was babbling now, but she simply couldn't stop herself. "And she threatened him. Someone overheard her telling him if he didn't leave Ellie alone, she would stop him." *I must stop talking.* A smirk spread over Fitzwilliam's face. "She just about confessed to me she killed him, and she looked so scary. I can well believe it." Her voice had reduced to a whisper.

There was an awkward silence.

"Yes, well, that's riveting Lady Rossex," Fitzwilliam said.

Spicer's face was pink, and she was looking down at her feet.

He continued, "I hate to burst your bubble, but Mrs Crammond has an alibi for the time of the murder. Someone saw her in the Rose Garden at eight thirty-five and again at eight forty-five. And guess who that was, my lady?"

Lady Beatrice's head spun. *Don't answer that. It can only make it worse.*

"It was Naomi, your own maid."

Lady Beatrice looked at the ground and muttered, "My mother's maid."

Fitzwilliam grinned like a Cheshire cat. Lady Beatrice wanted to curl up and die; she closed her eyes and sighed.

DS Spicer broke the silence by clearing her throat. Opening her eyes, Lady Beatrice saw Spicer was smiling now. "Lady Rossex, we must thank you and Mr Juke for bringing to our attention that someone moved the furniture in the Garden Room. We're now considering other theories."

Lady Beatrice gave her a curt nod and turned towards the door. *I need to get out of here.*

"Lady Rossex," Fitzwilliam called after her.

She swung round to face him but couldn't meet his gaze.

"I wonder if you can do something for me?" Unfolding his arms, he straightened.

She was expecting a warning to not meddle, to keep their theories to themselves, and to let the police carry on with their job. "Yes, of course." She lifted her chin, bracing herself for the onslaught.

Fitzwilliam looked down at his hands, turning them over as he examined them. Coughing, he put his hands in the front pockets of his black chinos. "It's Lady Sarah."

Lady Beatrice's heart raced. She suddenly felt lightheaded.

"I'm afraid she's looking like a credible suspect. She's the only other person who had access to the keys for the Garden Room, and we know she lied about her movements during the time someone killed Mr Sterling."

I know, I know. Lady Beatrice shook her head.

He paused. Taking his hands out of his pockets, he raked one of them through his short, brown hair. "I'm sorry. I've been putting off calling her in for a formal interview, hoping she would come forward voluntarily. But she's ignored all my requests to speak to her and there's only so much I can do." He shrugged and shook his head. "She may have vital information that will help us. I can't delay much longer."

It surprised Lady Beatrice that his concern sounded real. *What to do?* She'd made a fool of herself in front of the one man who already thought she was a pampered princess. The least she could do was try to redeem herself by co-operating with him. "What do you want me to do?" she asked.

"Can you persuade her to come and talk to me as soon as possible… please?"

She pondered for a moment. His hair was slightly messy, and she could detect a shadow of stubble on his square jaw. His complexion was sallow. He looked like he needed more sleep.

"I will do my best, chief inspector."

He smiled. Not a sneer. Nor a sarcastic grin. A proper smile. It transformed his tired face. "Thank you."

"Indeed. Fine. Well, thank you," she spluttered as she bolted through the door and out into the welcoming fresh air.

27

EARLY EVENING, WEDNESDAY 14 APRIL

Lady Beatrice knocked on the door of Francis Lodge, her sister's home, hoping she'd be able to talk to Lady Sarah alone before she sat down to dinner with her family. The door opened and Lady Beatrice's niece, Charlotte, squealed in delight.

"Aunty Bea, are you here for dinner? Mummy didn't say. What a lovely surprise." Beaming, she looked around at Lady Beatrice's feet. She raised her blue eyes to her aunt's face. "Where's Daisy?"

"I'm sorry, Lottie, but she's with some friends. I'm on my way to have dinner with them now, but I popped in as I need to talk to Mummy quickly. Is she around, darling?"

Lottie's shoulders dropped. "Oh, all right. I'll find her," she muttered as she turned away.

Lady Beatrice put her hand up to her mouth and swallowed hard. *I'll bring Daisy to see Lottie tomorrow*, she promised herself. She moved into the grand hall of Francis Lodge and closed the door behind her. Lottie had run off through a door on the right, leading to the kitchen. The butterflies in Lady Beatrice's stomach increased in activity as Sarah poked her head around the kitchen door.

"Are you coming in?" Lady Sarah asked in a clipped voice.

Normally, she would be eager to join her sister in the bright, welcoming room. She would grab a coffee from the coffeepot that was always on (John, her brother-in-law, was a coffee addict like her) and sit on a stool in front of the breakfast bar, chatting to Sarah. But not tonight. This would not be a cosy chat that they could have in front of John or Lottie.

"No, sorry, sis. I have security waiting for me outside. I just need a quick word." Lady Beatrice stayed where she was. Sarah strode through the door and stood in front of her.

"Why are security with you? Tell them they can go. Come in and have a coffee. When you leave, you can go via the back garden gate. You'll be straight onto the Estate, no press." She turned and walked back towards the kitchen, her black high heeled Chanel court shoes clicking on the stone floor as she moved.

It never ceased to amaze Lady Beatrice how her sister stayed looking elegant from the minute she got dressed until the moment she went to bed. The green Diane von Furstenberg ribbed-knit midi wrap dress she was wearing today was uncreased. Her long brown hair was still neat in its chignon. She looked as pristine as she had earlier that morning. Lady Beatrice looked down at her open brown suede jacket, her black Tom Ford T-shirt, which had 'Fabulous' written on the front in silver, her Holland Cooper biker jeans, and her chunky Gucci ankle boots. *I look like I've climbed off a motorbike after a gruelling cross-country ride.*

"Sarah, wait... please," she cried. Sarah turned. "I'm on my way out. I stopped off because I need to tell you about a conversation I had with DCI Fitzwilliam this afternoon."

Sarah stomped back to where Lady Beatrice was standing. Stopping in front of her, she crossed her arms. "I thought we agreed you weren't getting involved in this murder nonsense anymore. You promised to concentrate on getting my events suite completed before the deadline," she lectured, a warning tone in her voice.

"Perry and I are on it, Sarah. But I bumped into Fitzwilliam as I was leaving, and he asked me to talk to you." *Not quite true, I know*. But she wouldn't tell her sister that she'd stormed into Fitzwilliam's office, told him that Mrs C was a murderer and was shot down in spectacular style.

"It's serious Sarah. You're one of their only suspects for Alex's murder."

Lady Sarah threw her head back and laughed. "Oh, come on, Bea. Are you seriously telling me that the police think I killed Alex? Why on earth would I do that?" She stopped laughing. "*You* don't think I killed him, do you?" she asked, putting her hand up to her chest.

"Of course not," Lady Beatrice jumped in. Grabbing Sarah's hand, she held it in hers. "But, Sarah, they need to talk to you. You're one of the few people with a set of keys to the Garden Room. And they know that you're lying about where you were at the time of Alex's murder. The more you refuse to co-operate, the more you're forcing them to go down a formal route."

"And what exactly does that mean?" Lady Sarah barked, wrenching her hand out of Lady Beatrice's. "Are they going to arrest me, a member of the royal family?" Her eyes were blazing.

Well, this is going as badly as I feared. This requires tough love. She took a deep breath.

"No, not if they can help it. But someone murdered Alex Sterling and they have to follow up on all leads. That's how it works, Sarah, royal family or not. Their next step is to interview you under caution. You'll need a lawyer and there's a chance the press will find out!" Lady Sarah looked taken aback. "I'm worried for you," Lady Beatrice told her sister in a wobbly voice.

"Well, that makes a change. It's usually the other way around," Lady Sarah mumbled.

What does that mean? She sighed. Now wasn't the time to ask.

"Where were you, Sarah?"

"I had to come back to the house."

"Why?"

"That's none of your business," she snapped. Lady Beatrice stepped back. Sarah sighed. "I'm sorry, but it's private," she said in a softer voice. "Anyway, I think you're being overdramatic. They can't possibly think I'm a murderer."

One more try, then I'm giving up. Lady Beatrice reached for her sister's hand again. "Even if you won't tell me, tell Fitzwilliam, Sarah… please. You may have important information. Help the police end this for all of us," she begged.

Sarah stared at her sister, then lowered her gaze.

Lady Beatrice dropped her hand. "I have to go." She turned and moved towards the door. "Just think about it. Please." Opening the door, she walked out into the night on shaky legs. *I need a drink!*

Lady Beatrice entered The Ship and Seal. As the welcoming heat hit her, she unbuttoned her jacket. At the bar, Seth Padgett and Pete Cowley were sitting with a group of people she didn't recognise. Pete appeared to be telling a story as Seth handed him a pint of beer. They waved, and she waved back before heading straight to the dining area. Perry and Simon sat in a booth next to the one they'd been in the other night. A huge grin spread over her face. *There's my girl.*

Daisy, who had been lying next to Simon, jumped off the seat and ran towards her mistress. Her tail wagged so hard her whole bottom half was swaying from side to side and she could barely keep upright.

Scooping Daisy up, she cuddled the wriggling body. *I hate arguing with my sister.* She took a deep breath and returned Daisy to the floor. As she approached, Perry shifted so she could sit next to him, and Daisy jumped up and resumed her position next to Simon; she laid her head on his lap with a deep sigh.

Simon pushed a gin and tonic in front of Lady Beatrice, and she took a huge gulp.

"That bad, heh?"

She nodded and took another mouthful. "I needed that," she said, as she placed her now almost empty glass back on the table.

Simon slid a menu in front of her, saying, "Decide what you want to eat and then you can tell us all about it."

She chose the hot goat's cheese salad with garlic croutons. She hadn't realised how hungry she was until now.

Simon returned from placing their order with another gin and tonic for her. She took just a sip of her drink this time and relayed to them her confrontation with Fitzwilliam. As she told them, she realised that if she'd not been so keen on showing off her detective skills to him, she could've saved herself the embarrassment. And, she reflected, why had she thought that she could solve a murder that experienced and respected senior police officers like Mike and Fitzwilliam were struggling with?

Perry apologised for leaving her to face the ordeal on her own. Simon tried to make them both feel better by telling them about when CID had gone off on wild goose chases based on their own theories. He also pointed out that the new information about the furniture they had given them this morning provided the police with a new direction. Perry appeared to find comfort in that. Lady Beatrice didn't.

Sarah was right. I should have left it up to the police and focused on my job.

When the food arrived, Lady Beatrice ate her salad (which was lovely) in silence, absentmindedly feeding morsels of goat's cheese to Daisy. When they had finished, Perry asked if she had talked to Sarah.

"Yes, but I failed to make her understand that they'll have no choice but to go down the official route if she keeps ignoring them. She won't take it seriously."

"Hopefully, she'll think about what you've said and change her mind," Simon suggested.

"I hope so. I'm so worried about her."

They nodded in sympathy.

"Oh, and I asked her where she was at the time of Alex's death."

"And?" Perry asked, his eyes shining.

"She said she had to go home."

"Why didn't she say that in the first place?"

Perry exclaimed, throwing his hands up. "It's no big deal. I don't understand why she lied about it."

"Did she say why she went home?" Simon's head tilted to one side.

"I asked her. She told me it was private and none of my business."

Thinking about it now, Lady Beatrice thought it was a strange thing for her sister to have said. They told each other everything. *You haven't told her about James's letter.* She ignored the voice in her head. *What was so private that she couldn't tell me?* She hoped her sister wasn't in trouble.

"If Lady Sarah had told the police that she went home, then they would've asked her why, and clearly she doesn't want to tell them," Simon said.

The sound of a guitar being tuned drifted over from the bar, followed by a cheer. Lady Beatrice looked at Perry and Simon. "There's a band?" she asked.

"It's the monthly Open Mic Music Night," Simon explained. "Anyone can get up and sing or play an instrument. It's a fun night."

Not for me. "I think I'll leave now if you don't mind. It's been a draining day and I'm ready for an early night." She messaged for the security buggy to come and collect her and Daisy. Meanwhile, Perry and Simon debated whether to stay and listen to the open mic or call it a night too and go home to watch *Bake Off*.

Simon Lattimore was hurrying across the green, his hands deep in his pockets. He took one out and glanced at his watch - eleven-fifteen. He hoped he wasn't too late.

When he and Perry had arrived home ten minutes ago (the open mic option having won over another night in front of the television), he'd realised that he hadn't picked up his messenger bag with his laptop in it. He hoped it was still under the table in the booth where they'd eaten.

Oh god, what if it's gone? He couldn't bear to think about it. His laptop was indispensable. It held his book drafts, his ideas, and his outlines. His whole life as a writer was on that machine.

Breaking into a run, he reached the pub door. Relieved to find it still unlocked, he yanked it open and almost collided with a figure bundled up against the cold. Looking up, Simon recognised the man. "Sorry, Pete."

"No problem, mate," Pete slurred, unsteady on his feet.

Rushing past him, Simon entered the warmth

and light of the pub. Once inside, he unbuttoned his coat as he headed towards the dining area. Dylan, who was wiping down tables, asked if anything was wrong. Simon explained about the laptop, and they went to the booth together to see if his bag was still there. Simon breathed an enormous sigh of relief as he spotted it under the table. He laughed as he picked it up and thanked Dylan. Slinging the messenger bag over his body, he waved goodbye as he strode towards the door.

When the cold air hit him, he pulled his coat tight across his body and, head down, hurried across the road to the green. Hearing a loud *oomph*, he halted and looked around. There was another. It sounded like someone hitting a punch bag.

He followed the sound, his muscles tensing. Realising it was coming from the alleyway on the right-hand side of the pub, he ran towards it. His heart was racing, his ex-policeman's instinct telling him something was wrong. As he reached the entrance, he slid to a stop and activated the torch on his phone. Through the beam of bright light, he could see a person lying in a heap on the floor. A figure was standing over the body, kicking it.

Shouting, Simon thundered down the alley, the sound of his heartbeat thrashing in his ears. The figure froze mid-kick as they looked up, then quickly sped off in the other direction.

Simon gave chase, but a gurgling sound coming from the victim stopped him cold. He redirected his torch downwards. Blood and vomit stained the pavement beside the body. Taking a deep breath, Simon knelt to check the body for a pulse as he di-alled 999.

28

EARLY MORNING, THURSDAY 15 APRIL

The Society Page online article:

Crime Writer Saves Francis Court Mugging Victim While Murderer is Still on the Loose

Last night a member of staff at Francis Court was found badly beaten in an alleyway in the nearby village of Francis-next-the-Sea. It is reported that the attack, which took place next to the local pub, The Ship and Seal, was a brutal mugging.

The victim was found by Simon Lattimore (39), the famous crime writer and winner of last year's Celebrity Elitechef, who lives in the village. Mr Lattimore was commended for his efforts in helping the victim while waiting for the ambulance to arrive. A spokesperson for the ambulance service confirmed that without Mr Lattimore's fast response and first aid skills, the victim could have died at the scene. It is rumoured that the victim is Pete Cowley (46), a gardener at Francis Court and an ex-sergeant in the Royal Marines. Mr Cowley was drinking at the pub earlier in the evening with some work colleagues.

He was admitted to hospital with severe injuries and is currently unconscious. Doctors stress that the next twenty-four hours will be critical to his chances of survival.

The Fenshire Police issued the following statement: 'Our inquiries into this serious incident are ongoing and it is important we establish exactly what happened. We would urge anyone who may have witnessed the incident but has not yet spoken to the police to come forward.'

Francis Court continues to be the centre of a police investigation into last week's murder of the estate manager, Alex Sterling (44). Alex, like Pete Cowley, was a long-standing member of staff.

The popular press has raised concerns about how such a violent attack could take place whilst Fenshire CID and PaIRS officers are onsite at Francis Court, in the village where the incident occurred. They are renewing their call for reassurance from Gollingham Palace and PaIRS that the staff and members of the royal family who live and work at Francis Court are safe. After last night's incident, it appears they may have a point.

A buzzing sounded beside Lady Beatrice's right ear. She opened one eye. Her phone screen was lit up and flashing. Daisy turned her back on her mistress and resettled herself away from the intrusion. Lady Beatrice sighed. *I'd better have a look. It could be important.* Stretching for the phone, she removed it from its charger.

Sarah: *Have you seen the news about Pete Cowley? I like Pete, can't believe anyone would want to hurt him. You are right, this is serious. I am off to talk to DCI Fitzwilliam right now. Will come over to your apartment when I'm done. xx*

Lady Beatrice was wide awake. *What has happened to Pete Cowley?* Jumping out of bed, she rushed into the sitting room and bounded across the room to the desk in the corner. She flipped open her laptop. There was a notification that *The Society Page* had posted a new online article. She clicked the link and started reading. A few minutes later, she returned to the bedroom and texted Perry.

Lady B: *Oh my gosh, just read what happened last night. Is Simon all right? x*

While she waited for a reply, she sat on the bed and rubbed the soft belly of a deeply slumbering Daisy. *Poor Pete.* She didn't know him well, but he'd come across as a nice chap from her interactions with him. She couldn't believe he was lying in a hospital bed right now, fighting for his life.

Perry: *I was waiting for you to wake up! He said he's fine, he said he's seen much worse during his time in the police. I know he's made of stern stuff, but I want to be sure, so I'm going to stay and have breakfast with him. Is that Ok? x*

Lady B: *Yes, of course. x*

Perry: *I'll meet you in TSR as planned at ten. x*

Lady B: *See you later. Send Simon my love. x*

29

STILL EARLY MORNING, THURSDAY 15 APRIL

Arriving at the office of PaIRS, Lady Sarah hesitated at the door. She took a deep breath and knocked. Smoothing down her Alexa Chung fitted navy blue dress, she paused, then turned the handle and walked into the room. In the far corner of the office, hunched over a table, were DCI Fitzwilliam and DS Spicer. They straightened up as she entered.

"Lady Sarah, thank you for coming," DCI Fitzwilliam said, and introduced her to Spicer.

Lady Sarah smiled at them and cleared her throat. "Chief inspector, before we continue, may I apologise for not responding to your requests for a meeting until now. I have no excuse, I'm afraid. My sister came to the house last night and ticked me off for not taking your investigation seriously. That, combined with the Pete Cowley mugging, has made me realise she was right. I'm not sure how I can help you, but I'll answer any questions you have."

She ceased babbling and looked at DCI Fitzwilliam, waiting for his response. She raised her chin, expecting a scalding.

"That's quite all right, Lady Sarah. All that matters is that you're here now. Please take a seat." He gestured towards the chair that Spicer was pulling out from behind her desk. Placing it opposite Fitzwilliam's desk, Spicer popped over to close the office door, then returned to stand by Lady Sarah's side. She took out her notebook and pen and nodded to Fitzwilliam.

Sitting down, Lady Sarah crossed her legs at the ankle and rested her hands in her lap. "Can you tell me how Pete is? It said in the press it was touch and go if he'll make it?"

DS Spicer filled up a cup of water from the dispenser and put it on the desk for Lady Sarah, who smiled and mouthed, "Thank you."

"They have stopped the internal bleeding," Fitzwilliam informed her. "But he's still unconscious. It's a waiting game, I'm afraid."

Lady Sarah nodded. "Thank you. Please ask me whatever you need to." She smoothed down the skirt of her dress and returned her hands to her lap.

"Let's start with your movements from when you arrived onsite on the day of the murder until you appeared in the Breakfast Room to meet your sister and Mr Juke."

"I arrived at my office around eight. Perry, sorry Mr Juke, came in a few minutes after me and said hello, then went to his own office. I was working on the new brochure for the Events Suite. I had intended to meet my sister and Mr Juke for breakfast, but at about ten past eight, I received a call on my phone. This resulted in me arranging a meeting with someone at my house at eight-thirty. I left my office just before twenty past eight to walk home."

DS Spicer put her hand up. "Can I confirm you live at Francis Lodge, my lady?"

"Yes, it's on the southeast side of the estate and takes about five minutes on foot from the office. There's a locked back gate that offers a shortcut directly from the estate. It enters our property via the garden."

DS Spicer nodded. "Thank you. Please carry on, Lady Sarah."

"I arrived at my house with about five minutes to spare, and my visitor arrived a few minutes later. The meeting took about twenty minutes, then I left, going back the same way, and went straight to the

Breakfast Room." She paused and looked expectantly at DCI Fitzwilliam.

"Thank you, Lady Sarah. Can I ask you a few questions?"

"Yes, chief inspector, ask away."

He smiled. "Did anyone see you on your way to or from your house?"

"I'm not sure, chief inspector. I saw Pete Cowley a few minutes after I left my office. He was coming from the direction of the composting area and appeared to be heading towards the Old Stable Block. Presumably he was going back to the gardening shed. I don't think he saw me. He was quite a way away."

Before she could go any further, Spicer jumped in. "Excuse me, my lady, but are you sure it was Pete Cowley?"

"Yes, sergeant, I'm sure." Lady Sarah replied confidently.

Spicer persisted, "We have other witnesses seeing Alex Sterling in that area at about the same time. Did you see Mr Sterling as well, my lady?"

"No... but it's easy to mix the two up," she told them. "They look very similar from a distance and especially from behind."

DCI Fitzwilliam raised his eyebrows. "Really?"

Lady Sarah nodded. "I know I saw Pete Cowley, and I didn't see Alex Sterling."

Spicer and Fitzwilliam exchanged looks. "What was he wearing, my lady?" Spicer asked.

"Overalls. The dark-blue ones a lot of the estate workers wear."

"Thank you, Lady Sarah. That's very helpful," Fitzwilliam said.

Spicer was busily scribbling in her notebook. He waited for her to finish, then continued, "Can I ask you who you were meeting at Francis Lodge?"

Raising a hand up to her hair, which was pulled up into her signature chignon, she patted it in place.

"We'll need to contact them to confirm your statement. Purely routine, of course."

Closing her eyes, she took a deep breath. "I'm not sure that would be wise, chief inspector. I can assure you it has nothing to do with Alex's murder."

He shook his head. "I'm sorry, my lady, but I must insist."

"Then can we talk in private, please, chief inspector?" Lady Sarah opened her eyes and turned to give DS Spicer an apologetic smile.

Fitzwilliam nodded at Spicer, and she left the room, closing the door behind her.

Lady Sarah took another deep breath. *I'll have*

to trust him. "Have you heard of Desmond Brooke, chief inspector?"

"Isn't he the chief editor of the *Daily Post*, my lady?"

"Yes, that's him," she said, nodding. "Mr Brooke contacted our public relations team here at Francis Court ten days ago, asking for an interview with Lady Rossex. He spoke to my PR manager and told her he had new information about James Wilt-shire's accident, and he wanted to discuss it with Lady Beatrice."

Fitzwilliam raised his eyebrows. "Did he give any more details?"

"No, chief inspector. My PR manager told him if he had new information about the accident, then he would need to contact the police. That's our standard response. You wouldn't believe how many calls we receive about supposed new information and requests to interview Lady Beatrice. We don't share them with her, of course." She took a sip of water.

"Brooke contacted us again the next day. He reiterated he had information that would greatly interest the public. He told my PR manager he was going to publish it that week unless he could talk to Lady Rossex. She told him someone would contact him and called me. I discussed the situation with my mother, and we agreed I would talk to Brooke and find out what information he had. We decided not to tell my sister." Lady Sarah uncrossed her legs and recrossed them. "My PR manager contacted Brooke to arrange a call with me, but he refused, insisting he would only talk directly with Lady Beatrice. She told him it wouldn't be possible, and he hung up."

"When was this, my lady?"

"Last Tuesday, the day before the murder. I wasn't too worried at that point. I thought if he didn't get what he wanted, he would go away. But I was wrong."

Pausing, she took another sip of water.

"At about ten past eight on Wednesday morning, I received a call from security at the main gate. Desmond Brooke was there and told them he had an appointment to see me. He wasn't on their list, so they refused him entry. I instructed them to take his mobile phone number and inform him I would ring him straight back. I didn't want him on-site, so I called and arranged to meet him at my house at eight-thirty."

"That's most unusual, my lady."

"I'm aware of that, chief inspector, but it was an unusual situation. Brooke is an influential member of the press and not someone I could afford to ignore. If he was pursuing this story, then there was likely something in it. I thought if I invited him to Francis Lodge, he would be flattered and easier to deal with." She gave a short laugh. "Even hardened senior editors are a tad star struck when meeting members of the royal family on a one-to-one basis in their homes."

Fitzwilliam smiled and nodded. "Please continue, Lady Sarah."

"When I arrived at Francis Lodge, I checked the library looked presentable and ordered coffee. Brooke arrived on time." She paused, taking a deep breath.

"Lady Sarah, I know this is difficult and I appreciate you'd rather not share private details with me, but remember, I was there during the investigation into James Wiltshire's death. I may be able to help."

Of course. She had almost forgotten that he had been part of the team investigating James's death. *Maybe he can help.* "Yes, you're right, chief inspector." She swallowed. "So Brooke arrived. The library at Francis Lodge is spectacular, and he was suitably impressed." She smiled briefly, then her face clouded over. "He told me there was a letter written by James to my sister. He said someone found it in the overnight bag James had left in

London the night of his accident. Brooke claimed it only came to light a few years ago. He would not give me any more details about the letter or its contents. He said the letter had been handed over to Lady Rossex." Lady Sarah shook her head. "I know nothing about a letter, and I told him so. He was most insistent it exists, claiming his source was reliable."

She sighed. "If it's true, chief inspector, and he publishes the details..." Her voice trailed off. She looked at Fitzwilliam, her eyes wide and fearful. "My sister may look fine now, but it's taken her years to recover from James's death. The press intrusion during the investigation and the ongoing speculation since then... I can't let her go through it all again." She shook her head.

Fitzwilliam frowned. "Have you talked to Lady Rossex about this?" he asked gently.

"I don't even know if the letter is real. When I asked Mr Brooke if he had a copy, he refused to say. I don't want to talk to my sister about it and upset her. Surely if there was a letter, she would've told me or my mother?"

Detective Chief Inspector Richard Fitzwilliam studied her face for a few minutes in silence. A feeling of unease pooled in her stomach. *What does he know?*

"Lady Sarah, I can confirm there is a letter." She looked up at him, pain in her eyes. *Oh, no.* "But"—he put his hand up—"I can also reassure you your sister has the only copy, and no one knows of its contents except me and her." Lady Sarah's eyes were so wide, she felt she must look like a cartoon cat.

"Fenshire CID gave it to me unopened, and I handed it to Lady Rossex in the same condition. She gave me permission to read it in her presence to make sure the contents had no impact on the verdict of the inquest into her husband's death, which I did. There was nothing in the letter relevant to the verdict, so I left the letter with her. That is why, Lady Sarah, I can tell you with confidence only your sister and I know the contents. Unless your sister has shared the contents with someone, and I'm sure we can both agree, that's extremely unlikely." Lady Sarah nodded. "Then it's not possible the details are with anyone in the press."

Letting out a long sigh, she gave him a cautious smile. "Thank you, chief inspector."

"So, my lady, it appears Mr Brooke is bluffing. I imagine someone from Fenshire CID has told him about the existence of the letter, but I doubt he knows anything more about it than that." He smiled back. "And what's more, unless someone from here or the palace confirms there is a letter, he can't prove it even exists. My suggestion is to remind him Francis Court doesn't comment on private matters."

"Yes, you're right. I can't tell you how much better I feel about it now, chief inspector." She sat more upright, a weight lifting off her shoulders.

"One last piece of advice, Lady Sarah. Talk to your sister. Tell her about Mr Brooke and his claim. Make sure she's prepared for any press attention."

Oh Bea, how can I make this go away for you? Lady Sarah made to open her mouth in protest, but he put up his hand.

"Lady Rossex is stronger than you think, my lady. She'll cope just fine once she realises there's no story without her input."

Lady Sarah closed her mouth, looking pensive. *Will she really?* Bea certainly seemed bolder and more confident these days. *Look how she talked to me last night!* Making no comment, she rose from the chair, brushed herself down and looked at Fitzwilliam. "Thank you again, chief inspector." She moved towards the door, then stopped as she remembered something. "Oh, one last thing. I'm sure you already know this as you have Alex's phone, but I had a text exchange with him the morning he died."

Fitzwilliam's eyebrows shot up. Crossing the room, he opened the door and shouted, "Spicer".

DS Spicer rushed in. "Yes, sir?"

"Were there any text messages on the victim's phone from the morning of the murder?"

She shook her head. "No sir."

He turned to Lady Sarah. "Well, my lady, it looks like you have new information for us. What time was this?"

"It was about six forty-five. I asked him if he would come to my office early so I could double check some estate information with him for the publicity material I'm producing for the grand opening of the Events Suite. He said he was meeting someone before breakfast but would catch up with me in the Breakfast Room at around eight-thirty."

Spicer and Fitzwilliam stared at her, their eyes glistening.

"When he wasn't there, I assumed I'd missed him as I'd arrived late for breakfast. That was, of course, before I knew he was dead." She looked at DS Spicer, who was writing in a notebook, and picked up her mobile phone. "Would you like to see the text exchange?"

30

NOT LONG AFTER, THURSDAY 15 APRIL

Lady Beatrice opened the door of her apartment and Mrs Harris entered with a tray of tea, coffee, and pastries. Daisy ran around her feet, excited to see her mistress.

"Daisy, love, just let me put the tray down." Tottering over to the coffee table in the seating area in front of the windows, Mrs Harris placed the tray down and bent down to fuss Daisy.

The door opened and Lady Sarah breezed in. "Hello sis, hello, Mrs Harris. Oh, that looks good. I'm starving," she announced as she headed straight for the coffee table.

Mrs Harris curtsied and left the room.

Lady Beatrice padded over to join her sister.

"How did it go then?" she asked as she poured herself a coffee.

"Very well," Sarah replied. "In fact, I may have given them some useful information." She looked smug and then grinned.

She's in a much better mood. "Like what?" Lady Beatrice asked.

"Well, I surprised them when I told them I'd seen Pete Cowley just after I left my office," she said, sipping her tea.

"Pete? What time was that?" Lady Beatrice was surprised too. No one else had mentioned seeing him.

"About twenty past eight. I was walking home via the back way, but I don't think he saw me. He was quite a distance away."

"Are you sure it was Pete and not Alex?"

Sarah put her cup down and focused on her sister. "That's what DS Spicer asked."

"That's because Seth and Joe said they saw Alex at about that time," Lady Beatrice informed her.

"Yes, I know. But as I pointed out to her, they look alike, especially from the back. I've mistaken them for each other before. But they have different walks. Alex sort of bends forward and lollops, whereas Pete is more upright and marches. I expect it's because he's ex-military."

Lady Beatrice closed her eyes and tried to picture them. They were both about the same height. Both were stocky and muscular, but not fat. Both men had shaved heads. Pete had a beard and Alex was clean shaven, but Sarah was right — you couldn't see that from the back. Her mind raced with possibilities. "Was he wearing dark-blue overalls?" she asked, almost holding her breath while she waited for her sister to answer.

"Yes," Sarah replied.

Yes! I can't wait to tell Perry and Simon about this.

Daisy looked from Sarah to a croissant and back. Picking it up, Sarah broke off a piece for her.

"So what else did you tell them?" Lady Beatrice asked, trying to keep the excitement out of her voice. "Did you tell them why you went home?"

"Yes." Sarah poured herself another cup of tea, not looking at her sister.

Lady Beatrice leaned over and grabbed her hand. "Sarah, is everything all right at home? You know you can talk to me about whatever's troubling you, don't you?"

Sarah smiled. "Everything is fine at home, Bea. You don't need to worry about me. I'll tell you

what I was doing, but not today. Soon, I promise."
She squeezed Lady Beatrice's hand.

"Okay." Lady Beatrice smiled in return, then
breathed a sigh of relief. She could see Sarah
looked less on edge that she had earlier in the week.

"So do you want to hear what else I told
Fitzwilliam and Spicer that they didn't already
know?"

Lady Beatrice raised her eyebrows. *Do I? Of
course I do!*

Sarah laughed at the look on her sister's face. "I
had a text exchange with Alex on the morning he
died."

Lady Beatrice's eyes nearly popped out of her
head. *What?* "Tell me!" she demanded.

"I asked him if he would come and help me that
morning with some estate information I wanted
checking. He said he was meeting someone before
breakfast but would see me in the Breakfast Room
at eight-thirty."

"What time was that?"

"Quarter to seven."

"In the morning?" Lady Beatrice asked incredulously. Sarah nodded. "Sarah! Why were you texting staff at such a ridiculous time in the morning?"

A flush crept across her sister's cheeks. Lifting
her cup to her mouth, she took a sip of tea. "I'm

always up early, and Alex was an early riser too. We've had meetings at seven before, so it didn't seem inappropriate." She put her cup down and crossed her arms.

"Well, it is! People have lives, sis. Seven-thirty is the earliest you should contact staff unless it's an emergency. *And* no later than seven-thirty in the evening either!"

Lady Sarah was taken aback at her sister's outburst. "All right, all right. Point taken." Standing, she smoothed down her dress. "Right, well, I must run. I've lots to do today and haven't even started yet." She grabbed the last piece of croissant and popped it into her mouth before skipping out of the room.

When Lady Beatrice and Daisy entered the Old Smoking Room, Perry was already there, rearranging the cushions on a two-seater sofa overlooking the terrace. Daisy ran up to him and threw herself at his feet, flipping herself on her back, ready for tummy rubs. Perry dutifully obliged. Lady Beatrice smiled. Watching them, she couldn't tell who was enjoying it more. Perry looked up, an ample grin on his face.

"How's Simon?" Lady Beatrice asked as she walked across the room.

"He's okay. We had a lovely, relaxed breakfast. I left him working on the blurb for his latest book."

"What's a blurb?" Lady Beatrice frowned.

"It's like a summary of the book that goes on the back cover. It's harder to write than the book itself, according to Simon." He smiled. "So it's a welcome distraction for him today."

Lady Beatrice nodded. "So what happened last night?"

Perry told her about the open mic. "It's actually great fun. You'll have to stay next time. I was even tempted to have a go myself." He grinned. "Except I couldn't hold a tune if my life depended on it."

"So did Pete stay for it?"

"Yes, he was with Seth and a couple of locals. Turns out he and Seth are quite talented," he added. She raised an eyebrow. "Pete played the guitar while Seth sang some Irish ballads. They were top-notch. We all joined in the chorus, even though we didn't know the words."

He related to her the events of later in the evening as recounted to him by Simon.

"Poor Pete. He was lucky Simon had left his laptop. He could have died if he hadn't."

Perry nodded in agreement. "I can't help but wonder if that was someone's plan."

"What? I thought it was a mugging?"

"Think about it. We live in Francis-next-the-Sea. How many muggings do you think we've had in the last ten years? The most violence we see here is when there is a sale on Farrow and Ball paint at the posh interior design shop on the high street." He grinned, then his face clouded over. "From what Simon said, the assailant was kicking Pete even though he was on the floor and not resisting. That's not mugging someone; that's trying to kill them."

"Simon saw the assailant?"

"Yes, but they fled as soon as Simon shone a light into the alleyway."

"Do you think Pete knows something about Alex's death and someone was trying to shut him up?"

"Could be, Miss Marple."

Lady Beatrice swatted at him. He darted out of the way and grabbed Daisy, holding her in front of him as a shield. Daisy turned and licked his face. They both giggled.

After Lady Beatrice filled him in on Lady Sarah's testament about the morning of the murder, he asked, "So do you think she saw Pete and not Alex?"

"Yes, I believe her. She's very observant."

"It must be a family trait."

"So now I'm wondering if it was Pete that Seth and Joe saw, not Alex. If you think about how far they were away from him, it's possible they mixed the two up by mistake. We need to talk to them again."

"If they saw Pete and not Alex, then we don't know when Alex was last seen," Perry blurted out, his eyes shining.

"Indeed. He could've died any time after six-forty-five, when he was texting with Sarah."

"Didn't you say he told her he was meeting someone before breakfast?"

She nodded.

"Do you think it was the murderer?"

"Could be, Hercule," she responded, picking up a squirming Daisy for protection as Perry tried to swipe at her.

31

LUNCHTIME, THURSDAY 15 APRIL

Lady Beatrice entered the gardening shed, excited after her earlier conversation with Perry. They were getting somewhere again. *You were not getting involved anymore, remember? You were going to let the police do their job.* She sighed. *I should leave it alone.* She'd promised herself if she found out anything of interest, she would tell Fitzwilliam straight away. But then he already knew about the meeting, so she didn't really have anything new to tell him. Yet…

As Daisy ran in ahead of her, Lady Beatrice waited for her eyes to grow accustomed to the dark. She could just make out Joe Fox in the far corner. He had his feet up on a bench, a mug of tea in one hand and a sandwich in the other. He jumped up when he saw her and stood to attention.

"Sorry, my lady, Seth isn't here. He's gone home for lunch," he shouted as she advanced towards him.

"Please relax, Joe, and finish your lunch." Having reached Joe, Daisy sniffed him over. Sitting, she looked up at his sandwich. He bent down and patted her on the head.

Lady Beatrice smiled as she reached them. "Be careful, Joe. She's obsessed with food. You'd best keep an eye on that sandwich of yours." He laughed, moving it out of Daisy's way. Foiled, Daisy wandered off and started sniffing around the gardening shed.

Joe rubbed the back of his head. "Is everything okay, my lady?"

She smiled. "Yes, there's no need to worry. I just wanted to ask you a couple of questions, if that's all right?" He nodded slowly. "Last time we talked you said you were with Seth on your way to breakfast when you saw Alex walking over from his cottage towards the Old Stable Block." He nodded again. "Are you absolutely sure it was Alex?"

"Yes, my lady."

"And why did you think it was Alex?"

He rubbed his forehead. "Sorry, my lady. I don't understand."

"I mean, did you see the man and think, that's Alex, or was it something he did that made you realise it was him?"

He frowned. "I can't quite remember, my lady. I think Seth said something like, 'I wonder where Alex is off to', and when I looked over, I saw Alex walking towards the Old Stable Block."

"Could it have been Pete?" she asked. He looked puzzled. She continued, "Pete was coming back from the compost area, also in blue overalls, and heading here to the shed at about the same time." Joe's brow furrowed, and his head tilted to one side as he gazed into space. "They look alike, especially from the back," she added for good measure.

"Yeah, I suppose it could have been," he replied slowly. He nodded his head and shrugged. "Yeah, it could have been Pete on his way back from the compost bins. I'd never thought about that."

Lady Beatrice smiled. This was good. "Thank you, Joe. I'll let you finish your lunch in peace. Come on, Daisy."

She was half-way across the shed, Daisy at her heels, when Joe shouted, "Lady Rossex!" She turned. "It could have been Pete, but I still think it was Alex, my lady."

After her conversation with Joe, Lady Beatrice headed for the cafe to pick up a sandwich to go, but Daisy had other ideas. She dived through the roped-off entrance of the courtyard, disappearing around the corner. Rushing after her, Lady Beatrice called her name. She caught up with her in front of the garden centre. After calling Daisy to her side, she bent down and clipped her lead on. As she straightened, a female form collided with her, almost knocking her off her feet.

It was a blonde, long-haired teenage girl.

"Are you all right?" Lady Beatrice asked, bobbing down to see the face of her assailant. An impressive array of piercings and heavy black eyeliner met her.

"Oh, I'm so sorry, Lady Rossex. I wasn't looking where I was going." Her accent was local.

"Indeed," Lady Beatrice responded with a smile. "You look upset. What's wrong?"

A fat tear ran down the girl's pale face, leaving a trail of black mascara that ended at her lip. She sniffed. "I was just interviewed by the police, my

lady, and it freaked me out a bit. But I'll be fine."
The girl straightened up. She was only marginally
smaller than Lady Beatrice's five-foot-nine. A long
red and black checked shirt hung over a white T-
shirt, and black ripped skinny jeans were tucked
into black biker boots. *She looks like a younger
blonde version of me*, Lady Beatrice thought.

"I'm sorry, but I don't think I know who you
are."

The girl did a short curtsy and replied, "I'm
Cass Gunn, my lady. I work in the garden centre."

Lady Beatrice nodded and smiled at her.
"You're Ellie's daughter?"

"Yeah." She looked like she was going to cry
again.

"Well, it's nice to meet you, Cass. Shall we sit
down, then you can tell me all about it?" Cass
nodded as Lady Beatrice led her past the *Private*
sign and into the courtyard, stopping at the staff
picnic area in front of the courtyard offices. They
sat opposite each other at a table in the far corner.
Lady Beatrice let Daisy off her lead. The little
white terrier jumped straight onto Cass's lap and
licked her face. Cass laughed. *She's a pretty girl
when she smiles.*

"So what happened, Cass?"

Cass wiped her face and hiccupped. "The police

think I'm a suspect because I've no alibi for the time Alex was killed. I was in the garden centre, but no one saw me." She sniffed and Daisy licked her cheek.

I'm going to have words with Fitzwilliam, scaring the poor girl to death like that. But as she looked closer, there was something about how Cass didn't quite meet her gaze that made her ask, "So you were in the garden centre the whole time, were you?"

Cass looked around, then shook her head and whispered, "No, I went to see Joe." A crimson stain crept up her neck.

I see. Lady Beatrice nodded.

"I went to say hi and see if he wanted me to bring him a coffee. He was in the south gardens when I spotted him, but he was with Seth. It looked like they were going off to breakfast, so I turned round and went back to the garden centre."

"What time was this, Cass?"

"Not long after I got in."

"And did anyone see you?"

She shook her head. "I saw Pete Cowley in the distance coming back from the composting area, but I don't think he saw me, so I have no alibi." Her face fell again. She stroked Daisy, who was half sitting on her lap.

"Are you sure it was Pete you saw and not Alex?" Lady Beatrice held her breath while Cass thought about it.

"Yeah, it was definitely Pete. I could see his face."

Oh yes! Now they had another witness who'd seen Pete and not Alex. *Let me check before I get carried away.* Lady Beatrice curtailed the excitement bubbling up inside her. "So just to be clear, you didn't see Alex at all while you were on your way back to the garden centre, only Pete?"

Cass nodded and wiped her face. "I didn't see Alex, but I think I saw Lady Sarah heading towards the south side gate. She was ahead of me, but it looked like her."

"Can you remember what she was wearing?" Lady Beatrice was aware the answer could confirm Sarah's alibi, so it was important.

Cass snuffled. "A camel-coloured coat and a black dress, my lady."

Lady Beatrice smiled. Cass sniffed. She was still on the verge of tears.

"Cass, please don't worry. I'm sure the police don't seriously think you killed Alex. They're asking us all questions. Try not to let it worry you."

Cass burst into tears.

So much for my reassuring technique. Lady

Beatrice rose and moved to sit next to Cass. She put her arm around the young girl's shoulders. Daisy was on the other side, trying to lick Cass's face.

"It's not that," the girl gasped between sobs, her head in her heads. "It's my mum."

"What about your mum?"

"I think she may have killed Alex."

Well, I wasn't expecting that. "Why do you think that?"

Wiping her face, she turned to look at Lady Beatrice. "She told me she was in her office the whole time, but I saw the back of her as I returned to the garden centre." She hiccupped. "Mum was heading towards the Garden Room." After another hiccup, she threw herself forward onto the table, burying her head in her arms.

"Cass, I don't think your mum killed Alex."

She raised her head, tilting it sideways as she looked at Lady Beatrice. "But she was going to the Garden Room. Isn't that where he was killed?" Before Lady Beatrice could reply, she carried on. "Maybe it was self-defence. They were always arguing. It could've got out of hand."

"Did you like Alex?" Lady Beatrice blurted out. The question took them both by surprise.

Sniffing, Cass shrugged as she sat upright. "I didn't want him to be with my mum but, to be fair, he was okay with me. In fact, he arranged my job in the garden centre."

"You said your mum and Alex were always arguing. What did they argue about?"

"She wanted them to live together, but he wasn't keen," she replied. Then she paused, her well-shaped eyebrows creasing up. "Actually, now I think about it, the last argument they had wasn't about that at all. I only overheard some of it. She was asking him if he'd tampered with a car. He was furious and said something like, 'I wasn't going to let her just leave me.' I'd no idea what they were talking about, but a few minutes later he came flying out of the house, almost knocking me over."

Interesting. "When was this, Cass?"

"A few weeks before he died. I was coming back from the pub. Joe and Seth walked me home as Seth lives next door to Mum and Joe lives with his parents in the street behind us. We could hear them shouting through the open window of the sitting room. I was embarrassed, but they didn't seem to notice. Seth carried on up the path to his house and Joe carried on down the road." She looked exhausted and her face was a mess — eyeliner and mascara were on her cheeks and smudged around her eyes.

"Do you know what I think, Cass?" Lady Beatrice smiled. Cass looked at her expectantly. "I think the police will soon have new information that makes the time of death much earlier than they originally thought. It will mean neither you nor your mum are suspects anymore."

"Really?" The girl smiled for the first time and hugged Daisy.

"Indeed."

Cass looked at her phone and scrambled up from the bench. "I need to tidy myself up and return to work. Thank you, Lady Rossex. I feel much better now."

Lady Beatrice watched her leave. She'd told Cass a little white lie, but she *was* confident they could prove the murder had happened before breakfast.

32

STILL LUNCHTIME, THURSDAY 15 APRIL

Ellie Gunn popped her head round the door of Sophie Crammond's office. "Soph, do you have five minutes to spare?"

Sophie looked up from her computer. Ellie Gunn was looking tired; she had grey smudges under her red, sore eyes. Sophie had tried to persuade her to take some more time off, but Ellie wouldn't hear of it. She'd said she needed the distraction. Sophie smiled at her friend. "Of course. What's up, my lovely?"

Ellie sat down opposite her and gave a deep sigh. "I just lied to the police."

Sophie's eyebrows shot up.

"I feel so awful, Soph. I never lie to anyone."

She slumped in the chair, looking thoroughly miserable.

Sophie leaned over and gave her hand a quick squeeze. "I know. So tell me what happened."

Jumping up, Ellie paced in front of Sophie's desk. "Well, you know how they're re-interviewing everyone at the moment?"

Sophie nodded. They had interviewed her earlier this morning, an unpleasant experience as she, too, didn't like to lie, especially to the police.

Ellie continued, staring at her upturned hands. "Well, now they're asking about where I was between six-thirty and nine. I told them the same story as before. I had breakfast with Cass at the cottage, and we walked here together. She went off to the garden centre, and I came here to my office. I said good morning to you when I arrived and then I was in my office until we had our meeting at nine-fifteen." She dropped eye contact with Sophie and sat back down. Arranging her hands in front of her, she rested them in her lap.

"But I wasn't really in my office." She darted a glance at Sophie. "I realised when I went to retrieve my glasses from my bag that I still had Cass's purse. I thought I'd take it back to her." Her voice was shaky, and Sophie thought she was about to cry. She smiled at Ellie encouragingly. "I tried to find Cass, but she wasn't at work, so I left and came back. I was back in my office before twenty-five past eight."

"Did anyone see you?" Sophie asked.

"Not that I know of." Ellie shrugged her shoulders and moved her hands to the surface of the desk, her palms turned down.

Leaning over, the head housekeeper squeezed Ellie's hand. "Well, if no one saw you, then you're okay. No one will know you weren't in your office."

Ellie shook her head. "I'm worried about where Cass was. She told the police she was at the garden centre the whole time, but I know she wasn't there when I went looking for her. What do I do?"

They sat in silence for a few moments, contemplating her dilemma. Then Sophie Crammond had an idea. "How about you tell Lady Rossex? She seems to be involved in the investigation, but she's not the police. She may be able to help."

Ellie looked reluctant. "Oh, I wouldn't want to trouble her ladyship. I don't know her very well. She's always seemed a bit stuck-up to me. I can't believe she will condone me lying to the police."

"I don't think she's stuck up. She's just rather private. And don't forget, she is a mother. She will understand why you needed to protect Cass. I think she'll want to help."

Ellie shrugged. "Okay, I suppose it can't do any harm. Will you be with me when I tell her?"

Sophie smiled. "Of course I will. I'll radio her now and find out when she can see us."

33

FIFTEEN MINUTES LATER, THURSDAY 15 APRIL

Lady Beatrice walked into Ellie Gunn's office, Daisy following behind. Ellie sat at her desk, drinking from a mug. Sophie Crammond sat next to her, checking her phone. Ellie sprung up.

"Thank you for coming, Lady Rossex." She looked mentally and physically exhausted.

It was a look Lady Beatrice had seen in the mirror every morning in the weeks and months following James's death. She smiled kindly at Ellie.

"You're welcome. So what can I do for you?" Lady Beatrice asked as she took a seat opposite them, while Daisy went around the desk and jumped up on to Ellie's lap.

Lady Beatrice focused on Ellie, reluctant to look at Mrs Crammond sitting directly in front of her. *I can't believe I accused her of being a murderer. I just hope she never finds out.*

Ellie glanced at Sophie, and Sophie nodded.

"I have lied to the police, my lady, and I'm not too sure what to do about it."

"Indeed. And why did you do that?"

Ellie told Lady Beatrice about her movements the morning of Alex's death. She explained she didn't want to cause trouble for Cass, so she'd told the police she'd been in her office the whole time.

Lady Beatrice wanted to smile. A mother and daughter trying to protect each other, both worried the other was a possible murderer. *At least I can fix this.* She told Ellie about her conversation with Cass, leaving out the bit where Cass thought her mum was a murderer. Ellie sagged back in her chair, letting out a long sigh. She hugged Daisy, who licked her face.

"I have the impression she has a crush on Joe, but doesn't want anyone to know," Lady Beatrice told her. Ellie raised her eyebrows and nodded.

"And what should I do about lying to the police, my lady?"

"I suggest you talk to Cass, then go to the police together and tell them the truth."

Ellie looked at Sophie, who nodded. "I'll do

that, Lady Rossex, thank you." Daisy jumped down as Ellie rose from her chair.

Sophie Crammond stood up too. "Many thanks for your time, Lady Rossex. We appreciate your reassurance."

About to rise, Lady Beatrice remembered what Cass had said about the argument she had overheard between her mother and Alex. The reference to his tampering with a car had been niggling at her. *Now is my chance to find out more.*

"Ellie, can you clear something up for me, please?"

"Of course, my lady." Ellie sat back down.

Sophie Crammond hovered by Ellie's side.

"It's about an argument Cass overheard between you and Alex a few weeks before he died. You mentioned something about a car being tampered with."

Ellie blushed. Sophie looked at her with concern. Expecting one of them to tell her to mind her own business, Lady Beatrice didn't push.

After a while, Ellie looked up at Sophie and mouthed, "It's okay." While Sophie sat down, Daisy jumped onto Lady Beatrice's lap and lay her head on the desk, facing them.

"Are you sure you want to talk about this, Lady Rossex?" Ellie asked.

Stroking Daisy's head, Lady Beatrice nodded.

"Well, I suppose you know about my relationship with Alex?"

"You mean the worst kept secret at Francis Court?" Lady Beatrice replied, smiling.

Ellie smiled back and continued, "Yes, that's the one. Well, you may or may not know, but it started before Gill died." She shook her head. "It's not something I'm proud of, but we were both in unhappy marriages and—" She shrugged. "It just happened." Sophie patted her arm.

"On the day of Gill's accident, Alex was in Grantham looking at an irrigation system and I went with him. We had stopped off for dinner at King's Town and were driving back when Alex got the call from the police. They told him Gill had been seriously injured in an accident and was at the hospital. Alex was distraught, so I took over the driving, and he spent most of the journey with his head in his hands, mumbling to himself and shaking his head. I only caught some of what he said, but I heard him say, 'She can't have been in the car. It wasn't working'. Then later, he whispered, 'Oh my God, what have I done?'"

Ellie paused and took a sip of tea. "We went straight to the hospital, but by the time he arrived at the ward, she'd died. Not long after, he told me he couldn't continue with our relationship, and we never discussed it again." Her eyes welled up with tears and she paused. Sophie handed her a tissue, and Ellie dabbed at her eyes.

The poor woman has enough on her plate at the moment without me raking up the past for her.

Lady Beatrice was about to suggest they leave it for now when Ellie continued, "I won't bore you with the on-off relationship we've had since then, my lady. But recently I had come to the end of my tether. When it was clear Alex didn't want us to live together, I broke it off with him." She slowly shook her head from side to side.

Sophie patted her hand. "You did the right thing, El."

Ellie smiled sadly at her and took a deep breath. "Anyway, it turned out he didn't take well to me being the one to break things off this time. He tried to persuade me to carry on as we were, but I refused. He appeared at the cottage a few weeks ago, but by then I'd had enough. I accused him of refusing to accept that I wanted to leave him, in the same way he'd not understood Gill wanted to leave him."

She patted at her eyes with the tissue again. "I don't know why I said it. I didn't even know for sure she wanted to leave. But I had obviously hit a raw nerve, as he was the angriest I had seen him in fifteen years. He shouted back, 'Do you think I would have *let* her leave after everything I'd done for her?' and I asked, 'What do you mean, *let* her leave? She *did* leave you!' He said she couldn't have left him as he'd taken the starter from her car. I was shocked. I told him I couldn't believe he'd tampered with Gill's car."

She sighed. "He stormed out at that point. Later, he rang me. He had calmed down and said he was sorry. He admitted he felt like it was his fault Gill had died. I felt sorry for him; he believed if her car had been working, then she wouldn't have been in the earl's car and would still be alive." Her eyes shined with tears.

Lady Beatrice placed Daisy on the floor as she stood up. "Thank you, Ellie. I appreciate you being so candid with me. I'm so sorry for your loss."

Lifting her hand to her face, Ellie wiped under her eyes. She stood up and smiled weakly. "Thank you, my lady."

34

NOT MUCH LATER, THURSDAY 15 APRIL

Rushing across the marble floor of the Painted Hall, Lady Beatrice felt tears welling up behind her eyes.

It's my fault. I told her I wanted to know.

It was no good. As much as she'd wanted to, she couldn't keep it buried. Her husband had been having an affair with Alex's wife. Of course his death was going to open old wounds.

She slowed down as she reached the north side door. *Breathe!* For a few moments, she stood with her hand on the door, attempting to calm herself. *Coffee!* She needed coffee.

The low rays of the afternoon sun made her squint as she stepped out into the fresh air. Standing at the top of the steps, enjoying the unexpected warmth, she contemplated what Ellie had told her.

So is that why James came back early? To collect Gill because her car wasn't working? She felt a sudden stab of anger. If Alex hadn't tampered with Gill's car, then James would have been safely in London, not dead.

She clenched her jaw. *But he would have still left me.* He would be alive, but with someone else. And everyone would know about it. Her jaw hurting, she closed her eyes and took another deep breath, warm air filling her lungs. *What am I thinking?* Would she rather James was dead than face the humiliation of everyone knowing he didn't love her?

She opened her eyes. *Of course not!* Sam would have a father. She moved her hand to her chest, her heart aching. James would have been a great father.

Stop it! What's done is done. Letting her arm drop, she took one final deep breath and headed down the stairs. Daisy, who had been sitting, head angled towards the sun, eyes closed, jumped up and followed her.

From what Ellie had said, Alex had blamed himself for his wife's death. Lady Beatrice shook her head. She couldn't blame him as well. Ultimately, it was James who had returned for Gill. He'd sealed his own fate.

She reached the bottom of the steps, her sister's

words echoing in her head — *leave the investigating to the police, Bea, and concentrate on your job.* Maybe Sarah was right. After all, she'd hardly known Alex, so why did it matter to her who'd murdered him? She'd only suggested they investigate so she could show off to DCI Fitzwilliam. And that had backfired spectacularly so far. What did they say about pride coming before a fall?

So just leave it then!

But she couldn't.

Somehow, it mattered to her who'd killed Alex. If she helped find the murderer, would it allow her to put the past behind her and move on? *Only one way to find out.*

Suddenly, Daisy darted out in front of her, heading across the lawn. *Blast*! She had forgotten Daisy was supposed to be on a lead in the public areas. She looked around, but thankfully she couldn't see anyone. Neither could she see Daisy now. *Where did she go?* Lady Beatrice called Daisy's name, scanning left and right. Then she spotted her.

Over to the left in a coppice of trees, Daisy began to dig.

Calling her again, Lady Beatrice hurried along the terrace past the Smoking Room. As she reached the Garden Room, she caught sight of Daisy heading out of the trees.

What on earth is in her mouth? "Daisy!" she ran, shouting.

Changing direction, Daisy cut through the open side entrance to the back of the Old Stable Block.

Blast!

Lady Beatrice ran along the length of the terrace and down the stairs, turning left at the bottom and through the gigantic black double doors marked *Private*. As she entered the courtyard, she glanced around. Daisy was heading towards the temporary police offices. A door opened and DCI Fitzwilliam stepped out. Lady Beatrice carried on running towards them both.

"Hello Daisy, what have you got there?" Fitzwilliam asked the excited bundle of fur as she came to a stop in front of him.

Lady Beatrice, almost level with them, shouted, "Daisy, drop!"

Daisy dropped a glove at Fitzwilliam's feet.

***

Turning to his office, Fitzwilliam hollered, "Spicer! Evidence bags, please."

DS Spicer rushed out carrying some clear plastic bags and a pair of small tongs.

"Good girl, Daisy," Fitzwilliam stooped and patted her head. "Now, where did you get that from then?" He looked up at Lady Beatrice. "Do you know where she found it?"

Lady Beatrice shook her head. "Not exactly, but she came out of the trees on the other side of the lawn opposite the Garden Room."

Fitzwilliam took the tongs from Spicer and picked up the glove. Studying it, he turned it over. It looked like a standard gardening glove. That was, except for the large brownish stain on the front, which spread from the palm to the fingers.

Lady Beatrice gulped. "Is that blood?"

Using the tongs, Fitzwilliam put the glove in one of the evidence bags and handed it to Spicer. He wiped the tongs clean and put them and the remaining bags in the pocket of his blue gilet. "Okay, Lady Rossex, let's go."

As he strode across the courtyard towards the side doors, Lady Beatrice jogged a few steps to catch up with him. Daisy was already trotting beside him, her tail held high.

They headed towards the grove, crossing the perfectly manicured lawn at a military pace. As they arrived at the edge of the trees, Lady Beatrice pointed out where she had seen Daisy exit. As they started walking under the canopy of trees, Daisy shot ahead, and they hastened after her.

"Daisy, leave!" Lady Beatrice cried out and Daisy halted ahead of a pile of leaves and twigs in front of a hole. She sat, her tail wagging. Rushing over to her, Lady Beatrice patted her head. "Good girl, Daisy."

She surveyed the clearing. It was a sizeable area; the trees providing a screen for the substantial space behind them. Fitzwilliam took the tongs out of his pocket and poked around in the dirt. Daisy lay down and watched him intently. He retrieved a plastic bag and lifted something off the ground with the tongs. It was another glove. He raised his radio to his face.

"Spicer, this is Fitzwilliam, over."

"Yes, boss, this is Spicer, over."

"Call Fenshire CID, please, and arrange for forensics to come back out."

35

SOON AFTER, THURSDAY 15 APRIL

"Let's go back to the office, Lady Rossex." Once again DCI Fitzwilliam didn't wait for her consent before he started marching towards the courtyard, Daisy by his side. Lady Beatrice followed them as he talked over his shoulder. "You can have the Garden Room back tomorrow, my lady."

She suppressed 'About time' before it came out of her mouth and instead thanked him.

"Chief inspector, are you still sure your witnesses saw Alex Sterling and not Pete Cowley the morning of the murder?" she asked as she caught up with him.

Looking straight ahead, he replied, "You believe they actually saw Mr Cowley?"

"I know my sister is adamant it was Pete, so

yes, I do." *Should I tell him Cass also saw Pete?* She hoped Cass and Ellie would come forward soon, then Cass would tell him herself.

But she didn't need her to.

"I think you're right, Lady Rossex."

"Well, that's a first." It came out of her mouth before she could stop it. She laughed, hoping he would join her, but there was no response, so she cleared her throat. *With any luck, he didn't hear me.*

Fitzwilliam carried on, striding through the open gates and into the courtyard. *Phew, he sets a pace. Just as well I run regularly.*

"So does that mean you are expanding the time of death window?" She asked as they reached the door of his office.

Spicer was on the phone and smiled at her as they entered. Fitzwilliam dumped the tongs and the bag holding the other glove onto Spicer's desk. Daisy, still glued to Fitzwilliam's side, followed him to his chair. Sitting down, he reached over to a plate of biscuits on the far end of his desk. He broke off a small piece of rich tea biscuit and gave it to the white terrier.

Lady Beatrice stood in front of his desk, her arms folded.

Looking up at her, he gestured for her to take the seat opposite him. "Yes, Lady Rossex. We now believe the time of death was between six forty-eight and eight o'clock."

She smiled. She had not expected him to tell her at all, let alone that easily. *I may as well try another question.* "So why eight?"

He paused. She was sure he would tell her to mind her own business.

Shaking his head, he said, "Well, to start with, Alex told Lady Sarah via text he was meeting someone *before* breakfast. We think this was probably the killer. There's no sign he went to his office at all and, from the background work we've done, he was normally there by eight. And finally, there are too many staff arriving onsite from eight onwards. It would be too risky for the murderer to move the body at that time."

"Indeed, chief inspector." She paused, remembering what Simon had said. "You said *move the body*. Does that mean you now believe someone killed Alex elsewhere and moved his body to the Garden Room?"

"No." He looked at her guardedly, clearly knowing something she didn't. Before she could ask, Spicer ended her call and walked over to place a piece of paper in front of Fitzwilliam. Lady Beatrice craned her neck to read it without success.

"I don't understand why the text exchange between my sister and Alex wasn't found on his phone." It sounded more like an accusation than she'd intended. He bristled. *I may have blown it.*

"It was deleted," Spicer piped up, ignoring Fitzwilliam's glare. "Our IT people are working to retrieve all deleted messages in case there is something else there of interest."

"So with the change in the time of death window, my sister, Sophie Crammond, Ellie Gunn, and Cass Gunn are all no longer suspects. None of them were on-site that early."

"How do you know that?" Fitzwilliam interrupted. Lady Beatrice ignored him, turning instead to Spicer. "Unless someone could have sneaked on site without security seeing them?"

Spicer shook her head. "Security here is excellent."

"Then that only leaves the gardeners — Seth Padgett, Joe Fox, and Pete Cowley. And none of them have an alibi."

"Again, how do you know that?" Fitzwilliam stared at her with open hostility.

She returned his gaze. "Seth was about the estate clearing up the remaining debris from the storm that weekend. Joe was in the south gardens, and Pete was over in the compost area getting ready to burn the collected debris." She tried not to look smug. "They are Francis Court staff, chief inspector. They talk to me."

She looked away from Fitzwilliam to catch the eye of Spicer. "Well, we can rule Pete out, can't we?" Spicer gave a barely perceptible shake of her head and tilted it sideways towards Fitzwilliam.

"And why do you think that, Lady Rossex?" he asked dryly.

Oh dear, he sounds really miffed now.

"Someone beat him up last night, chief inspector."

"I'm well aware of that, Lady Rossex," he replied, a note of sarcasm creeping into his voice.

"If the murderer tried to kill him, then it must have been to stop him from talking. He must know something." *Isn't it obvious?*

"The incident is being treated as a mugging," Fitzwilliam stated with a sigh.

"In Francis-next-the-Sea, chief inspector? It's hardly a den of iniquity, is it?"

"We have no evidence to suggest otherwise at the moment." He sounded bored now.

Knowing she'd get nowhere with him, she turned back to Spicer. "How is Pete?"

"He's still unconscious, my lady."

Poor Pete, fighting for his life while this arrogant know-it-all thinks he's the prime suspect.

Lady Beatrice couldn't ignore the nagging feeling that there was some link between Alex's murder and James's accident. *Should I tell him about the argument between Ellie and Alex, and what Alex had said on the night of Gill's accident?* She glanced over at Fitzwilliam. He was feeding Daisy another piece of biscuit. Lady Beatrice smiled. *Maybe I should swallow my pride and give him a chance.* "Chief inspector?" She waited for him. He looked up. "Can we have a word in private, please?"

He stared at her for a few seconds, then turned to his sergeant. "Spicer, forensics should be here soon. Can you meet them at the gate and point them in the direction of the grove of trees opposite the Garden Room, please? I left a marker where they need to start." Spicer nodded. Smiling at Lady Beatrice, she left the room, closing the door behind her.

Standing up, there was a quiver in Lady Beatrice's stomach. She was alone with DCI Fitzwilliam. Daisy stirred, looking up at her mistress, her head tilted to one side. Moving around the chair she had been sitting on, Lady Beatrice put her hands on the back and faced him. Daisy settled back at Fitzwilliam's feet.

"Thank you, chief inspector." She smiled, hoping he would warm to her.

"What can I do for you, Lady Rossex?" he asked. He leaned back in his chair, watching her.

She sighed. *Get on with it, Bea.*

She described the background to Ellie and Alex's relationship, explaining she had recently discovered they were a couple at the time of Gill's death. She told him what Alex had said in the car on the way to the hospital and of his and Ellie's argument a few weeks ago when he'd admitted to tampering with Gill's car. Lady Beatrice paced across the room as Fitzwilliam listened politely, his expression giving nothing away. When she had finished, he looked down at Daisy. The silence stretched.

"Please sit down, Lady Rossex." He gestured to the chair opposite him. She nodded and sat down. Leaning forward, he put his elbows on his desk and brought his hands together in front of his mouth, his fingers intertwined.

"Interesting," he remarked.

Is that it? She crossed her legs and waited, hoping there was more to come.

"But why do you think it's important to this case?"

"I have a feeling there's a link between Gill's accident and Alex's murder."

"A *feeling*, Lady Rossex?" Shaking his head, he sighed.

"Yes, a *feeling,* chief inspector. Call it a woman's intuition if you prefer."

He smirked and shook his head harder. "Not really," he quipped.

Ignore him. He is an idiot who wouldn't know a feeling if it came up and bit him! "Have you checked if there is any connection between Alex and Seth, Joe, or Pete? Something from the past, perhaps?" she snapped, ignoring the smirk still resting on his face.

"We're working on that." He uncrossed his arms and shifted in his seat. She could tell this was going nowhere.

"I don't believe there is a connection between this murder and your husband's accident."

She shook her head. "So why *was* Alex murdered, chief inspector?"

"We're working on that, too. We have a witness who confirms Pete and Alex had recently fallen out, something to do with Ellie Gunn. That appears to be a promising line of enquiry and a likely motive to me. In my experience, Lady Rossex, men only ever fall out with each other when there is a woman involved." He rose from his chair and grinned.

Beastly man! Lady Beatrice jumped up, her hands on her hips. "Well, I think you're taking the easy way out, chief inspector."

"And I think you need to stop interfering and leave the investigating to the police, Lady Rossex. Despite what you think, we know what we're doing."

Stop interfering? How dare he! Anger coiled in her stomach. With a curt, "Come on, Daisy," Lady Beatrice stormed out of the office, slamming the door behind her.

36

MINUTES LATER, THURSDAY 15
APRIL

She stormed into Perry's office to find him sitting at his desk, reading something on his computer screen. Daisy ran straight to him for her usual fuss.

"That hateful man! Well, whether he likes it or not, I won't stop interfering." She threw her phone down on Perry's desk, pulled out the chair opposite him, and plonked herself down. "We will find out who killed Alex, and then he will have to thank us. I can't wait to see his face when *that* happens," she blurted out as she crossed her arms.

Perry stopped fussing with Daisy and looked at Lady Beatrice, a smile on his face.

What's so funny?

"I assume you're talking about Detective Chief Inspector Fitzwilliam?" he asked, still grinning.

"Yes. Is it obvious?" she cried.

He threw his head back and laughed.

Taking a deep breath, she moaned. "I don't think I have ever wanted to slap someone so much in my life, Perry."

He looked at his watch and turned off his screen. "Well, you'll have to tell me about it later, as I need to leave in a minute. Simon wants me to pick up a few things at the supermarket so he can start cooking."

"Fine," she huffed. "Oh, remind me to tell you later about the blood-soaked glove Daisy found."

"What? You couldn't have started with that?" he yelled.

It was her turn to laugh. "Go." She pointed to the door. "And I'll tell you and Simon about it later. Can you do one quick thing for me? You're friends with one of the human resources team, aren't you?" He nodded. "Will you ask them to check if there's a link between Alex and any of the gardeners, please?"

"Yes, of course. I'm sure you'll explain why later?"

She nodded.

Patting Daisy on the head, he walked towards the door. "Right, I need to go. They will clear the Garden Room tomorrow at ten. I've finished marking up everything except for two items I wasn't sure about, so I've left them for you." He grinned. "I'll see you both later."

Lady Beatrice entered the house via the north side door and walked through the Painted Hall, her footsteps echoing as she crossed the black and white checked marble floor. She turned right into the Salon, its rich terracotta-coloured walls providing the perfect backdrop for the family portraits on display. At the far corner of the room, she opened an unobtrusive wooden door and let Daisy go ahead of her into a corridor. Straight ahead was the door to the Blue Dining Room, newly improved and now able to sit fifty. Rounding the corner, she heard voices. As she drew closer, she saw Seth Padgett and Joe Fox outside the Smoking Room, talking to Daisy, who was jumping up at them, her tail wagging.

"Seth, Joe, I'm so sorry." Lady Beatrice approached them. "I always seem to have to apologise to you for my dog's appalling manners. Daisy, get down!"

"It's fine, Lady Rossex. She's such a lovely little dog, we don't mind." Seth patted Daisy on her head as she stood next to him, sniffing his leg.

"We were just checking the weight and size of some pieces ready for the move tomorrow," he said, nodding towards the Garden Room further down the corridor.

"I'm going to mark the last few items up now," she told them. "Is there an update on Pete?" she asked Seth.

His face clouded over, and he ran a jerky hand through his hair. "He's still unconscious, my lady." He shook his head. "I hope they can sort him out. He's a great bloke is Pete."

Next to him, Joe looked down at the floor and nodded.

"Indeed. I'm sure they will do everything they can. Try not to worry too much."

"Thank you, my lady." Seth replied, and with a shrug, he followed Joe down the corridor. Lady Beatrice watched them leave. Seth looked like someone with the weight of the world on his shoulders. *Poor man.* Pete was obviously a friend, as well as a colleague. He must be worried sick.

Ahead of her, Daisy was sniffing at the bottom of the Garden Room door. Reaching the room, Lady Beatrice turned the handle. It was locked. *Of course, it is.* She looked down the empty corridor. She should have asked Seth for the keys.

"Mrs Crammond, can I have the keys to the Garden Room, please?" Lady Beatrice asked as she entered the head housekeeper's office.

"Of course, my lady." Mrs Crammond twisted round and unlocked the key safe behind her desk. She sorted through the keys mumbling, "They're here somewhere." After what seemed like an age (but was probably only thirty seconds), she exclaimed, "Ah, here they are!"

"Sorry, my lady, it's my fault," she said as she turned and handed them to her. "Mr Juke gave them back to me, along with the Smoking Room keys earlier, and I seem to have mixed them up." She shook her head. "It's been a long week."

"Indeed," Lady Beatrice agreed. "Thank you for these, Mrs Crammond. I won't be long. I've a couple of items to mark up and then I'll bring them straight back. Will you still be here?"

Mrs Crammond looked at her watch. "Yes, I'll be here until at least five, my lady, so you've plenty of time."

A sea of neon yellow stickers greeted Lady Beatrice as she walked into the Garden Room. Smiling, she strode over to the sideboard where Perry had left the room inventory. She picked up the list. There were only two items Perry had not highlighted. One was *ugly blue lamp on side table by door* and the other was *hideous purple patterned dish on tray by window.* She laughed out loud. He'd obviously decided what should be done with them. Picking up two *get rid* stickers, she marked them up. Sighing, she looked around the room. *I hope we can finally clear it tomorrow. Third time lucky.*

37

EVENING, THURSDAY 15 APRIL

"This is so moreish, Simon. I can't stop eating even though I was full ages ago," Lady Beatrice said, breaking the silence that had descended on the three of them as they ate.

"Thanks. It's called *bolognese ragu* in Italy," Simon replied. "It is my Nonny's recipe."

"Well, that was the best bolognese I have ever had." Lady Beatrice pushed away her plate and rubbed her extended stomach.

"It's the combination of beef and pork mince that makes it taste so good," Simon told her.

"And the homemade tagliatelle," Perry added. "You can't beat freshly made pasta." He leaned towards Simon. Resting his hand on his partner's arm, he said, "It was absolutely amazing, love." They gazed into each other's eyes, smiling.

Lady Beatrice looked over at Daisy, hoping to have a similar moment with her girl, but the little white dog was curled up tight in her favourite armchair, her eyes closed, snoring gently.

After Lady Beatrice brought Simon and Perry up to date on the afternoon's events, Simon sent a text to CID Steve to see if he could find out more. Sitting back, sipping their red wine and letting their food settle, Perry asked, "So what happened between you and Fitzwilliam that prompted you to come storming into my office with a flea in your ear?" He winked at Simon.

"It was nothing important. You know how that man irritates the hell out of me. Let's not spoil our evening by talking about him," she said, hoping to evade the issue. She wasn't ready to share her theory of a link between Alex's murder and James's accident. To her relief, he let it drop.

"How did talking to Seth Padgett go?" Simon asked Perry.

"He said the same as Joe. He thought it was Alex he saw, but admits it could have been Pete, although he doesn't think it was. I guess it doesn't matter now as Sarah and Cass Gunn have both confirmed they saw Pete and not Alex." Simon and Lady Beatrice nodded in agreement.

"Even the police now accept it was Pete everyone saw at eight twenty-two rather than Alex," she confirmed.

"The only new thing Seth told me was that Pete and Alex had a blazing row last week. He said he wasn't exactly sure what it was about, but he thinks it was to do with Ellie Gunn."

Lady Beatrice nodded. "That's why the police have made Pete their prime suspect."

"I just don't believe it," Perry cried. "Why was he beaten up then? It makes no sense to me." He raked his hand through his spiky strawberry-blonde hair.

"Indeed, but Fitzwilliam said they're still treating it as a mugging. They don't think it's connected to Alex's murder." She shook her head in disbelief.

Simon's phone beeped. He picked it up and read the text message.

"It's CID Steve," he reported. "He says forensics have the gloves but haven't been able to pull any prints off them yet. He confirms it's human blood on them. They're waiting to find out if it matches Alex Sterling's. He says they still haven't been able to retrieve the deleted text messages from Alex's phone."

"Well, that's disappointing," she responded. "I suppose we will have to be patient."

"He also confirms that Alex's brother inherits any money. So we can rule that out as a motive for our suspects. I'll text Roisin later and see if she has anything more up to date," Simon told them.

"So, to clarify, our original suspects are now in the clear as none of them were onsite before 8am?" Perry asked.

Lady Beatrice nodded. "But I can't see Seth, Pete, or Joe as murderers. And where's the motive? Seth and Pete have been here for a few years. Why would either of them suddenly decide to kill Alex now? Joe's so new, he can hardly have known Alex."

Perry cocked his head to one side. "It makes no sense."

"What about this argument between Pete and Alex?" Simon asked.

"It was one argument. Seth didn't even know for sure what it was about." Perry shook his head. "I'm stumped." He sighed and took a sip of wine.

"Me too. I like them all and can't picture any of them as murderers," Lady Beatrice agreed.

"Is there a connection we don't know about?" Simon asked.

Perry turned and looked at Lady Beatrice. "Is that why you wanted me to ask Claire in human resources if there's a link between any of them and Alex?"

"Indeed. It's something that occurred to me as an avenue we've not explored yet. Although, I feel as if I'm clutching at straws."

"Well, I'm waiting for Claire to get back to me. It'll probably be in the morning."

Her phone vibrated. "Well, I'd best be off," she said. "Our security carriage awaits us. Come on, Daisy." Daisy reluctantly jumped off the armchair and trotted over to her. "Dinner was lovely, as always. Thank you both. I'll see you in the morning."

38

LATER THAT EVENING, THURSDAY 15 APRIL

Lady Beatrice yawned as she walked into her apartment. The food and wine had made her drowsy. She padded to the dressing room, while Daisy ran into the bedroom. Alfie, who had been asleep on the chaise at the end of the bed, rose and greeted his canine companion. They sniffed each other and once the catch-up was complete, Alfie crawled back onto the antique lounger and resumed his sleep. Jumping onto the bed, Daisy fluffed up the duvet to make a nest. Circling twice, she found the perfect position before curling up and closing her eyes.

Lady Beatrice climbed into bed but couldn't settle.

After thirty minutes of lying there restlessly,

with her eyes closed, willing herself to sleep, she gave up. *Maybe a bath will help me relax and fall asleep?* Trying not to disturb Daisy, she carefully pulled the duvet off her legs and eased herself out of bed. She tiptoed past Alfie and made her way to the bathroom.

Turning on the bath's taps, she struggled to achieve the right temperature. She huffed. *This is why I prefer showers!* Adding some bath soak, which had been a Christmas gift from Grandmama, the scent of lavender filled the bathroom.

Easing herself in slowly, she waited every few centimetres for her body to grow accustomed to the heat. Eventually, she submerged herself fully and gave into its warmth. *And relax...*

Who am I fooling? She'd never been less relaxed. There was too much going on in her brain.

She'd read somewhere recently that the trick to relaxation was to empty your head of all thoughts by allowing them to flow through your mind, acknowledging them as they went by, then letting them move on and out. This would be the perfect time to try it. If she could remove all the thoughts and questions from her head, then maybe she could sleep. She closed her eyes.

Alex meeting his murderer before breakfast... work overalls... Seth and Joe being sure it was Alex walking towards the Old Stable Block... the Garden Room door unlocked on the day of the murder... the clearing behind the grove of trees where Daisy found the gloves... Pete in the pub with his mates last night singing Irish songs... the Garden Room door locked this afternoon... Alex tampering with Gill's car...

Thoughts came and went in her mind, but nothing made sense. She opened her eyes as she heard her phone vibrating in the other room. The water was getting cold. She gave up.

Perry: *Lovely Claire in HR just got back to me. Alex recommended Pete for his job 3 years ago through Friends and Family Scheme! Could that be the link? x*

Lady B: *Could be. Let's have breakfast in TBR at 8:30 and discuss. x*

Perry: *Sure, see you then. Sleep tight. x*

39

FIRST THING, FRIDAY 16 APRIL

Sarah: *Morning Sis, are you awake yet? xx*

Bea: *Yes, just out of the shower. xx*

Sarah: *You're early! Can I pop up to talk? I'm in my office, so 5 mins? xx*

Bea: *Yes, although I've not had my coffee yet, so be warned! xx*

. . .

Sarah: *I'll ask Mrs Harris to bring some up. See you shortly. xx*

As Lady Beatrice left her dressing room and entered the sitting room, a knock sounded on the door. Hurrying over, she opened it. Mrs Harris padded in, holding a tray. "Lady Sarah ordered coffee and tea for you both, my lady, and I have added some toast."

Trotting out from the bedroom, Daisy and Alfie arrived at the coffee table at the same time as Mrs Harris. She placed the tray on the table and patted each of them.

Strolling in, Lady Sarah said, "Thank you, Mrs Harris, you're a gem."

"You're welcome, my lady." The family house-keeper looked at Lady Beatrice. "Would you like me to take young Alfie with me, Lady Beatrice?"

Lady Beatrice smiled and nodded. "Thank you, Mrs Harris."

"Come on, Alfie," Mrs Harris called, and Alfie obediently paced over to her. She curtsied and walked out, Alfie following, and closed the door behind her.

Moving to the sofa facing the window, Lady Beatrice sat and poured herself a large coffee. Her sister followed her, sitting opposite, and poured herself a tea. She added milk and grabbed a slice of toast before crossing her legs at the ankle. She stared at the teacup in her hands.

"You wanted to talk?" Lady Beatrice prompted her.

Sighing, Sarah lifted her gaze, a worried expression marring her face. "Bea, Desmond Brooke, the chief editor of the *Daily Post*, has been in contact. He claims there's a letter from James that was given to you by the police."

Lady Beatrice struggled to breathe. *The press knows*? With clammy hands, she gripped the handle of her coffee cup. *This cannot be happening.* She put the cup down. Her hand automatically went up to her mouth to stifle the cry building up behind it. She was aware of the sofa dipping as Sarah sat down beside her and grabbed her other hand.

"Are you all right, Bea?"

Lady Beatrice let out a long breath. *Focus!*

Something was pushed into her hand. "Drink this."

The strong black coffee did the trick. Lady Beatrice turned and looked at her sister.

"Oh, Bea, I'm so sorry. I didn't want to tell you. I knew it would disturb you," Sarah said in a shaky voice.

Lady Beatrice looked at their hands, still entwined. Her chin wobbled. She took another deep breath. *Come on, Bea. You are not a child. You're an adult, and you have to face this.* She squeezed her sister's hand, then let it go. "I'm fine, Sarah. I'm just shocked," she said with as much confidence as she could muster.

Rising, she moved over to the picture windows. The sun was already peeping above the trees, and the sky was clear of clouds. She closed her eyes for a few seconds, then turned and sat back down, taking the seat Sarah had vacated a few minutes ago. Jumping down from the sofa opposite, Daisy climbed up to be by her mistress. She laid her head on Lady Beatrice's lap.

"Did Brooke tell you what he's going to do about it?" she asked in a muffled voice.

"What he wants is an interview with you to discuss it," Sarah whispered.

When Lady Beatrice shook her head, her sister nodded quickly. "And of course I've told him that's not possible."

"And so he threatened to publish what he knows?" Lady Beatrice finished for her. Sarah nodded again. "So what does he know?" Lady Beatrice braced herself.

"That's it, Bea, I don't know. He won't tell me

anything other than there's a letter and you have it. He says his source is reliable." She tilted her head to one side and wrinkled her nose. Lady Beatrice remained silent, trying to work out what he knew.

"Fitzwilliam thinks Brooke is bluffing." Sarah continued, "He said only you and he know the contents of the letter. Is that true, Bea?"

"Fitzwilliam?" Lady Beatrice gasped. "How does he know about this?" She rubbed her forehead. *Of all people.*

"I had to tell him, Bea. It was Brooke I was meeting at my house on the morning of Alex's murder. I didn't want to tell anyone, but you insisted. And then there was the attack on Pete. I had no choice..." Her voice trailed off as she hung her head.

"Sorry. Of course you had to tell him." Lady Beatrice nodded slowly.

"I told him in private if that helps." She raised her head and gave Lady Beatrice a tentative smile.

"Thank you." Lady Beatrice smiled back. "Just give me a minute, please." Taking another sip of her coffee, she let her mind catch up. She looked down at the black and white geometric rug beneath her bare feet. *He has a point.* She and Fitzwilliam were the only people who had read the letter. *So even though someone else, probably from Fenshire CID, knows of the existence of the letter and has told Brooke, neither of them can know the contents.*

"He also said I should tell you. He said you're stronger than I think." Lady Beatrice looked up at her sister and frowned. Sarah smiled. "And I think he might be right."

"He's right about one thing," Lady Beatrice replied. "No one other than me and him knows the contents of the letter. I'm confident about that. The worst Brooke can do is publish that he has a source who claims there is a letter."

"That's what Fitzwilliam said too," Sarah agreed. "So there *is* a letter then, Bea?"

She had expected the question. "Yes," she admitted. "It came to light five years ago. Fitzwilliam brought it to me."

"You never told me." Her sister's voice was soft.

"Because it was deeply private and tremendously upsetting. I just wanted to pretend it didn't exist." Lady Beatrice's vision blurred with tears.

The eyes that looked back at her were bright and watery, too. Sarah nodded. "I understand." Rising, she opened her arms to Lady Beatrice, who jumped up and gratefully accepted her big sister's hug. Daisy, displaced by the sudden movement of her mistress, jumped down too and sat by them, her tail wagging.

"Thank you," Lady Beatrice whispered into Sarah's hair.

As they separated, Lady Beatrice glanced at the clock on the wall. *Is that the time already? Pull yourself together, Bea.* She wiped her fingers under her eyes and sniffed. "Sarah, I'm so sorry, but I'm due to meet Perry for breakfast in a few minutes. I promise we'll finish this conversation later."

Sarah dabbed at her eyes with a napkin. "What shall I tell Brooke?" she asked.

"Tell him to publish and be damned!" Lady Beatrice hissed.

Her sister laughed in astonishment. "How about I tell him I can't confirm there's a letter? I'll tell him if he goes ahead and publishes his story, there'll be no comment from Francis Court or Gollingham Palace."

Lady Beatrice smiled. "I prefer my version."

40

BREAKFAST TIME, FRIDAY 16 APRIL

Lady Beatrice and Daisy headed to the Breakfast Room. The meeting with Sarah had left her shaken, and she hoped they were doing the right thing by calling Brooke's bluff. *We'll find out soon enough.* All she could do in the meantime was to concentrate on finding out who murdered Alex.

She still didn't want to believe Pete was a murderer, but she couldn't ignore the fact that they now had a link between him and Alex. If Alex had secured Pete's job for him three years ago, then they had a history beyond that of mere work colleagues. They needed to find out what that connection was. She stopped in the corridor and sent a text.

Bea: *Do you have the keys to Alex's cottage? xx*

Sarah: *Yes. I've finished organising his personal effects for his brother to come and collect. Why? xx*

Bea: *Could I borrow them after breakfast? I want to take a quick look at the cottage and see what state the furniture and furnishings are in. xx*

So, it was a little white lie, but she *would* have a look while she was there.

Sarah: *Sure. I'm off to a meeting at the Orangery shortly, so will leave them in the top drawer of my desk. xx*

Bea: *Thanks sis. xx*

<hr>

The Breakfast Room was quiet when Lady Beatrice arrived. Daisy ran over to where Simon and Perry were sitting by the window overlooking the outside terrace. Even though it was sunny, it was too cold to sit outside. As she approached the table Nicky appeared, and she ordered a coffee and a pineapple juice. She couldn't face food right now. As she sat down, Simon was still bent over, stroking Daisy's exposed tummy, but Perry was staring at her, his coffee cup half-way to his mouth. "What's wrong?" he cried.

How does he know? She ran her fingers through her hair. *Do I tell them about the letter?*

Simon had stopped fussing Daisy. They were both gazing at her now. In their eyes, she didn't see curiosity or excitement, she only saw concern. *They care. They want to help. I can trust them.*

Lady Beatrice took a deep breath and told them all about the letter. It was hard admitting her husband had been leaving her to run away with Gill Sterling. It was difficult to tell them he'd loved her but had never been in love with her. Her heart ached when she told them he'd hated his life in the public eye, and he hadn't been able to cope with their families' expectations. She assured them she'd never realised how unhappy he was. She then admitted to them that DCI Fitzwilliam was the only other person who knew the contents of the letter, and she despised him for it.

Perry and Simon listened to her intently. When she'd finished, they each reached over and grabbed one of her hands. Tears welled up in the back of her eyes.

"Oh my giddy aunt." Perry shook his head, his eyes shining with tears as well.

"Indeed," Lady Beatrice replied, looking down at their entwined hands.

Simon squeezed the one he was holding. "It must've been awful dealing with this on your own for so long."

She gave them a weak smile. "It was, but I feel much better now I've told you both."

Noticing Nicky was approaching, they all released each other. She unloaded their drinks and placed two plates of scrambled eggs and smoked salmon on toast in front of Perry and Simon. As they ate their breakfast, Lady Beatrice told them about Desmond Brooke and his threat to publish a story about James's letter. They told her to try to not worry about it until it happened and, if it did, they would figure it out together. *Together.* It sounded so much easier when they said that.

"Indeed, we should concentrate on finding out what the connection is between Alex and Pete," she agreed.

"Yes, we really need to crack on." Simon nodded.

"Do what?" She frowned.

"We need to crack on. It means get on with it," Simon explained. "It's an Irish saying. Roisin says it all the time. I must have picked it up from her."

"Ireland!" Lady Beatrice hollered. Perry and Simon jumped.

"That's it," she declared. "It's been in my head for the last twenty-four hours. Gill was Irish, or at least had family in Ireland. In James's letter, he said Gill was going to tell Alex she was leaving him and going back to her family in Ireland." They met her statement with blank stares. She tried again. "Perry, you said on Wednesday night Pete and Seth were playing and singing Irish ballads at the open mic event." He nodded. "Well, what if the connection is Ireland? Pete could have been an old friend of Gill's from Ireland. That could be the link with Alex."

Simon tilted his head to one side.

A smile slowly crept over Perry's face. "It could be." His eyes were shining. Then he dropped his shoulders and sighed. "He doesn't have an Irish accent, though." He looked over at his partner. "In fact, I don't think he has an accent at all."

"That's often the case with people in the military," Simon reassured him. "They travel so much and mix with so many people from different places, they lose their original accent."

"Well, it's worth exploring," Lady Beatrice said. "I'm going to Alex's cottage to see if I can find anything there of interest."

"And I'm going to talk with Roisin and CID Steve," Simon offered. "I want to see if they have anything else on the gloves, Alex's deleted text messages, or how they think the killer got in through the French doors."

"Talking about doors," Perry added. "I'm going to go back to see Mr Ward. I've worked out there's a flaw in the key cutting system."

Simon and Lady Beatrice turned to him, their eyes wide.

"Remember how I said if someone wanted a key cut, then they would hand the key over to Mr Ward along with the authorisation slip from the key holder?" They nodded. "And then he records it in the log and gets them to sign for it." They nodded again. "Well, what if I turned up with a key and said it was for the Old Stable Cafe, for example, but actually it was for the Garden Room? In the book, it would look like I'd had a key cut for the cafe but in fact I'd given him the key for the Garden Room to cut."

"Nice work," Simon said, patting Perry's arm.

"I'm going to have another look at the log and check all the keys that were cut in the weeks leading up to the murder."

"Well, that sounds like a plan," Simon agreed. "Do you think we should let Fitzwilliam know about Pete and his connection to Alex?"

Lady Beatrice shook her head. "He dismissed my ideas yesterday. We need something more concrete before we give him any more of our theories.

Even if we establish the connection, there's still the motive to consider."

Plus, I don't want to make a fool of myself in front of him again.

41

THIRTY MINUTES LATER, FRIDAY 16 APRIL

Walking to Keeper's Cottage, where Alex had lived, Lady Beatrice had a warm, tingling feeling in her limbs. The sun was shining, and she felt invigorated. Walking from the main house to the staff cottages took her past the garden compost and clearing area on the right, then along the path running next to the tree-lined long drive, which was originally the main entrance into Francis Court. The dappled shade from the coppice created moving shadows on the grass, and as she looked over to the left, she glimpsed a solitary male deer grazing on the edge of the woods.

Daisy trotted by her side. Occasionally, she'd dart off to follow the trail of a scent she had caught, but she'd always return to her mistress once she'd finished.

Lady Beatrice smiled to herself, remembering Perry and Simon's reaction to her tale of woe at breakfast. They'd been so supportive. She felt cared for. *I'm truly fortunate to have two such amazing friends.*

Although what Sarah had said about Fitzwilliam was puzzling. He'd told Sarah she was stronger than Sarah thought she was, yet he treated her like a spoiled child. *Why do I have such a short fuse with him?* Was it because she detested his awareness of James's feelings about her and their life together? Was it because he knew her private business, which made her feel vulnerable? She sighed. He was the one person who could tell the press her husband didn't love her and wanted to be with someone else, and yet, with him, she was childish, rude, and uncooperative. Admittedly, he was also churlish and unpleasant, but was this a reaction to her treatment of him?

I will make more of an effort to be pleasant and co-operative with him in the future.

In fact, as soon as she'd finished at Alex's house, she would tell him everything they had learned so far.

Lady Beatrice unlocked the front door to Alex's cottage and stepped inside. Unlike Perry and Simon's cottage, which was so much bigger on the inside than she'd imagined it would be from the outside, Keeper's Cottage was as small inside as it looked outside. She remembered Sarah had offered Alex an apartment above the Old Stable Block after Gill had died, but he'd refused, saying he preferred the peace the little cottage offered.

Throughout the narrow hallway boxes were stacked up, presumably ready for Alex's brother to collect. Lady Beatrice examined them. They had also been marked up: *Photos, Paperwork, From Attic, Glasses & Mugs, Kitchen stuff, Clothes, Shoes, Bedding,* and *Bathroom Stuff.* It was sad to see someone's life boxed up so neatly, ready to be taken away. *Another sign that life goes on regardless.* Soon, this would be someone else's home.

Walking around the boxes and moving further along the hall, Lady Beatrice followed Daisy into a small kitchen. Daisy sniffed at an area on the wooden floor, her tail wagging. *No doubt someone has dropped some food recently.* Lady Beatrice scanned the empty room. With nothing of interest for her to look at, she returned to the hall.

Paperwork was a sensible place to start. She opened the box and started rummaging through the papers inside. There were recent bills, bank statements, and payslips. She ignored them and took out a clear plastic folder. Inside were travel insurance documents, a couple of airline loyalty cards, and two passports.

Lady Beatrice took out the passports. One was Alex's. It looked quite new, one of the red ones. She checked the expiry date. It was valid for another seven years. The older one was Gill's. She checked and saw it had expired ten years ago. Putting them back in the folder, she returned the lot to the box and closed the lid before moving on to the box marked *From Attic*. Peering inside, she frowned. It appeared to be full of Gill's belongings.

Lady Beatrice had struggled when it had come to disposing of James's personal effects, not knowing what to keep and what to let go. She'd wanted to retain some items to show her unborn child when they were older — their father's schoolbooks, sports medals, and trophies. She'd kept a hip flask, which had belonged to James's grandfather, and some books he'd treasured. It had been painful to go through it all, memories flooding back of happier times. She'd kept a selection of photographs, passing some on to his devastated parents. *I'm so glad they never knew how James felt about this life.* Even now, Sam loved going through the photos and mementos, asking questions about his father from the memories they represented.

So it didn't surprise her Alex had kept some of Gill's belongings. It was *what* he'd kept that was strange. The box was an eclectic mix of half used bottles of perfume, some rather cheap looking jewellery, earrings (not all pairs), makeup bags, and sunglasses. It was as if he'd simply scraped everything off the top of her dressing table and straight into the box. She shook her head as she picked out the makeup bags. There were three of them. One was small and full of nail polishes and lipsticks. Another, slightly larger one, (which she could barely open, it was so full) contained eyeshadows and blushes. *Who has this many?* The largest one was packed with small sponges and brushes. Had Gill ever been a makeup artist? Surely it was too much makeup for one person? Returning the bags to the box, she closed the lid.

She was dismayed when she removed the lid from the box marked *Photos* and found it contained a massive pile of loose photographs, along with two thin albums. She picked up the box and moved down the corridor, towards the sitting room. As she passed the open door to the kitchen, she saw Daisy lying on the floor in the spot where she'd been sniffing earlier.

"Come on, Daisy. Let's find somewhere more comfortable to sit." Daisy jumped up, gave the floor a final sniff, and followed Lady Beatrice into the sitting room.

The space was flooded with natural light from a bay window overlooking the front garden. Lady Beatrice picked a leather armchair by the window to sit in, putting the box down beside it. Daisy had already made herself at home, curled up on the floral two-seater sofa facing the fireplace.

Sitting down, she removed the box lid and picked out the two albums. One had a cream cover. It was Alex and Gill's wedding album. She looked at the photographs of the young and happy couple smiling at the camera. She almost didn't recognise Alex. It was a long time since she had seen him with hair. He looked smart in his dark-blue suit, standing tall and straight. Dressed in an off-the-shoulder white lacy wedding dress, Gill's mid-length brown hair was curled to within an inch of its life. She held a bouquet of pink and white flowers to her chest.

They look so full of love and hope.

They didn't yet know that less than five years later they would be so miserable that he would start an affair with someone at work and she would attempt to run off with another man.

Lady Beatrice sighed deeply and carried on looking through the album. There was a picture of Alex with a proud looking older couple — presumably his parents. There was another of him with the same couple and a younger man — his brother, maybe? It appeared to be a small wedding. Most of the photos were of Gill and Alex, very few were of guests. There was a single photo of Gill standing next to a woman in her forties. They looked alike, so she guessed it was Gill's mother.

She closed the album and returned it to the box. Taking out the second, smaller one, she flicked through it, recognising Drew Castle, her mother's family estate in Scotland. Closing the album, she hoped Alex's brother might allow her to keep hold of it for a short while. Grandmama would love to see the photos. Thinking she would ask Sarah later, she returned the album to the box.

Now faced with the daunting task of sifting through the pile of single photographs, she looked at her phone. It was nearly nine-fifteen. At nine-thirty, she needed to leave so she could help Perry clear the Garden Room at ten.

Puffing her cheeks, she exhaled loudly and picked up a handful of photos. They were a mix of local landscapes, deer, and the Fenshire coastline. She put them on the floor and grabbed another handful. There was one of Alex standing with his arm around the shoulders of his presumed brother. Looking closely, she recognised the lion, crown, and laurels on the cap badge of the man's green beret. It was that of the Royal Marines. She frowned. Something rang a bell with her.

Ah, that's it. Yesterday's article in *The Society Page* had reported Pete Cowley was an ex-marine. *Could that be the connection between Pete and Alex?* She would check with Sarah or HR when she returned to Francis Court. Putting the photo to one side, she sifted through three more handfuls. There were more photos of the estate, wildlife, and scenery — nothing of any interest. She was running out of time, so she delved deeper into the box and stirred through the remaining photos to see if she could see any with people in.

Then she spotted it.

A photo of four people standing together at what looked like a family function. Picking up the photo, she turned it over. Written on the back, in faded pen, was *Ma, Da, Me*. She couldn't quite make out the fourth name. *Was it Hollie or maybe Ollie?* Turning it over again, she recognised Gill. She looked about thirteen years old. She was smiling and holding her flowery red dress as if she was about to drop a curtsy. The older woman next to her, standing proud in a green tea dress and heels, was the same woman as in the wedding photo — Gill's mother. Lady Beatrice looked at the other two people. One was a man in his forties. He looked uncomfortable in a brown ill-fitting suit and was staring at the camera, stony-faced. The other was probably in their late teens, their green eyes gazing into the camera. Lady Beatrice gasped. Recognising the person immediately, she shuddered as an icy shiver ran through her body. She was looking into the eyes of Alex Sterling's killer.

42

ABOUT THE SAME TIME, FRIDAY 16 APRIL

Entering the PaIRS office, DS Spicer made her way to her desk and reaching it, dumped her handbag on the top.

"So? What did Mr Cowley have to say?" DCI Fitzwilliam asked, looking up from his laptop.

"I missed him, sir. They discharged him first thing."

"What?" he asked incredulously.

"I know," she said, shaking her head. "He was most insistent, apparently. Said he was fine, that it was only a few cuts and bruises, and he would rather be at home resting."

"And is he?"

"I've tried ringing him but can't get a reply, so I don't know, sir. I was just going to drop off the car and pop to the loo, then walk over to his house in the village."

Fitzwilliam nodded. "Okay, then you'd best take someone with you, just in case. He's still our prime suspect."

Simon Lattimore ended the call on his mobile phone. His friend Roisin in forensics had come up trumps again. He must tell Lady Beatrice and Perry about the gloves. Looking at his phone, he noticed one unread text message. He opened it.

Lady B: *Have found evidence. I think I know who the killer is! Just tidying up here, meet me in TBR in ten mins x*

His eyes widened, and a grin broke out on his face. *Perfect*, he thought. *I can tell them when I get there.* Grabbing his leather jacket, he headed out of Rose Cottage.

DCI Fitzwilliam put the phone down, "Spicer!" he shouted.

She poked her head around the office door. "Yes, boss?"

"Good, you're still here. They've recovered the deleted text messages from Alex Sterling's phone."

Spicer walked into the office. "And?"

"They've found the text exchange with Lady Sarah. More interestingly, though, there was another text exchange, this time between Alex Sterling and Seth Padgett, that took place the night before. They arranged to meet at Alex's cottage at seven the next morning."

Spicer raised her eyebrows. "Seth Padgett? So, he's our killer, not Pete Cowley?" She smiled.

He looked at her sharply, remembering how she'd agreed with Lady Rossex that Pete Cowley was not their murderer. "Not so fast, sergeant. We don't know for sure if the person who Alex met was the killer. They could have been meeting for something work-related or for any number of other reasons."

"But why wouldn't Padgett have told us, sir?" she asked.

"You should've realised by now, sergeant, people don't always give us the full story. Sometimes they're hiding secrets; sometimes they're protecting others. Often they think it's not relevant. They lie or omit information for their own reasons. So let's not jump ahead of ourselves. I need to talk to Padgett and see what he has to say for himself." He rose from his desk.

"Do you want me to come too, sir?" Spicer asked.

"No." He shook his head. "Let's stick with our original plan. You go and interview Pete Cowley. I'll try to find Padgett."

Nodding, she turned and left the office. Fitzwilliam followed her out.

Immensely pleased with himself, Perry Juke was on his way back from the workshop where he'd been studying the key cutting log. He'd found some interesting information to share with the others. But first, he needed to check on a couple of things to be doubly sure he was on the right track. As he scooted around the outside of the lawn, towards the main entrance of Francis Court, his phone beeped.

Lady B: *Have found evidence. I think I know who*

the killer is! Just tidying up here, meet me in TBR in ten mins x

Excited, he changed direction. Cutting through the Old Stable Block courtyard would be the quickest way to the Breakfast Room.

As Fitzwilliam crossed the courtyard, Joe Fox emerged from the gardening shed. Locking the door behind him, he jumped onto the gardening quad bike and started it up. Fitzwilliam ran over.

"Mr Fox," he shouted, "can I have a quick word, please?"

"I'm in a bit of a hurry, sir," Joe replied, fidgeting in his seat.

"It won't take a minute. I just want to know if you have you any idea where Mr Padgett is?" Fitzwilliam asked.

"He's gone off to the compost area." Joe looked at his watch and added, "He'll be back soon. We're due to move some furniture at ten." He revved up the bike.

"Thank you," Fitzwilliam replied.

Joe nodded his head, and putting the machine into first gear, sped out of the courtyard.

As Perry hurried through the side doors into the courtyard, DCI Fitzwilliam was walking towards his office. They met in the middle of the cobbled area, but Perry was reluctant to stop. He wanted to get to the Breakfast Room as soon as possible.

"Is everything okay, Mr Juke? You seem to be in a hurry," Fitzwilliam said.

Perry paused. *Now what do I do?* Should he tell Fitzwilliam what was going on or wait until they had something concrete to share, as Lady Beatrice had suggested. He glanced at the text message again. She said she had evidence. *Maybe this is the right time to share with Fitzwilliam?*

"Mr Juke?" Fitzwilliam prompted him.

Perry turned his phone round and showed him the screen. "I've had this text from Lady Beatrice. I'm off to meet her now."

Fitzwilliam scanned the message. "Have you any idea who she thinks the killer is?" Perry shook his head. Fitzwilliam scratched his chin, a frown forming on his brow.

"We found a link between Pete Cowley and

Alex Sterling," Perry told him. "Alex recommended Pete for the gardener's job three years ago. Lady Beatrice went off to Alex's cottage to do some digging." He was bouncing from one foot to another.

"Is there something else, Mr Juke?" Fitzwilliam asked.

"Only that I found a flaw in the key cutting system," Perry blurted out.

"Go on."

"Well, when someone gets a key cut they need a permission slip from the key holder, but it doesn't say on the slip which key it is for. When Mr Ward logs it in the book, he *asks the person* who is requesting the key."

"I see," Fitzwilliam responded. Immediately, his brows rose. "Yes, I see." He nodded.

"So when I examined the log this time, I looked to see if any of the suspects had keys cut for *any* room around the time of the murder," Perry continued.

Fitzwilliam raised his eyebrows. "And?"

Lady Beatrice put her phone in the back pocket of her jeans and picked up the pile of discarded photographs. She threw them back in to the box marked *Photos* and returned the box to the hall, dumping it down by the others. She called Daisy, who came trotting out of the sitting room. "Well, I think we have what we came for," she said to her as they moved to the door, the photo of Gill and her family grasped firmly in her hand. "Now we need to go, Daisy, and get help."

Daisy dashed off through the half-open door, but as Lady Beatrice opened the door further, a person was standing there. She froze, the picture in her hand suddenly feeling heavy.

It's them!

"Seth Padgett was the only suspect who had keys cut in the last three months," Perry said. "They were supposedly for the gardening shed, cut a week before the murder. There wasn't a permission slip because he's the key holder of those keys, so he doesn't need one."

"That's excellent work, Mr Juke." Fitzwilliam's face cracked into a smile. "I'll ask DS Spicer to follow it up with you, if that's all right?"

Perry nodded. "Yes, fine. Well, if you'll excuse

me, I need to go to the Breakfast Room to meet Lady Beatrice," Perry reminded him, already moving in that direction.

Fitzwilliam followed. "Can I tag along, Mr Juke? I'm interested to hear what she has to say."

Perry shrugged. "By all means, chief inspector."

I hope she won't kill me for this.

"Lady Rossex, is everything all right?" the killer asked, moving forward to stand on the threshold, effectively blocking the doorway.

Lady Beatrice's brain had stopped working. She should say something, but nothing came through the fog that had descended inside her head. She nodded.

"It's just, I saw you heading this way earlier and when you didn't come back, I came to see if you were all right."

Say something! They don't know that you know, she reminded herself, creeping her hands behind her back. "That's very kind of you," she stuttered, looking down at her feet. "I'm fine, thanks," she added, feeling a wave of heat travelling up her neck.

"So what are you doing here, my lady?" They moved forward slightly.

She backed into the hall. *Think,* Bea. *Say something.* "Um, I came to check everything was ready for Alex's brother to pick up."

The killer tilted their head to one side and stared over her shoulder at the pile of boxes behind her. "Really? Because we packed up the boxes for the kitchen a few days ago, and when Lady Sarah came to check, she said that was everything ready to go."

Rats! Why did I say that? Sarah had already told her they had packed everything, and it was ready for Alex's brother to collect.

"Um..."

"Are you looking for something?"

She looked up at the face in front of her; steely eyes stared back. Shrugging, she looked down at the floor.

Why isn't my brain working? Think!

"Er, no," she mumbled. *Well, that's not much help, is it?* She needed to get out of the cottage and find Fitzwilliam. She inched forward, but the person in front of her didn't move.

"I only ask because it looks like someone has been searching through those boxes." The figure moved forward again. Her heart raced. She couldn't get past them. Moving backwards, she stumbled over her feet. She stopped and turned around to make sure she wouldn't trip over anything else.

Too late, she realised what she'd done. A sharp intake of breath came from the person now behind her. "What's that you have there in your hand, Lady Rossex?"

She jerked around, keeping her hands firmly behind her back. "Er, nothing." Pulling one hand from behind her back, she looked at her watch. "In fact, I really need to be going," she blurted out, quickly giving a half smile.

The eyes looking back at her didn't blink. "It looks like a photo to me." Without warning, a hand reached out and grabbed her arm. Twisting it forward, they snatched the photo from her. They stared hard at it, rubbing the back of their head. Then they reached behind them and closed the door.

It clicked shut.

At the sudden sharp sound of barking, Perry quickened his pace. He wanted to be the one to tell Lady Beatrice of his discovery about the keys before Fitzwilliam agitated her.

Stepping out of the courtyard, he looked around

for Lady Beatrice, but he couldn't see her any-where. He frowned as he spotted Daisy hurtling along the long drive towards them, barking. A cold chill raced down his spine.

"Where's your mum, Daisy?"

43

MEANWHILE, FRIDAY 16 APRIL

The killer pushed Lady Beatrice backwards, through the hall and into the sitting room. They shoved her towards the armchair she had recently vacated. Stumbling, she fell back into the chair. Her heart was beating out of her chest. She looked directly into the eyes of the killer, trying not to flinch as, eyes blazing, they returned her gaze.

"That's you Seth, isn't it? You're Ollie." Lady Beatrice said, her throat clenching as she pointed to the photo.

The corner of his mouth kicked up into a sneer as his face turned puce and blotchy.

Perry gradually became more anxious. Daisy ran backwards and forwards in front of him, barking, and Lady Beatrice was nowhere to be seen. *Where is she?*

"Where's your mum, Daisy?" he begged the barking, jumping little dog in front of him. She ran ahead, looking back as she went. When he didn't move, she ran back and started barking again.

"Does Daisy normally bark?" Fitzwilliam questioned as he joined him. "I've never heard her bark like this before."

Perry shook his head frantically. "No, neither have I. Something's wrong."

Seth Padgett rocked from one foot to the other, staring at Lady Beatrice. She swallowed and whispered, "Was Gill your sister?"

Stopping, he nodded. "She was my little sister." His shoulders drooped, and he stared down at the photo in his hand. "I always looked out for her," he said in a quiet voice. "I remember the first day she started school. Ma was working, so I dropped her off on my way to high school. Her hand was so tiny in mine. I swore I would protect her and make sure she was always safe."

He shook his head. "There was this one boy, Ronan. He was a proper show off and liked to pick on the little ones. She said nothing at first, but I heard her crying in her room one day, and eventually she told me he was calling her names and teasing her in front of his mates." He looked up. The knuckles on his now balled fists were white. "She was so tiny and vulnerable. What kind of person does that?" His mouth turned into an ugly glower. "He didn't find it so funny after a bloody nose and no front teeth."

The muscles in her legs tightened. She wanted to jump up and run, but he was blocking the doorway. She needed to keep him talking while she tried to figure a way out.

"So did you kill Alex, Seth?" *Will he admit it?* She held her breath.

Rocking his head side to side, he cried, "No! Pete Cowley killed him! They had a big argument about Ellie Gunn. Pete's been in love with Ellie for years. He was so mad that Alex wouldn't leave her alone after she broke up with him, that he..." His voice trailed off as he stared down at the photo again.

She let out the breath she had been holding in a rush. *Pete?* Could she have been wrong? Was Alex's murder nothing to do with Gill and James, after all? She watched the tall man in front of her. His dishevelled curly brown hair made him look a bit like a mad professor. As he slowly raised his head, tears ran down his face.

"He killed my sister and ma," he said in a faltering voice, as he wiped the tears away with the back of his hand. Pain distorted his face.

What's he saying? Her stomach turned rock hard. *Oh, no. Maybe I was right after all.*

"Is that why you killed him, Seth?" she asked gently. Grasping her hands together, she tried to stop them from shaking. *I need to look in control.*

"He killed them, so I had to kill him," he stammered.

I need to escape, but how?

She nodded, "Of course. I understand. If anyone killed a member of my family, I would want to do the same."

Taking a deep breath, he looked down at the floor. "When my father died, I went into the Navy. I sent money back to Ma for her and Gill, looking after them, you know?" He looked up, his eyes still wet with tears. Lady Beatrice nodded. "I spent a lot of time at sea and couldn't afford to travel back to Ireland often, but Ma wrote to me every other week. She told me Gill had met someone who worked on the king's estate in Scotland, and they were getting married. I couldn't make it to the wedding, but I wrote to Gill to say congratulations. I was glad she had someone to look after her." He winced. "I didn't realise he was a monster. I really didn't." He jerked his head from side to side.

"It broke Ma's heart when Gill died. She gave up on life. I left the Navy to go home and look after her. I did odd gardening jobs locally. Ma was overcome with guilt. She said Gill had been unhappy ever since they left Scotland. Gill's letters in the months before she'd died talked about Alex becoming increasingly controlling and abusive. But Ma had done nothing. She went to her grave blaming herself." He put his head in his hands and sobbed.

If I can push him aside now, I might get out of the door, Lady Beatrice thought. *Right. Here goes.* She placed her hands on the seat of the chair, one on either side of her legs, and pushed herself up.

Seth whisked his hands from his face and glared at her.

Pretending she was crossing her legs, she slumped back in the chair. *Blast!* "Is that why you came to work at Francis Court? So you could kill Alex?" she asked quickly, hoping to distract him from her bungled escape.

He sniffed and brushed his hand over his face

as if he was removing an invisible cobweb. He bent his head, his gaze fixed on the carpet. "After Ma died, I had no one left, so I came over here. I wanted to find the man who had hurt my sister and caused my mother to worry herself into an early grave. I applied for a temporary job in a false name as a gardener." Looking up, he glanced around the room before settling his gaze on her. "I liked it here, you know. After years shut up in a tin can under the sea, I enjoyed being outside. I settled in quickly and they offered me a permanent post after a few months. As I got to know Alex, it seemed to me like he was a hard worker. No one really had anything bad to say about him and he didn't come across as a bully. So I thought maybe Ma had become confused in her grief, you know?" The green eyes staring at her were red and puffy.

She nodded again, slowly. *Just keep him talking.*

He shook his head. His gaze moved to over her shoulder and into the garden beyond the window. He continued, his voice stronger and clearer. "So I kept my head down and worked hard. I rented a cottage in the village and when my boss left two years ago, they made me head gardener. I was right chuffed." He sighed and shook his head again.

"So what changed?" she asked in a mollifying voice.

His face clouded. "I heard the rumours about Alex having a fling with Ellie Gunn, but by then, I was enjoying my job and didn't really care." His nostrils flaring, his voice becoming louder, he said, "Then a couple of weeks ago, Joe and I were coming back from the pub with young Cass Gunn, making sure she got home safe. At her house, I heard shouting. Cass said it was her mum and Alex, that they were always arguing. I walked up my drive and I heard Ellie say something about Gill wanting to leave him, so I waited on my porch to hear what else they would say." His face reddened even deeper, and he rubbed his forehead as if trying to remove a stain from it.

He looked about to burst, like a big, red, angry spot. She pushed herself further into the back of the chair. *Am I doing the right thing by keeping him talking? Or am I making him mad enough to want to kill me?*

"And that's when I heard him admit he'd tampered with my sister's car to stop her from leaving." His voice wavered as he paced in front of her. Twisting his hands together, he didn't seem to notice he was crumpling the photo. "I knew then that he was responsible for Gill's death. I had to do something about it. He had to die." He turned to look at her, his eyes cold like steel.

Lady Beatrice rubbed her clammy palms together. She didn't have a clue how to get out of this situation, and now he was looking scarily calm. A shiver ran down her spine.

"I don't want to hurt anyone else," he told her, his gaze not leaving her face.

Well, that's a relief.

"I'm all packed and ready to go. I only needed a few more hours, and I would have left. But you've mucked that all up, Lady Rossex, and now I need to decide what to do with you."

Rubbing his forehead, Perry stared down at a frantic Daisy running around by his feet and barking.

Fitzwilliam suddenly grabbed his arm. "Where did you say Lady Rossex was?"

"Meeting us in the Breakfast Room." Perry's head flinched back slightly. He frowned.

"But from where, man?" Fitzwilliam shouted. "Where was she coming from?" His voice had an urgency to it that made Perry feel nauseous.

"From Alex Sterling's old cottage. Why?"

They both looked in that direction. Daisy sprinted off towards the long drive, her barking sharper. Perry followed her, but a sudden beep behind him caused him to stop. Turning, he looked back at Fitzwilliam.

"Blast!" Fitzwilliam cried as he ran past Perry, heading towards Daisy's retreating back.

Breaking into a run, Perry followed.

"What's going on?" he shouted. His shoes, not made for walking fast, let alone running, were pinching his toes. *Should I take them off and continue without them?* He sucked air through his teeth as he shook his head and carried on running. *No time.*

"They've pulled Seth Padgett's fingerprints from inside the gardener's gloves," Fitzwilliam shouted back. Daisy was still ahead of them, looking behind to make sure they were following her. "Joe Fox told me Seth had gone to the compost area," he continued.

"Oh my giddy aunt!" Perry exclaimed as he fell behind. Puffing hard, he wheezed, "That's in the same direction as Alex's cottage!"

Fitzwilliam lifted his radio to his mouth. "This is DCI Fitzwilliam. All police units and security to Keeper's Cottage immediately, over."

Simon arrived at the north side gate of Francis Court. He tapped his pass on the access pad and pushed through. There was a loud bang, and he sprung back as the door to the security office flew open. Adrian Breen, head of security, came rushing out, followed by two uniformed colleagues.

"What's going on, Ade?" Simon called after him.

Breen jumped into the driver's seat of one of the security buggies. "We've had an urgent call to go to Alex Sterling's old cottage," he shouted.

Simon's blood ran cold. Alex's cottage was where Lady Beatrice was looking for clues.

"Wait!" he shouted as he sprinted towards the buggy. "I'm coming too."

44

AT ABOUT THE SAME TIME, FRIDAY 16 APRIL

"Seth," Lady Beatrice said, trying to keep her voice calm. "I can't imagine how hard it has been for you to lose your father, your sister, and then your mother in such a short time." She paused. *Can I make him see sense?* She took a deep breath. "But I have a thirteen-year-old son who has already lost his father. Do you want to be the one to take away his only remaining parent from him?"

Her stomach dropped. Seth didn't appear to be listening anymore. He was staring somewhere above her head, as if in a trance.

Will he notice if I move? She shifted her weight to one side.

Immediately, his attention was on her, his eyes wild as he scanned the room. *What is he looking for? Crikey, is he looking for something to kill me with?* She held back the scream wanting to escape from her throat.

Suddenly, he stopped and tilted his head to one side. Lady Beatrice could hear it too — the sound of a dog barking in the distance. *Daisy!*

Seth's eyes frantically searched the room again. "Where's your dog?" he shouted, leaning towards her. She shrugged. He lunged for her, his hands closing around her throat. Her head snapped back against the chair's headrest.

No, this can't be happening to me.

Shaking her head madly from side to side, she squirmed in her seat, trying to loosen his grip.

Beads of sweat ran down her back. She struggled harder. His hands relaxed from their vice-like grip. *It's working.*

But then he adjusted his hold, and she thought her back would break as he slammed his body on top of hers.

He's too strong for me.

She tried to shove him away, smacking at his arms and chest, but it seemed to have no impact on him.

Is this the end?

No, I'm too young to die!

She curled forward, using her stomach muscles

to round her back, and with one enormous effort, she arched strongly, trying to flip him off her. Momentarily taken by surprise, he lifted his weight from her battered body for a few seconds. Then he spread his legs further apart. Leaning in again, he pushed her further into the chair, his hands still around her throat. Her limbs felt heavy, as if someone had flicked her energy switch off.

What about Sam?

What about Daisy?

I can't leave them...

Her arms floundered. It was getting hard to breathe. She couldn't fight much longer.

What will they do without me?

The pressure under her throat intensified as his thumbs pushed harder.

The Society Page will love this.

And just as I'm making friends...

Her eyes fluttered. Her arms sagged.

I can't...

45

A FEW MINUTES LATER, FRIDAY 16 APRIL

DCI Fitzwilliam burst through the door of Keeper's Cottage shouting, "Lady Rossex?"

Daisy, who had finally stopped barking, flew past him, running down the hall towards the room at the end of the corridor. Darting forward, Fitzwilliam raced after her.

His eyes scanned the room as he burst through the door. Lady Beatrice was sitting in an armchair by the window. Breathing heavily, she laughed as she tried to escape the pink tongue darting out from the over-excited bundle of fur on her lap. The light shining on her pale face made her look like a ghost. She squinted in his direction.

Perry almost tripped over as he exploded through the doorway, his face purple and his breath laboured. He held onto the wall to stop himself from falling, then staggered into the room.

The smile disappeared from her face as she looked from them to the body on the floor in front of her.

"Is he dead?" she croaked.

Lady Beatrice watched Fitzwilliam pad over to the motionless body and place his fingers on Seth's neck. She held her breath. There was blood on Seth's left temple. A small wooden display table lay shattered next to him. He'd hit his head as he'd fallen backwards. *Oh, the irony!*

Fitzwilliam let out a sigh as he stood up. "He'll live," he said, turning towards her, a look of relief creeping over his face.

Lady Beatrice let out the breath she'd been holding. Suddenly, something knocked her back in her seat and thin bony arms enveloped her, over-powering her senses with a mixture of expensive aftershave and sweat. A muffled voice cried, "Are you okay? I've been so worried." The tension leaving her body, she leaned into the hug, while Daisy whined and tried pushing her nose between them.

"Mr Juke, please unhand Lady Rossex. I need to talk to her."

Fitzwilliam's command had Perry leaping up, still grinning at her. He retrieved a neatly folded white handkerchief from his suit pocket. Flipping it open, he wiped the sweat from his brow.

"Perry, did you run?" she rasped. He nodded, and they both laughed. *Ouch, that hurt.* She put her hand up to her neck; it was sore to touch.

"Lady Rossex, are you hurt?" Fitzwilliam leaned in and removed Daisy from her lap. He placed the little terrier gently on the floor by the chair, murmuring, "Good girl". Standing up, he towered over Lady Beatrice, his brows creased as he stared at her neck.

Lady Beatrice put her hand down and sunk back into the chair. "I'm fine." She smiled to reassure him. Footsteps sounded in the hall. Within a few moments, the room was full of people. Mike Ainsley and DS Spicer had been the first to enter, closely followed by Adrian Breen, two uniformed security officers, and Simon. The small sitting room was full to capacity.

Heading straight towards them, Simon looked from Perry's red face to Lady Beatrice slumped in the chair. "Are you both okay?"

Perry nodded, and Lady Beatrice smiled up at

Simon. "Perry ran, so you may need to find him some oxygen." Her gravelly voice sounded alien to her. Laughing, Simon pushed his way out of the room. Mike Ainsley moved to join Fitzwilliam, who was still standing in front of Lady Beatrice. She cleared her throat and winced. "I did the split and kick manoeuvre, Mike. You would've been proud of me," she croaked.

After a look of astonishment, he broke into a huge grin. "Well done, my lady. I'm glad it came in handy."

Simon returned with two glasses of water and handed one to Lady Beatrice. She smiled and thanked him. The cold water slid down her throat; she winced again.

"Breen," Fitzwilliam said, "will you and your team please wait for the ambulance? They'll need directing. Spicer, can you take some pictures of the scene and bag up any evidence? Mike, he"—he pointed to Seth—"will come round any minute. Can you cuff him and keep an eye on him? Mr Juke, can you and Mr Lattimore give me five minutes with Lady Rossex, please? Maybe you can wait in the garden?"

Perry and Simon looked at her. When she nodded, they left. Daisy jumped back onto Lady Beatrice's lap. She wasn't going anywhere.

"Lady Rossex," Fitzwilliam continued, "are you well enough to move to the kitchen with me, please?" She nodded. After scooping Daisy up again, he placed her on the floor and offered Lady Beatrice his arm. She wanted to refuse, but a wave of weakness hit her. Clasping his extended arm with one hand, she used her other to push herself up and out of the chair.

"Thank you, chief inspector." She released his arm and headed towards the door. Her legs felt like they were made of lead. *The photo!* "Sergeant," she whispered, turning back towards Spicer. "There's a photo. Seth had it in his hand when he fell. It shows Gill Sterling, her parents, and Seth, although his real name is Ollie. He's Gill's elder brother."

"It seems I owe you an apology, Lady Rossex"

Now that wasn't what I was expecting. She frowned. *What exactly is he apologising for?* She leaned forward and kissed the top of Daisy's head (the little dog had climbed onto her lap as soon as they'd sat down at the kitchen table) and waited for him to continue.

DCI Fitzwilliam stood up, found a glass in a cupboard above the cooker and filled it with water from the tap. Placing it on the table, he returned to his seat. "It seems you were correct about there being a link between Alex's death and your husband's accident. I shouldn't have dismissed your woman's intuition." He smiled, his eyes sparkling. She smiled back. "We'll need to take a full statement at some stage, but for now, I'm more concerned about your health. Are you sure you're all right?" He nudged the glass of water towards her.

Nodding, she took a sip. He opened his mouth, but closed it again when she jumped up. Daisy tumbled off her lap. The sirens of an ambulance were growing louder. "I need to go, chief inspector," she told him, holding on to the edge of the table to steady her wobbly legs.

"I'd rather you waited to be checked out by the paramedics," he said, getting up.

She shook her head. "I don't want my involvement getting into the papers. The more strangers here, the more likely that'll happen." She pleaded with him. "Please let me go."

To her surprise, he nodded. "Okay, come on." He escorted her out, Daisy trotting by his side.

As soon as she got outside, she carefully breathed in a lung full of fresh air. *That feels splendid.*

"Breen," Fitzwilliam called over to the man

who was talking to a uniformed police officer on the driveway. "Please take Lady Rossex, Mr Juke, and Mr Lattimore to the Breakfast Room." He turned to Lady Beatrice and smiled. "I think Lady Rossex needs a large coffee." Adrian nodded and hurried over to fetch the security buggy.

Before she could thank him, Fitzwilliam's phone rang. He moved away to answer it.

"Are you sure you're okay?" Simon and Perry asked as they surrounded her, concern written all over their faces.

She nodded. "He's right. I could do with a bucket full of coffee."

46

TEN MINUTES LATER, FRIDAY 16 APRIL

Back in the Breakfast Room, alternatively sipping coffee and water to keep her throat lubricated, Lady Beatrice relayed to Perry and Simon everything that had happened at Alex's cottage while they told her about the keys and the fingerprints. Just as they'd finished, DCI Fitzwilliam entered the restaurant and came striding across the room towards them. Nicky, who must have been hovering close by, followed him to their table. He pulled out the empty chair and sat down. Daisy scrambled up, stretched, and went to sit beside him. He patted her head.

"She's all done in." Lady Beatrice told him.

He looked down at Daisy and smiled at her. "You've had a busy morning, little girl. All that barking must have taken it out of you." He ruffled her head, and she wagged her tail in response.

He smiled at Nicky and ordered a large black coffee, then asked if it was too late for toast.

"I'm sure I can sort something out for you, chief inspector," she purred.

Oh my goodness, did she really purr?

"Thank you, Nicky. I'd really appreciate that." He smiled at her again. "It's been a long day already!"

She scampered away, giggling.

Lady Beatrice had never heard Nicky giggle before.

Still smiling, Fitzwilliam turned to them. "I don't know if you've heard already, but Pete Cowley regained consciousness last night. Although groggy, he can talk and move. He has an array of cuts and bruises and no recollection of what happened, but the doctors are confident he'll make a full recovery. They released him from hospital a short while ago."

Perry clapped his hands. Lady Beatrice sighed. *Thank goodness for that.*

"That's great news." Simon's voice broke, and he put a hand up to his mouth. Perry grabbed his partner's other hand and beamed at him.

"We're hoping Mr Padgett will give us a full

confession when we're able to interview him. Our theory is that he incapacitated Mr Sterling at the cottage and used the tractor and trailer to move the body to the Garden Room, where he killed him."

Lady Beatrice remembered Daisy sniffing obsessively at a spot on the kitchen floor. She told Fitzwilliam in case it was relevant. He pulled out his pocketbook and made a note.

"Thank you, Lady Rossex. Mr Juke has also given us some useful information about keys that we'll follow up. Mike and his team are on their way to Padgett's cottage now to see what they can find there."

Nicky arrived with Fitzwilliam's coffee and an enormous pile of toast.

His eyes shining, Perry leaned over to Lady Beatrice. "So tell me all about this kick and split manoeuvre, and—"

Lady Beatrice rubbed her fingertips in small circles on her forehead. *It's as if someone has unplugged me.*

Perry stopped talking. Looking at his watch, Simon rose from his seat. "I think we should go," he said to Perry. "Don't you need to find Joe to see what we can do to get the Garden Room cleared? I'll give you a hand." he offered. Perry nodded and got up.

Looking up at them, she smiled. "Thank you, that would be a weight off my mind."

Perry squeezed her shoulder as he walked past, and they left.

Lady Beatrice watched Fitzwilliam work his way through a mountain of toast while she sipped her coffee. She wanted to leave too, but she couldn't find the energy to move.

Fitzwilliam tore a slice of toast in half and offered a piece to Daisy. She wasn't interested. He chuckled, putting it back on his plate. "She really has run out of juice, hasn't she?"

Lady Beatrice nodded. "I know how she feels."

"Are you sure you're well?" he asked, his eyes full of concern.

"Yes, I'm fine. Just tired." She cleared her throat and took a sip of water.

"It's normal to feel like that after you've been through a traumatic experience. It's something to do with the adrenaline released during a fight-or-flight situation," he told her.

"Well, thank you, Dr Fitzwilliam," she replied. She smiled so he would know she was joking.

He laughed. "They warned us about it during special protection training. To be honest, I wasn't listening carefully enough to give you a more detailed explanation."

As he carried on eating, her thoughts turned to Gill Sterling. There was still the same dichotomy to contend with. Was she the sweet, unassuming victim, ignored and abused by her husband, as believed by her family and James? Or was she the moaning, stuck-up woman who disliked her life and her husband's job that everyone at Francis Court saw? *Who was the real Gill Sterling?*

Recalling Gill's expired passport and the makeup bags she'd found in Keeper's Cottage, her skin tingled. *Could that be it?* To be sure, she would need some information about Gill's financial status when she'd died, and any injuries noted during the post-mortem. She looked over at Fitzwilliam, who was spreading jam on his last piece of toast. *He seems almost bearable at the moment. Is this the right time to ask him a favour?*

"Chief inspector, can you find out for me if Gill paid a substantial cash sum into her account just before she died? Also, did she have any external injuries, maybe old scars, or anything consistent with being beaten or attacked?" The request rushed out of her. She swallowed and took a sip of her now cold coffee.

He raised his eyebrows. "Can I ask why?"

"Let's just say I'm curious. I have a theory, and

if what you tell me supports it, then I'll share it with you."

"More woman's intuition, Lady Rossex?" He grinned.

"Yes, and you said you should have taken more notice of it. So now you can put your money where your mouth is," she said, grinning back.

Sarah: *I've spoken to Brooke. The deed is done, not sure what will happen now. Police and sirens all over the place again. Please don't tell me there's been another murder? xx*

Bea: *No, no one is dead. Will tell you all about it later. xx*

47

MID-AFTERNOON, FRIDAY 16 APRIL

The Society Page online article:
Letter from James Wiltshire to Lady Beatrice - Fake News?

The popular press has been reporting all morning on the existence of a letter from James Wiltshire, the Earl of Rossex, to his wife, Lady Beatrice. It is purported to have been written before the accident that killed him fourteen years ago.

The Daily Post *broke the news this morning, claiming the letter came to light five years ago because of an evidence move at Fenshire CID. Although there has been much speculation about the contents of the letter,* The Daily Post *could not provide any further details, other than repeatedly state their source is reliable.*

Francis Court, which responds to all enquiries regarding the Astley Family, has released a statement saying they do not comment on private matters. Gollingham Palace has released a similar statement. A little dickie bird tells us no one at Francis Court knows of the existence of such a letter, let alone of its contents. Here at TSP, we wonder if this is a case of an over enthusiastic member of the press jumping the gun before they have verified their 'reliable' source.

No doubt it won't stop the paparazzi from descending on Francis Court en-masse later today looking for the non-story.

Sarah: *Well, we knew this might happen. Are you all right? Did you speak to Sam? I'll come up and see you when my call has finished. Hugs. xx*

Ma: *Darling, are you all right? Sarah said you told them to publish and be damned! So proud of you. Come for afternoon tea with me and Pa, 3pm. x*

Fred: *Hey little sis, are you okay? I'm in a meeting all day but will ring you as soon as we have a break. TSP seems to think it's a non-story. I agree with them. x*

Perry: *Just seen the news. Are you okay? Come to dinner tonight. Simon is making sourdough pizzas. Yummy! We give great hugs here... PS if Simon asks if you like anchovies, please say no, I can't stand them. xx*

Fitzwilliam: *Lady Rossex, this is Richard Fitzwilliam. Sorry to see Desmond Brooke went ahead. It's a non-story. They have nothing more to say, no details. It will die quickly. Kind regards.*

Simon: *Glad you are coming over for pizza later. Do you like anchovies? x*

Sam: *Mum, they've given me and Robbie the evening off. No homework!! We're off to cricket nets. Love you. xxx*

Caro: *Sorry, been on a plane and only just seen the news, cuz. What a load of b**l. It will blow over soon. It's the past, Bea. Let it go and concentrate on your glorious future in interior design. Will call later. Lots of love. xx*

48

EVENING, FRIDAY 16 APRIL

Lady Beatrice waved Jeff off as she walked up the path of Rose Cottage. Daisy trotted beside her, her tail up, as she whined with excitement. The familiar smell of rosemary followed them up the path. Lady Beatrice knocked on the door and waited.

She put her hand up to the black and orange patterned Hermes scarf (hastily borrowed from her mother's extensive collection) that was tied loosely around her neck. She'd wanted to cover up the vivid bruises Seth had left there. Shifting on her feet, she tugged at the scarf. She wasn't a wearer of scarves; it felt alien to her. *And I look like an air hostess from the 1960s.*

The door opened and Perry stood to one side, beaming at her. Daisy threw herself in front of him, her tail wagging, demanding his attention. He chuckled and made the obligatory fuss. She accepted it for a short while, then darted past him, following the smell of roasting tomatoes wafting from the kitchen. They watched her go, both smiling. Then Perry turned to Lady Beatrice and opened his arms.

She stepped into the gentle hug. Perry smelt clean and familiar. His cashmere jumper was soft and warm. "Thank you," she whispered. He hugged her a little tighter. They stood there for a few minutes before detangling themselves and moving into the cottage.

Simon stood in front of the kitchen island, pizza bases laid out before him. Spreading a tomato topping on each one, he looked up and smiled at her. "Perfect timing, Lady Bea. What would you like on your pizza?"

"You're the expert, so you choose. Surprise me." She patted him on the arm and headed for the table, passing Daisy, who was already in her favourite armchair by the window, curled up and asleep. Perry stood by a chair, holding out a large glass of red wine.

"I want to talk to you both," Lady Bea announced when Perry returned to the table, having cleared away the remains of their pizza feast. She cleared her throat and tugged at the scarf around her neck. "I'd like it if you would call me Bea. Lady Bea is too formal now that we know each other so well."

Perry put his hand to his chest. "I'm touched, thank you," he replied, his eyes shining. He picked up his glass of wine and took a huge glug.

"It's what my family calls me." She swallowed, her eyes stinging slightly.

Simon smiled and raised his glass to her, an enormous grin on his face. Perry fanned his eyes.

"So how are you feeling, Bea?" Simon asked.

"About being strangled or about being plastered all over the news?" she joked. Perry spat out his wine. She laughed as he wiped his chin with his napkin. "I'm relieved the murder investigation is over and we can finish the Events Suite. I'm happy Pete Cowley is home and will make a full recovery. And as much as I hate all the press attention, I expect it will blow over soon." She pulled again at the stupid scarf. *How does my mother cope with having one around her neck all day? It's so hot.*

"Why don't you take it off, Bea?" Perry jumped in. "You've been fiddling and tugging at it all night."

"I had to put something on in case I bumped into the press and they took photos." She untied the scarf from her neck and threw it down on the table. "That feels much better." They both looked at her neck, but thankfully said nothing. Heat rising in her cheeks, she said, "I received an unexpected text message from DCI Fitzwilliam this afternoon commiserating with me. He said the letter was a non-story and would die soon."

"I think he has a soft spot for you," Perry said, surprising her.

What? She shook her head.

He grinned. "He was super worried when Daisy ran around barking and we couldn't see you. And when he realised you were in danger, he shot off like an Olympic sprinter. I couldn't keep up, and I have ten years on him."

She snorted. "I doubt his concern was about me personally. It's more likely he was worried about his reputation. Imagine if someone murdered a member of the royal family on his watch!"

Perry raised his brows at her.

She shifted her gaze to Simon. "Anything more about Seth from your contacts?"

"Actually, yes. When he arrived at the hospital, he asked about Pete Cowley. When they told him they had discharged Pete and, with rest, he would make a full recovery, he collapsed into a sobbing heap."

There was a loud knock at the door, making them all jump.

Detective Chief Inspector Richard Fitzwilliam walked into the kitchen of Rose Cottage with a smirking Perry following behind.

"DCI Fitzwilliam came over to see you, Lady Beatrice," Perry announced and winked at her.

"Mr Juke, Mr Lattimore, sorry to disturb you. I'm leaving to go back to Surrey shortly, and I have some information for you, Lady Rossex. Security told me you were here," he explained.

"That's quite all right, chief inspector," Simon responded. "Please come and sit down. Can I pour you a glass of wine?" He held up the bottle.

Fitzwilliam shook his head, standing awkwardly in the middle of the room. "I'm driving, I'm afraid."

"Coffee!" Perry shouted, heading towards the coffee machine.

"That would be great, thank you. Black please, no sugar."

"Please take a seat, chief inspector," Simon

said, pointing to the chair next to Lady Beatrice. She glared at Simon, but he took no notice. *I'll be having words with him and Perry later!*

"Thank you, and please call me Fitzwilliam," he said, sitting down. "All of you." He turned to look at Lady Beatrice. "Chief inspector is a mouthful. And, after all, we've been working on this case together," he chuckled, "even if I didn't realise it."

Perry placed a cup of coffee in front of Fitzwilliam. Lady Beatrice was sure he winked at Simon as he went to sit next to him.

"So, Fitzwilliam," Simon said, "is there an update on Seth Padgett?"

"Well, he's sore." Fitzwilliam looked at Lady Beatrice and grinned. "And not just where he hit his head."

She ducked her head as heat moved up her bruised neck.

"Mike warned me not to mess with you," Perry said, grinning. "I can see he knew what he was talking about!" He reached over and took her hand. "We're so proud of you," he said, giving it a squeeze.

Her heart sang. *I'm proud of myself, too.*

"We've charged him with the murder of Alex Sterling. We may add the attempted murder of Pete Cowley to the charges, but we'll need to see if we can prove it. And, of course, there's the attempted murder of Lady Rossex to consider as well."

What? Her heart raced. "Does that mean I'll have to testify in court?" she asked. "In public?" *The press will love that — attempted murder of a member of the royal family; off with his head!*

"We'll see what happens when we interview him over the next few days. If he's prepared to plead guilty, which I think he will, then we may drop one or more of the charges if it will secure a quick conviction. He'll take legal advice, of course. It's early days, but we will do everything we can to keep your involvement out of the press." He smiled at her and sipped his coffee.

Perry and Simon leaned forward, gawping at him from across the table; they wanted more. He sighed and smiled. "His real name is Oliver Hanratty, and he's Gill Sterling's elder brother. Since we last spoke, CID has found a set of keys at his house that included ones to the front door and French doors of the Garden Room." Leaning back, he turned to face Lady Beatrice. "Oh, and that patch that Daisy was sniffing on the kitchen floor at Keeper's Cottage shows traces of ketamine."

"Well done, Daisy." Perry raised his glass in her direction.

"What's your current theory of what happened,

chief inspector?" Her voice still sounded unsteady to her. He glanced at her neck. She raised a hand to it. He looked troubled.

"Call me Fitzwilliam, please, my lady," he insisted.

"Indeed, sorry, Fitzwilliam."

"We won't know for sure, of course, until we question him, but we believe Padgett met Alex at Keeper's Cottage at seven that morning. He drugged Alex in his kitchen, then transferred his unconscious body to the Garden Room, accessing it via the French doors. When Seth moved the body into the room, he lost a button from Alex's overalls on the way; as you had worked out, there was one missing when you found the body. We're confident he used the table to kill the victim. After that, he unlocked the front door to make it look like Alex had entered that way, before exiting the way he went in."

"That was smart," Simon interjected.

Fitzwilliam nodded. "Especially since he manipulated Pete into a position to give him an alibi. Later, he must have been worried Pete would connect the dots when we interviewed him again, so he attacked him before we could talk to him."

"What about the gloves?" Simon asked.

Lady Beatrice straightened, her thoughts

whirling. "I think I can answer that, if you don't mind, chief insp — sorry, Fitzwilliam?"

"Go ahead, my lady."

"Perry, do you remember when we were waiting for security to arrive the morning we found Alex's body? We saw Seth driving the tractor and trailer. He was coming from the trees opposite the Garden Room; he almost mowed down Adrian Breen and one of his team."

"Yes, now you mention it, I do. Some stuff fell off the back of his trailer, and he tried to clear it up." His eyes widened. "Do you think the gloves were on there?"

She nodded. "Yes, and I think they fell off and then Alfie got hold of them."

"Who's Alfie?" Simon asked.

"He's my parent's border terrier. He's obsessed with burying things."

Fitzwilliam nodded. "There was dog slobber on the gloves, but we assumed it was Daisy's. Thank you, that's helpful. I'll pass it on to Mike."

He drained his coffee cup and rose from the table. "Lady Rossex, can we have a word, please? I have the information which you requested this morning."

She rose to her feet. "Do you boys mind if I leave? I need to talk to Fitzwilliam." At their enquiring looks, she added, "I'll tell you all about it tomorrow, I promise."

When they nodded, she turned to Fitzwilliam. "Are you in your car?"

"No, I came on foot via the north side gate. The press have surrounded the main gates, and I didn't want them following me."

"Perfect. Daisy and I will walk back with you then, and you can tell me on the way."

Lady Beatrice turned to give Perry and Simon a big hug. "Thank you both so much," she said, then turned and followed Fitzwilliam out into the night.

49

LATER THAT EVENING, FRIDAY 16 APRIL

DCI Fitzwilliam and Lady Beatrice sauntered along the side of the green, with Daisy trotting between them. The evening was cooling down, and Lady Beatrice was grateful for her puffa jacket, the soft warmth keeping out the chilly night air.

"So, Lady Rossex—"

"Fitzwilliam," she interrupted, "if I have to call you Fitzwilliam, then you'll need to call me Lady Beatrice. It's only fair." She smiled at him, and he nodded.

"So, Lady Beatrice, you realise I'm breaking all kinds of rules by giving you the information I'm about to share, don't you?" She nodded. "I've looked at the post-mortem report for Gill Sterling.

There was no trace of any old injuries when they examined her. She died of internal bleeding resulting from the car crash." As Daisy took the lead, he continued, "I can also confirm a week before the accident, she received a large cash deposit in a bank account which was in her name only."

Feeling Fitzwilliam peering at her in the darkness, she nodded. She'd expected that.

"Interestingly, one of the bank transactions she made a few days before she died was to a train company. She'd booked a one-way ticket from London to Aberdeen and was due to leave the afternoon after she died." He paused.

"You don't seem surprised, Lady Beatrice," he commented as they approached the brightly lit north side gate.

Lady Beatrice waved at Jeff as they reached the entrance. "I have a foot escort tonight, Jeff," she shouted.

He waved from the security office and shouted back, "I've checked you both in. Have a pleasant evening, Lady Rossex, chief inspector." The gate clicked and Fitzwilliam pushed it open.

As they headed towards the main house, Daisy ran off towards the Old Stable Block, barking madly. A few minutes later, a brown dog came running out to meet her. "That's Alfie." Lady Beatrice pointed in their direction. "And to answer your question, you're right, I'm not surprised. I checked James's personal bank account statement. Nine days before his death, he took out ten thousand pounds in cash."

"And you think he gave it to Gill Sterling?"

She nodded. "I'm sure of it. I think he gave it to her to buy a ticket to fly to Mexico. You may remember in his letter he said that's where he was going and that she would join him a few days later."

"But she bought a one-way ticket to Scotland."

"And she left her passport at Keeper's Cottage. I found it when I was searching through Alex's belongings. I don't think she ever intended to go to Mexico with James."

"I see," he responded. It was too dark for her to see his expression, but she imagined he was making the connections she herself had already made.

They arrived at the north side door. The external security light clicked on, flooding them with light. Lady Beatrice retrieved her keys from the pocket of her jacket. She called Daisy and Alfie, and they sprinted towards her.

"And James didn't know?" Fitzwilliam asked.

She shook her head. "I don't think so. I think he genuinely thought she was in love with him, but I suspect she just needed someone to give her the confidence to leave Alex. What she wanted was a new life in Scotland, and James facilitated that by giving her the money."

Daisy and Alfie arrived, panting. Alfie ran over and sniffed Fitzwilliam.

"I also came across three bags of makeup in Alex's cottage. At first I was confused. It looked like way too much makeup for one person. She had many shaped sponges and a range of brushes in all sizes. Then this afternoon, I remembered an occasion when James and I had visited a television studio and they showed us round the makeup department. They used those sponges and brushes to build realistic injuries for the actors."

Fitzwilliam's eyes opened wide. A look of astonishment crossed his face.

"The thing is, I couldn't make James's version of Gill, covered in bruises and cuts inflicted by her bullying husband, fit with what everyone here had to say about her. Someone, I think it was Mrs Crammond, said she liked to play the victim to get attention. So when I found the makeup and remembered the studio visit, it occurred to me she could've used it to create some false injuries to attract James's attention."

Fitzwilliam was still for a moment, leaning on the stone balustrade leading to the ancient wooden side door. He leaned down and patted Alfie on the head, then nodded and said, "You could be right, Lady Beatrice."

"I know this may sound strange, but I feel a little sorry for James. I think she duped him into helping her because he had fallen for her when all along she clearly had no intention of escaping to a new life with him." She shook her head and sighed.

Daisy and Alfie sat in front of the side door, waiting for someone to open it for them. Climbing up the remaining two steps, Lady Beatrice turned the key in the lock. As she opened the door, they bounded in, then she turned back. "Oh, and one last thing, Fitzwilliam." She needed to tell him what she'd done earlier that evening. "I've destroyed the letter."

His eyebrows shot up, then his face cleared, and he nodded. "I think that was a wise move."

"Thank you, Fitzwilliam. Have a safe trip back to Surrey."

"You're welcome, my lady. I hope all goes well with finishing the Events Suite."

She smiled at him as he turned and walked

away. She stood there, watching his retreating back. He turned and caught her eye.

"Oh, and Lady Beatrice," he shouted into the night, "try not to find any more dead bodies."

***

Fitzwilliam climbed into his car and started the engine. He set the temperature to twenty degrees and reclined in his seat as the car started warming up. Should he make a call? He had information that could be important, but would anyone care after all this time?

Picking up his mobile phone, he slid it into the holder attached to the dashboard. He scrolled through the numbers until he found the one he was looking for.

"Richard, this is a surprise." The voice at the other end sounded hesitant. "Is everything all right?"

"Hello, sir. Sorry for ringing so late. I have some information that may interest you."

"Well, fire away then, man. Let's hear it."

"It's about the Earl of Rossex's accident, sir. I have new information that may be relevant to the investigation, if there still is an investigation?"

"It's still officially dead and buried, Richard.

The letter that was found only seemed to offer further evidence that James Wiltshire's death was just an unfortunate accident. Like you, I wasn't one hundred percent convinced, but those more senior than me felt it didn't warrant any further resources."

Fitzwilliam sighed, "Well then I'm sorry to have troubled you, sir."

"Wait," the man cried, "I said *officially* it's dead and buried. Unofficially, I'm still keen to hear what you have to say. Tell me what you have."

Fitzwilliam gave him a brief update on the arrest of Gill Sterling's brother for Alex's murder, then told him about Lady Beatrice's theory.

"I see. So what exactly about this concerns you?"

"When I told Lady Rossex that there was a large cash deposit made into Gill Sterling's bank account a week before the accident, that was true. But there were also other substantial cash deposits going into that account that I didn't tell her about. In the four months leading up to the accident, these amounted to just over fifty thousand pounds. Not just that, sir, but the balance on her account prior to that was over thirty thousand pounds. Lady Rossex told me the earl had taken ten thousand pounds in cash from his account nine days before the accident. She assumed that he'd given it to Gill Sterling, but even if he did, where did the other payments come from?"

"That's an interesting point, Richard. I don't believe we checked her bank account as part of the investigation. In fact, we did very little checking on Gill Sterling at all. It seemed unnecessary when it appeared her being in the car was just an unfortunate coincidence."

"Another thing, sir. If, as Lady Rossex believes, Gill Sterling made herself out to be a victim of abuse so she could attract the attention of James Wiltshire, then why? If she had the money and means to escape, why involve him at all?"

"What are you suggesting, Richard?"

Fitzwilliam took a deep breath. *I've come this far. I might as well share my thoughts.*

"What if someone was paying Gill Sterling to get close to the earl?"

"Um, now that would put a different spin on things." He paused. Fitzwilliam could hear his breathing down the line. He waited patiently for a response. "So if someone paid her significant amounts of money in the four months leading up to the accident, then who paid her? And why? And most significantly to us, was it related to James Wiltshire? Leave it with me, Richard. I will do some digging into the late Mrs Gill Sterling and see what I can find out. Let's keep in contact."

"Yes, sir. Goodnight."

The line at the other end had already gone dead by the time Fitzwilliam cut the call. He waited for a few minutes, staring out into the darkness. Then he turned the radio on, put the car into drive and started the long trip back home.

50

MID-MORNING, SUNDAY
2 MAY

The Society Page online article:

The Recently Refurbished Francis Court Events Suite has its Grand Opening on Time

Last night the Astley Family and guests attended the grand re-opening of the Events Suite at Francis Court, the family's sixteenth century stately home in Francis-next-the-Sea.

Francis Court, and its 25,000-acre estate on the North Fenshire coast, is the seat of Charles Astley, the Duke of Arnwall (63) who was in attendance with his wife, Her Royal Highness Princess Helen (62). The princess looked sophisticated in a mint green Dolce & Gabbana silk belted evening dress paired with nude Louboutin Rosalie leather sandals.

Escorted by her husband, John Rosdale (40), their eldest daughter, Lady Sarah Rosdale (38), who manages the Events Suite, looked elegant in a Talbot Runof metallic cape gown in gold, and black suede Jimmy Choo sandals.

Their youngest daughter, Lady Beatrice (35), the Countess of Rossex, was chic in an Alaia fringe-detailed black dress paired with Valentino Rockstud sandals also in black. Lady Beatrice, who has a degree in Interior Design, managed the interior design project for the Events Suite.

Also in attendance at the Grand Opening was Simon Lattimore (39), the crime writer and celebrated chef, wearing a black Burberry mohair dinner suit. Mr Lattimore was there supporting his partner, Perry Juke (33). Mr Juke, looking stylish in a Tom Ford Shelton satin trimmed black tuxedo, worked with Lady Beatrice on the interior design for the Events Suite.

Champagne and canapés were provided for guests as they previewed the newly remodelled Events Suite. The suite comprises four interconnecting rooms — the Salon, the Blue Dining Room, the Garden Room, and the Smoking Room. Accessed via Francis Court's magnificent Painted Hall, the suite can accommodate parties of up to fifty people. One guest described the atmosphere as 'elegant, opulent, and intimate'.

For larger events Francis Court has a wedding and conference facility, which includes a stunning cast iron orangery, built in 1845, at its centre.

The redesign and refurbishment of the Events Suite was completed on time, despite the murder of the Estate Manager, Alex Sterling (44), three weeks ago. Seth Padgett (45), also a Francis Court employee, has pleaded guilty to the murder and is due to be sentenced later this month.

A little dickie bird tells us Lady Beatrice and Perry Juke have been asked to redesign and refurbish Fawstead Manor, located just outside Fawstead Town, dubbed 'the Knightsbridge of Fenshire'. The newly acquired fourteen-bedroom country house was purchased by Sir Hewitt Willoughby-Franklin (68), whose wife, Lady Grace (61), is a close friend of HRH Princess Helen. Lady Grace's daughter Sybil (36) is due to marry Otis Trotman (40), the American heir to the Fortune hotel chain, in a lavish ceremony at Francis Court in September.

I hope you enjoyed *Spruced Up for Murder*. If you did, then please consider letting others know by writing a review on Amazon, Goodreads or both. Thank you.

Will the redesign and refurbishment of Fawstead Manor go ahead without a hitch? Of course not! Read the next book in the A Right Royal Cozy Investigation series *For Richer, For Deader* available in the Amazon store or wherever you get your paperbacks.

Want to know how Bea and Perry solved their first crime together without knowing it? Then join my readers' club and receive a FREE novella, *A Toast To Trouble* at https://www.subscribepage.com/helengoldenauthor_bmatttrm or if you'd prefer you can buy the ebook or paperback in the Amazon store.

For other books by me, take a look at the back pages.

If you want to find out more about what I'm up to you can find me on Facebook at *helengoldenauthor* or on Instagram at *helengolden_author*.

Be the first to know when my next book is available. Follow Helen Golden on Amazon, BookBub, and Goodreads to get alerts whenever I have a new release, preorder, or a discount on any of my books.

CHARACTERS IN ORDER OF APPEARANCE

Perry Juke — Lady Sarah's executive assistant seconded to work with Lady Beatrice for the duration of the refurbishment project.

Lady Beatrice — The Countess of Rossex. Seventeenth in line to the British throne. Daughter of Charles Astley, the Duke of Arnwall and Her Royal Highness Princess Helen. Niece of the current king.

Sam Wiltshire — son of Lady Beatrice and the late James Wiltshire, the Earl of Rossex. Future Earl of Durrland.

Daisy — Lady Beatrice's adorable West Highland Terrier.

Ward/Mr Ward — the Astley family's driver and overseer of maintenance at Francis Court.

Charles Astley — Duke of Arnwall. Lady Beatrice's father.

HRH Princess Helen — Duchess of Arnwall. Mother of Lady Beatrice. Sister of the current king.

Lady Sarah Rosdale — Lady Beatrice's elder sister. Twin of Fred Astley. Manages events at Francis Court.

Robert (Robbie) Rosdale — Lady Sarah's eldest son.

James Wiltshire — The Earl of Rossex. Lady Beatrice's late husband killed in a car accident fourteen years ago.

Earl and Countess of Durrland — the late James Wiltshire's parents and Sam's grandparents.

Gill Sterling — the late wife of Francis Court's estate manager. Passenger in car accident that killed her and James Wiltshire.

Alex Sterling — Francis Court's estate manager.

Naomi — Princess Helen's maid.

Lady Caroline (Caro) Clifford — Lady Beatrice's cousin on her mother's side.

Mr Watts — manager of exclusive restaurant The Station in Fawstead.

Frederick (Fred) Astley — Earl of Tilling. Lady Beatrice's elder brother and twin of Lady Sarah Rosdale. Ex-Intelligence Army Officer. Future Duke of Arnwall.

Queen Mary The Queen Mother - wife of the late King. Mother of HRH Princess Helen and grandmother of Lady Beatrice.

Adrian Breen — head of security at Francis Court. Ex-Fenshire CID.

Ellie Gunn — Francis Court's catering manager and on-off lover of Alex Sterling.

Seth Padgett — head gardener at Francis Court.

Pete Cowley — gardener at Francis Court. Ex-marine.

Simon Lattimore — Perry Juke's partner. Bestselling crime writer. Ex-Fenshire CID. Last year's winner of cooking competition *Celebrity Elitechef.*

Jeff Beesley — late shift lead security officer at Francis Court.

King James and Queen Olivia — King of England and his wife.

Joe Fox — apprentice gardener at Francis Court.

Charles — contractor managing restoration work at Francis Court.

Nicky — server in the Breakfast Room restaurant at Francis Court.

Sophie Crammond — head housekeeper ay Francis Court.

Alfie — The Duke and Duchess of Arnwall's five-year-old border terrier.

Mike Ainsley — detective inspector at Fenshire CID.

Eamon Hines — detective sergeant at Fenshire CID.

Mr Hutton — executive chef at Francis Court.

Richard Fitzwilliam — detective chief inspector at *PaIRS (Protection and Investigation (Royal) Service)* an organisation that provides protection and security to the royal family and who investigate any threats against them. *PaIRS* is a division of *City Police*, a police organisation based in the capital, London.

Nigel Blake — superintendent at *PaIRS*. Fitzwilliam's boss.

Carol — DCI Fitzwilliam's PA at *PaIRS*.

Tina Spicer — detective sergeant at *PaIRS*.

Mike Reed — detective inspector at *PaIRS* who headed up investigation into the car accident that killed James Wiltshire fourteen years ago.

Harris/Mr Harris — butler at Francis Court and valet to Charles Astley, the Duke of Arnwall.

Roisin — Simon Lattimore's friend who works in Forensics at Fenshire Police.

Steve/CID Steve — ex-colleague of Simon Lattimore at Fenshire CID.

Dylan and Janet Milton — landlord of the pub The Ship and Seal in Francis-next-the-Sea and his wife.

Cass Gunn — works in garden centre at Francis Court. Daughter of Ellie Gunn.

Mrs Cutter — lives in Francis-next-the-Sea, Perry's old neighbour.

Peter Tappin — owner of Tappin's Teas in Francis-next-the-Sea.

Ross Gunn — Ellis Gunn's husband (separated) and Cass Gunn's father.

Jasmine — server in the Old Stable Block Cafe at Francis Court.

John Rosdale — Lady Sarah's husband.

Charlotte (Lottie) Rosdale — Lady Sarah's daughter.

Desmond Brooke — Chief Editor, The Daily Post.

Mrs Harris — Astley family housekeeper at Francis Court. Wife of Harris/Mr Harris.

Claire — friend of Perry Juke. Works in Human Resources at Francis Court.

A BIG THANK YOU TO...

I have always wanted to write, ever since I picked up my first Agatha Christie book many years ago. But life got in the way, and although I remained an avid reader (moving more towards the cozy end of crime when I discovered M. C. Beaton), writing a novel moved to the 'if I won the lottery what would I do with my time' list, and there it stayed. Then recently, an unexpected change in circumstances, although painful to deal with, opened up an opportunity for me to take some time out of the business world and explore other options. So I followed my dream and began to write. Now I have everything crossed that I can earn a living doing what I love and not have to wait to win the lottery.

I would like to mention a few people who have

been critical in helping me along this journey, who've offered practical help as well as support and encouragement. Without them, I don't think I would have had the courage or the tools to follow my dreams.

First, I have to thank my marvellous husband Simon, who has been unwavering in his support. I sort of wish he hadn't told everyone we know that I'm writing a book (oh, the pressure!), but I love that he is so proud of me. When I needed to disappear to our caravan for weeks on end to have peace to write in, he stoically smiled and let me leave all the washing and household chores to him.

To my amazing stepdaughter, Ellie, for popping in to the caravan regularly to see how it was going and for understanding that sometimes I needed to keep writing because I was on a roll and therefore couldn't make our week-day date to watch *House of Games* together.

To my parents Ann and Ray, whose love of reading rubbed off on me at an early age. Thank you for being as excited as me when my first draft appeared on your kindles and for your promise to buy lots of copies for your friends.

To my niece and best girl Emma, for listening patiently as I explained my characters, my plot, and plans for how the series would develop. Your enthusiasm kept me buoyed up to carry on. I will hold you to your promise of reading this now that it's finished, even though you 'don't normally do books'.

For all my friends (and everyone in our village who Simon blabbed to about me writing a book in order to explain the caravan parked on our drive for weeks on end) who regularly checked in to see how I was getting on, especially Nicky Evans and Emily Burns-Sweeney, thank you so much. Your faith in me has been heart-warming.

To my beta readers, Lesley Catterall-Price and Lelia Wynn, thank you for your insightful and encouraging feedback. Your constructive approach made me happy and excited to take your thoughts and suggestions on board and make changes that have no doubt improved the final version.

To Peter Boon (the author of the Edward Crisp murder mysteries — check them out; you will love them), thank you for taking time out to help a first-time novelist. Your support and encouragement have been invaluable.

A big shout out to Abbie Emmons, author (her book *100 Days of Sunlight* is a must read) and enthusiastic provider of writing tips and advice through her YouTube series, *Writers Life Wednes-*

days. Your suggestions and help have been enormously useful to a newbie like me.

To my editor, Marina Grout, whose patience, humour and exceptional skills have made the editing experience a pleasure rather than a chore. Thank you for everything you have done to contribute to my debut novel. I look forward to working with you on the rest of the series.

To Georgiana Hockin, my wonderful long-time friend, thank you for your proof-reading services. It was so exciting working with you.

To my lovely and supportive friends Carolyn Bruce and Jo Skinner, thank you for being an additional set of eyes for me before publication.

To my ARC team — Lisa, Kerry, Karen, Tia, Michelle, Robyn, Zoe, Charlotte and Hannah — thank you for your support.

I have to give a special mention to Wagtail Country Park in Lincolnshire where I have escaped to in the caravan to write much of this book. It's a very tranquil place to get lost in my writing, and everyone there has been so welcoming. A special shout out to Mandy and Sue for all your help and support.

I may have taken a little dramatic license when it comes to police procedures, so any mistakes or misinterpretations, unintentional or otherwise, are my own.

To you, my readers, thank you for giving a new author a chance and reading this book (especially if you got this far!). I hope we can continue to enjoy Lady Beatrice, Perry, Simon, and Fitzwilliam together as the series unfolds.

And finally, thank you to my caravan dogs - Alfie, Margot and occasionally, Bourbon. Except when you were barking at passersby or demanding treats, you have been very good boys and girls, and your companionship has been priceless.

ALSO BY HELEN GOLDEN

A novella lenght prequal in the series A Right Royal Cozy investiation series. With Perry and Bea working against each other, can they still save the party—or will it be ruined beyond repair along with Francis Court's reputation as a gold-standard venue?

A short prequal in the series A Right Royal Cozy Investigation. Can Perry Juke and Simon Lattimore work together to solve the mystery of the missing clock before the thief disappears? FREE novelette when you sign up to my readers' club. See end of final chapter for details.

Second book in the A Right Royal Cozy Investigation series. Amateur sleuth, Lady Beatrice, must once again go up against DCI Fitzwilliam to find a killer. With the help of Daisy, her clever companion, and her two best friends, Perry and Simon, can she catch the culprit before her childhood friend's wedding is ruined? Also in Audio format.

The third book in the A Right Royal Cozy Investigation series. When DCI Richard Fitzwilliam gets it into his head that Lady Beatrice's new beau Seb is guilty of murder, can the amateur sleuth, along with the help of Daisy, her clever westie, and her best friends Perry and Simon, find the real killer before Fitzwilliam goes ahead and arrests Seb? Also in Audio format.

A Prequel in the A Right Royal Cozy Investigation series. When Lady Beatrice's husband James Wiltshire dies in a car crash along with the wife of a member of staff, there are questions to be answered. Why haven't the occupants of two cars seen in the accident area come forward? And what is the secret James had been keeping from her?

When the dead body of the event's planner is found at the staff ball that Lady Beatrice is hosting at Francis Court, the amateur sleuth, with help from her clever dog Daisy and best friend Perry, must catch the killer before the partygoers find out and New Year's Eve is ruined.

Snow descends on Drew Castle in Scotland cutting the castle off and forcing Lady Beatrice along with Daisy her clever dog, and her best friends Perry and Simon to cooperate with boorish DCI Fitzwilliam to catch a killer before they strike again.

A murder at Gollingham Palace sparks a hunt to find the killer. For once, Lady Beatrice is happy to let DCI Richard Fitzwilliam get on with it. But when information comes to light that indicates it could be linked to her husband's car accident fifteen years ago, she is compelled to get involved. Will she finally find out the truth behind James's tragic death?

An unforgettable bachelor weekend for Perry filled with luxury, laughter, and an unexpected death.
Can Bea, Perry, and his hen's catch the killer before the weekend is over?

Bake Off Wars is being filmed on site at Francis Court and everyone is buzzing. But when much-loved pastry chef and judge, Vera Bolt, is found dead on set, can Bea, with the help of her best friend Perry, his husband Simon, and her cute little terrier, Daisy, expose the killer before the show is over?

Even in a charming seaside town, secrets don't stay buried for long as Bea and Perry discover when they uncover the remains of a chef who disappeared 3 years ago. As they unravel a web of professional rivalries and buried grudges, they must race against time to solve the murder before the grand opening of Simon's new restaurant.

Lady Beatrice's peaceful holiday in Portugal is shattered when a Hollywood star's husband is found dead. What appears to be an accident soon reveals itself as murder. Tasked with clearing an innocent woman's name, Bea and Rich must untangle a web of lies to uncover the truth before it's too late.

PAPERBACKS AVAILABLE FROM WHEREVER YOU BUY YOUR BOOKS.

www.ingramcontent.com/pod-product-compliance
Lightning Source LLC
Chambersburg PA
CBHW031735180726
48283CB00005B/1516